Brancusi's Head and the China 12

Hope it great

Paul W.

Brancusi's Head and the China 12

Raoul Morris

Three Heads Inc.

For the three who matter most

The China 12

Dr Xi Liang	Chemist- Toxicologist
Dr Erasto Dialo	Engineer
Ms Koura Aripe	Designer- Ergonomist
Dr Lopez-Real	Pathologist- Biochemist
Dr Catherine O'Shea	Forensic psychologist
Dr Wolfgang Schult	Forensic Archaeologist
Dr Zhang Xin	Mathematician—Statistic and Analysis
Dr Rahul Patel	Mathematician Computationalist
Dr Himura Hoshika	Mathematician Probability

Operatives

Milo Talbot
Joanna Baines (deceased)
Kevin Twomey (deceased)

CHAPTER ONE

He knew he was putting it off. He had spent the evening walking along the bookshelves, pulling out the occasional book, mostly mathematical theory, mostly probability theory.

Then he just sat on the long couch in the middle of the room staring at them. He triggered the cranial implant and began to calculate the number of words on the shelves in front of him followed by the number of theories, the number of single hypotheses whose workings had changed how people saw themselves and each other when they were worked out in full. Then he reached out to his memory core to see, by comparison, how many were contained in it and then in the core at CERN where he worked.

He reflected on how being the 'sum of our memories' had changed, chewing his cheek, worrying the trauma, a small lump caused by a careless belt in the mouth he had received on a night out years earlier. It was what he did when he was stressed, when he put things off.

He was about to do something, or at least set in train something he had hoped never to do, a meeting he didn't want to have and a program he never wanted to run. It would cause havoc, well, perhaps not havoc, but a lot of disruption. It would prevent tyranny, not exactly but people he didn't like, controlling something he cared a hell of a lot about. He had given them the keys to the kingdom. Maybe he hadn't actually done so himself, but he had been part of it and now he had to hide them. Yeah, that was what he was doing. He was hiding the keys to the kingdom from the evil barons and orcs. He smiled.

He got up off his largish – he was sensitive about it – rump and walked over to the machine that was sitting on the desk at the end of the room. This place, this house in the tiny town of Cassis, was his haven, and this desk was his very centre of peace. He had no connection to anything here, except via that old-fashioned cable. Pull that from the machine and he was as isolated as a man from the middle of the last century, the 1940s, say. No, earlier, because they had had phones back then.

He pushed back the old screen and read the message. It was simple enough, a meeting. They would know where, 'the other place', and they would be equipped with their parts of the puzzle. He signed off with 'Three Heads'. He set the encryption to high.

His head began to throb. He suspected the worry and the number of times he had rewritten the message was taking its toll. He should have drunk more water. He always forgot to do that. The pain became more intense. He clutched at the side of his head, which was burning. He knew then that it wasn't a headache. It was something else but what?

He looked at the screen, which began to blur, and reached for the send button. There was another wave of pain and he grabbed his head with both hands. He turned trying to see if he could make out what was happening. There was a shape. He pitched forward, catching his knee on the corner of a chair, and fell to one side. The pain was blinding. The shape moved towards him, the vague outline of something. He couldn't make out who, or what it was. A man? It wasn't big or heavy, it was lean and taut. He tried to push up off the ground, see who it was but he couldn't and he didn't and he never would.

She stood over his body, looking at his hair which was matted around the point where she had burned out his implant's main processor and memory and, in effect, the surrounding tissue of his right lower lobe and part of the amygdala. She reached down and felt for a pulse. It was faint. She was thorough and she broke his neck.

He had been right, she was lean and dangerous. Dressed in black, her long hair tied back, she moved like a predator through a forest. She searched the house. She was unobtrusive, never turning on a light in a room where there wasn't already one lit.

She replaced everything she moved so it was exactly as it had been. It would have taken a real expert to notice the interference. That and a scan, and there were no scans of this house. As she moved through the rooms, she tried to remember the last time she had been anywhere so low-tech. She knew of only one place.

She walked towards his bedroom and stood at the door. Everything had been laid out on the bed ready for him to leave. She scanned the items, retrieved what she needed and returned to the study. She stood over the desk and looked at the screen. The system was old-fashioned and she didn't really understand it. The file hadn't contained any briefing on this kind of tech, though she had expected the house to be like this, the information had been very complete. They didn't think it was information she needed, they liked complete control. She pushed the screen back and looked at it. It was blank. He probably hadn't begun whatever it was he had been doing.

It was time to clean up. Getting him up into that fridge had been the toughest part of the gig. Who knew?

Out on the street, the town was just rubbing the sleep from its eyes and stretching. She had time for a slow breakfast overlooking the harbour before she went for her train. The wind had died down and it was turning out to be a nice day. Her hair was down and she was wearing a pretty summer dress, a young woman enjoying everything life had to offer. In the bag over her shoulder the head shifted about, settling into the space beneath her arm.

*

He had just hit the Paris Web on the shuttle from the Orly-Trans Airport hub when the message came in. The Euro-net ban on commercial traffic on Sunday meant he was getting the message late. That meant he was heading to Paris instead of back to Beijing, knowing he had been stood up. There's nothing like modern transport systems to get you to where you don't want to go, faster than you never wanted to get there.

Average height, his light brown hair curled if he let his hair grow. He never let his hair grow. Broad-shouldered, he carried an air of being able to take care of himself without exuding the menace of a dancehall bouncer or a lounge-bar lout. When he moved he did so without effort, with the ease of one comfortable with his physical abilities. He looked to be in his late thirties, but something about him suggested he was older. His grey eyes were sharp and tended to meet people square on, eye to eye, even when he was actually looking inward at the screen on his contact.

The message lit up his com, part of the neural net implant in his head that could access the other electronic elements in his system. They hadn't yet got the interface right but it was less clunky than it had been in the early days and had a huge memory. The net was an ultrafine filament injected into his head and had grown into his organic system, offering it immediate access to countless electronic services and information. Others in his line of work had similar systems, but the technology hadn't yet caught on with the squeamish general population.

Thinking 'Answer', the message appeared in his lens, straight in front of him. It recognised that he was in a public space and kept the message private, audible only through his ear implant. The image, a friend of his, played through the ocular implant in his less dominant eye. Her American drawl cut through the suppressed background noise,

"Hi, I hope this catches you before you leave. I can't be there this evening. The office buzzed me and . . . something's come up. Nothing big . . . I hope not anyway. I'm in conference for the rest of today, so there isn't much point in you coming here unless you want to be part of the holomeet. I'll call you when I'm done."

It had been planned as a bit of light R 'n' R after the trauma of Brazil. They had never met socially before, only through work. Well, that was, as they say, that.

He looked up at the commercial screen over his seat and it sprang to life with products he had bought, products like ones he had bought, and products recommended by friends that could be bought in Paris. From the outside it was a dull, flat, dark patch on the wall of the carriage, but he hadn't thought 'Off' so the commercial system had kicked in. He hated that. It spooled out a "Breaking News" item, which was hardly "breaking", about the recent US midterms. They had produced a result very favourable for the Americorp group, which would not have been predicted only eight months ago. A week is a long time in politics they say. Eight months is an eternity.

He called up a menu of Parisian bars he might like. As he did so, the commercial screen flickered and turned blank, then suddenly he was looking at a map with the three bars closest to the next station glowing red. He shrugged. Looking around him at the other passengers in the car he could see they were looking at similar screens, or possibly the same screen, except he couldn't see, as no one could, anyone else's page visible only to them. It was an illusion of course, as the 'screens' communicated directly with whatever connection device they were using, but somehow people found it less intrusive to view things outside of themselves. A stranger from an earlier time would have thought they all looked dead.

That was why he was in the bar, that was how he met her. Of course there was a her. There was always going to be a her. There always is.

He leaned into the booth: "Is this seat taken?"

She glanced up. "Why?"

He stopped, surprised at the pushback. "Well, I'd like to use the table screen."

The implant was great, but if privacy wasn't strictly necessary the screen was less tiring.

She looked at him steadily then shrugged. It was that kind of day she thought to herself. "If you have to."

Her voice gave out the hint of an accent, indefinable, but different. She was using the whole screen, monitoring group traffic, crime groups. He ran his finger down the centre of the screen, which covered the whole top of the table, dividing it into two discrete desktops. Her screen shuffled all of its content across to fit and she gave him an irritated look.

He winced. "Sorry."

He dismissed the instant appearance of the "Breaking News" which was same as before, and he flicked to hotels, making a quick reservation from the list of recommendations. Provisional payment was taken automatically from his account. A menu of entertainment showing at the hotel flashed up, but he waved them away. He tapped on holo to see what was on at the cinemas, but he knew he would have seen whatever it was before, Europe being days behind Beijing.

When he looked up, she was watching him. He looked back emotionlessly. She was tall, lithe and smartly dressed, in the type of silk that could be recycled in your home and printed out in the latest designer style, depending on the individual's subscription. The 'silk' was of course just a name, as most fabrics were reconstituted by machine, but the process mimicked the way worms and spiders produced silk, and any base material could be used to achieve a similar effect. Her face was lightly made up, suggesting she had not come out for the whole evening and that perhaps her visit to the bar was unplanned.

He tapped his chest lightly, forcing a smile: "Been stood up."

"I didn't ask," she responded, looking away.

He nodded, doing his best to maintain the conversation. "You like the crimes?"

"No."

"Ah." He looked back down at his screen.

A waiter came across with a drink, his usual. Unless told otherwise, each customer's 'usual' would be brought to them within five minutes of your taking a seat in any establishment. As the drink was placed on the flat table screen it glowed yellow beneath the glass.

"Single malt whisky? You've gone up in my estimation."

He smiled, surprised, and looked down at the glass, "That's nothing. You should be with me when I order wine."

He raised his glass to her first kind words. She double-tapped the screen with her glass and a waiter came over within a few seconds.

Handing her the drink, he said: "You're nearing your blood alcohol driving limit. If you want more, you'll have to sign for it."

She had clearly been there a while.

She rolled her eyes. "Like I'm likely to be driving, and . . . Whatever."

It was one of the world's anomalies. Despite the fact that every car was self-driving there was still a blood alcohol limit. The waiter spoke in French, and, though Milo spoke no French, he understood perfectly. One of the other features of his system was the ease with which it slipped between languages. He couldn't even tell whether she had replied in French or English. There were of course occasional slips, with the occasional embarrassing result.

She lifted her drink and they clinked glasses.

"So why'd you pick my table?"

"It was the easiest."

"That one was nearer the door," she said, pointing with her glass.

"Dead pixels."

"Dead pixels?" She frowned and looked over at the table "How old is that screen?"

He shrugged and she considered the bar anew.

"You could have been alone at that one," she said, picking out another table.

"Not for long. That woman at the bar is just biding her time."

"Still . . ."

"Ok, you looked like a nice sort of person. I don't want anything but to pass a quiet evening when I should have been out having fun with a girl."

She nodded, taking in his words, and sipped her drink. Then she stopped and looked at him. "How would you describe yourself?"

He frowned, confused by her shift in tone. "Why?"

"Humour me. You described me as 'nice'. I want to know who I'm with."

"I don't know . . . A pretty straight kind of guy. Not too bright, but not dumb either, you know . . . Average."

"The kind of guy you could rely on? The kind you could trust?"

"I guess."

He wasn't sure where this was leading, not sure he wanted to go there, not sure he didn't want to go there.

"And I'm a 'nice' kind of girl, am I?"

"I said you looked like a nice person."

"Fair enough." She took another sip weighing up the situation, weighing up his potential. "What would you say if I told you I had a head in my bag?"

Now she had his full attention. But then, she'd always had his full attention.

"I would tell you that I'm part of the China12 crime group and I would tell you not to tell me that."

"The China12, eh? They cracked that south-eastern pirate group, didn't they?"

He nodded.

"So you're not too bright?"

He shrugged "They let me in the back door . . . My boyish charm."

Since the second collapse of the Western banking groups, a number of countries had gone into meltdown, in spite of the best efforts of the international community or possibly because of them. These countries had become failed states. Chief among them was Italy, which had broken apart. Anywhere south of Rome was bandit country, it had gradually engulfed the whole Mediterranean Basin. After the war, Egypt had calmed down North Africa, but southern Europe was still a mess. This made shipping in the Mediterranean dangerous and the China12 had been instrumental in bringing one of the most dangerous pirate cartels to book.

Like all professional businesses that needed thought rather than simple action, the 'China12' was a collaborative company, a mastermind group. In this instance they were detectives, connected through the web, an expansion of the 'open source' movement. Economists, lawyers, even politicians had set themselves up as groups, solving problems collaboratively. Some of the groups had several hundred members, others as few as fifty.

The China12 was a very exclusive group, with few members and a big rep. Its membership was usually as the name implied, but the tough gig in Brazil had changed that. The boffins in the company were still trying to work out whether it was operative impulsiveness or intellectual arrogance that had walked them into a disaster. It was why he had needed the R 'n' R.

'Look, I'm in a bind and I need help," she continued.

He shook his head "This is my night off."

"Good, then what I tell you won't matter."

He sighed and leaned back into his seat. She had looked like such a nice girl.

"It goes back a few years. I'm part of the Meridian group."

"A lawyer! You should know better, carrying heads around!"

"Yeah. I'm also an art collector. I'm passionate about early-to-middle twentieth-century art, one or two artists in particular. I spend most evenings in holo exhibitions and, when work allows, going to see the real thing."

"Why? The holo programs are just as good."

"Do you examine a crime scene in holo?"

"That's different."

"So is art. You can't smell a hologram, you miss things, you can't . . . It's just not the same, all right?"

"All right."

"A friend of mine, a psychology lecturer in Paris, a few years back he messaged me that he had come across a tiny gallery, private, not in the guides or anything. It had a spectacular collection of late Nineteenth, and early Twentieth-century art. I had my train ticket that evening and was with him the next morning."

She stopped.

"And?"

". . . and?"

"Was it any good?"

She sighed. "It was stunning. A private collector, George Dawson, died about thirty-five years ago. He had incredible taste. The gallery was so intimate. We spent hours there and we were completely alone, apart from two old guards. They weren't really guards at all, they had been gardeners when Dawson was alive but they were too old for that by then."

Her mind was back in the gallery that first time, her eyes glowing. Then she came to and was in the bar again, the smile fading.

"We went to a cafe and we were brimming over with what we'd seen. One piece in particular had taken my eye. I minored in art history and my specialist topic focused on a Romanian artist called Brancusi. There was a piece of his in the collection and I was overwhelmed by it."

"Let me guess, a sculpting of a head. It's been on your mind ever since and you went back earlier today and took it. You've been monitoring the crimes ever since to see how close they are to you."

He looked at her and shook his head. "They will get you, you know. The gallery cameras will have you and those pictures will already be on the net. Recog will have your address. More than one of the crimes will have claimed salvage on it by now and a rate agreed. What's it worth?"

"About seventy million dollars."

He was stunned by this and laughed. "You're toast. Are you *sure*? That's a lot of money."

"I'm sure that's at least what it's worth. The last Brancusi to come up on the market was a small sculpture, nothing like as good as this, and it took twenty-seven million dollars. That was forty-two years ago."

He whistled and took a sip.

She looked at him steadily not nearly as worried as she should have been. He was paid to notice things. He should have noticed.

"There's not a lot I can do for you, lady. The crimes will have fed your face to the street net and the system will have picked you out. The solving of any crime is the weaving together of tapestry threads and you've left too many. You should know how this works. They'll be in here any second. In fact I'm surprised . . ."

He looked about him expecting to see people coming in

through the door and then realised that he had already been in there more than long enough. He looked back at her, puzzled. He should have noticed. She smiled gently.

"It's not that simple. I won't bore you with the details, but I acquired the piece, got it back home and it sat on a small stand in my living room. That was . . . a few years ago."

"I would have seen it reported."

"Apparently not."

"That isn't the kind of thing I would miss."

"No, but they don't seem to have reported it missing."

He looked at her and smiled, took a drink. He was sure he knew what had happened. "It's not real."

"It's real."

"Don't feel bad. You wouldn't be the first intelligent, knowledgeable art collector to be taken in."

"I haven't been. It's real."

"It wouldn't be the first gallery in Paris to put good fakes on display . . ."

"It's real."

"Honestly, there are syndicates that do this."

"Honestly, it's real."

"Why wouldn't they report it? They can't collect on it without reporting it."

"That I don't know. It surprised me too. I was terrified for the first year."

"Do they know it's gone?"

"Yeah, they know."

"You're sure?"

"I was there earlier today. The spot where they had it, it has been replaced by a different piece. That's how I know it's real."

"Ah. If it were fake they would have just had another one put there."

She nodded.

Playing with his glass he accidentally ordered another but went along with it. "You should thank your lucky stars. Say nothing, do nothing and go home."

11

"Can't do that."

He looked at her quizzically, knowing that she would tell him.

"When I moved to London, I was living in one of those houses built long enough ago to still be called eco houses."

He nodded "I remember those."

"Three months ago I got a big promotion."

"Congratulations."

"I decided to move to a new place, river view and all that. But the new place has a scanning system."

"Those are great. They save a ton of paperwork and avoid you having to argue with the insurance company."

"Thanks for the pitch, but that was the problem. My stuff was moved and unpacked while I was away. The insurance company, 'in the interests of being sure that I had enough cover', queried the piece."

"Tell them it's a copy."

"I did. They told me its exact provenance, that no authorised copies had been made and that it was still listed in the Dawson collection. The gallery had said nothing."

"And now your insurers want to send an assessor?"

"Bingo!"

"You know this town has a big river, right?"

"I could never do that."

"You're in quite a bind."

Leaning back, he took in what was happening in the bar. The screens on the walls near him were running through a personalised menu of things he might like to do, see or buy and people in town he knew, who he might like to see or buy things for. The screens farther away were showing 'frees', pop song promos and mash-up films made to show off the talent or point of view of the people who had made them and licensed free. His net, set to silent, could pick up the track of whatever he looked at or the bar's muzak, but he was content simply to listen to the gentle burble of voices. He turned back to face her as she examined the almost empty glass in her hand.

"They haven't reported it missing. Why not go back there and just hand it over?"

"I've got too much to lose if they decide to make a fuss now."

"We could just repeat the process you used to steal it."

She shook her head. "They have cameras, scanners and proper guards now. Four of them."

"So we can surmise they did notice their stuff had gone missing."

She nodded.

"Ok, I know what we need to do but you'll have to trust me."

"Why?"

"Because you're going to give the head to me."

"I can't. When the assessor comes round and I don't have the head they scanned, they'll go back to the gallery. At that point, they won't be able to lie."

"They won't have to."

"Would you like to let me know what you're going to do?"

"No. The less you know the better."

"China 12?"

He smiled.

She held out a hand "Julia Church, by the way."

He took her hand "Milo."

She waited for the rest, but he stood up and they left together. Paris has always been a city for people who just hit it off . . .

They went to dinner, nothing too fancy. They enjoyed real food grown in fields that saw the sky, by farmers who made decisions about crops and planting and harvesting, so it was expensive enough to reassure them both. He had an omelette, mushroom and cheese, with a mixed salad, while she had ribeye steak with a side of green beans. When the bill came, each offered to pay, neither was cheap. To prove it, they split the bill.

They shared his hotel room and indulged in an intense night of lovemaking. He was surprised at her need, her passion. The connection was something he had not experienced before, or not for a long time, at least, and it swallowed him whole. Perhaps it was his surprise at meeting her or his driving need to be taken out of himself, away from himself, to lose himself in another person who wasn't China12 and wasn't connected in any way with Brazil.

She slept the sleep of innocence beside him, he thought. She slept heavily, in any case. He was thinking. He couldn't remember his mind being so involved with someone, so consumed, and now he had a headache, dull and throbbing. He could have asked his system to supply a suppressing chemical, but he didn't want that. He had taken too much lately. At least this was real.

That was how he came to be sitting in a small office in a building built long before they had dreamed of calling their houses 'eco' anything. In the courtyard outside, a small fountain played host to the local birds while a cat watched, waiting for a slip. The house was old, even by Paris standards, having been built in the early seventeenth century. The gallery's founder, George Dawson, had been the first person, outside of the family who had built it, to own it and live in it, and he had kept it as only a lover of the beautiful will.

Milo was sitting in silence, evaluating. Opposite was a young woman dressed in a way Parisians and New Yorkers managed and everyone else tried for and didn't. Her jewellery was understated, except for a small silver pin. Art nouveau, a woman's head in profile. A cross on a silver chain lightly ornate and obviously old, dangled from her neck. Striking, full-lipped and dark-haired, she carried herself with the poise of someone used to telling people what she wanted and having them do it.

Ms Dawson forced a smile "You say you have something that might interest me?"

"I do."

She waited, the smallest tilt of her head indicating that she might be curious.

"A few questions first if you don't mind."

She raised her eyebrows. "You're from China12. Is this an investigation?"

"No, but I need to know one or two things. I promise it won't take long."

She moved her head, her chin giving a slight flick that Milo took as proof she was willing to go along with it.

"How long have you been the director here, Ms Dawson?"

"About seven years. Ever since my father died."

"The gallery is owned by a board of trustees?"

"No, I own it, but it's run by the board. I am paid by a trust fund, which the board oversees."

"So the board can replace you?"

"Yes, but only if they can show that I'm unfit to be in charge of the collection. My grandfather wanted this to be an accessible place for travellers and lovers of art to be able to spend a quiet time, simply being in the presence of great art. For that reason, though I own it all, I can't sell it. The board is entrusted with its care and to act as his conscience."

"It's very nice . . . not very well known."

"No, we opt out of the search results. If you want us, you must find us with your eyes and ears." She smiled, happy to appear out of place in a world of electronic nets and databases.

"Is it not hard to keep out of the guide books?"

"We have our allies."

He believed he had judged the situation just right, that he knew the whole story.

"Six years ago you were reasonably fresh in the post?"

"Yes."

"If something had gone wrong, would the board have kicked you out?"

"Well, it depends on what it was. They could only have stopped me being the curator."

"A serious humiliation nevertheless."

"I wouldn't have been happy."

Seventy million dollars! What was the salvage on that? he wondered. He would collect the salvage if he handed the head into the insurance company. Julia would be dumped from her job, but he could pay her off. It would be more than she would normally earn in five years. This heiress would be *unhappy*, but that would be all. He'd be made for life. He would have to leave the group on principle, but that wouldn't matter. There would be no more holo holidays. He could go to the real places, pay the quota fees, buy a bigger carbon allowance.

"Mr . . . um?"

He shook himself back to the job in hand.

"Six years ago, something happened here. Something that would have made you look bad."

She coloured, frowned, but said nothing.

"I don't know, but maybe there was an argument with the board about your old-fashioned security and because you were staying true to your grandfather's ideals. Then something happened. I've been made aware of what happened. Fortunately, I can also put it right."

She looked at him, appearing a little fidgety.

He smiled. "I know where it is." He kept his options open, all seventy million of them.

She was thinking, her face losing a little of its colour, then: "I think . . . you are mistaken."

Unexpected. He gave her a long, steady look. She met it and he could detect a slight rise in body temperature and heartbeat.

He decided to reassure her. "This won't cost you anything, Ms Dawson."

"You're right, because I don't know what you're talking about."

He watched her intently. She was all poise, but he caught a flash of light in her eye as the edge of a tear crept in. A Mexican stand-off. He realised that this was outside of her experience. ('A pretty straight kind of guy. Not too bright, but not dumb either . . .' 'The kind you could trust?')

"This is your lucky day."

"How so?"

He picked up his bag and put it on the table, tore open the Velcro and sat back. He nodded towards the bag.

Leaning forward, she pulled lightly at the edge of the bag and peered inside.

She sat back abruptly. "Mister, um?"

"Milo."

"Mr Milo . . ."

"No, just Milo."

She looked at him, judging him a little. "Mr . . .uh . . . Milo. What do you expect from me?"

He was knocked back, confused. "I thought you'd be . . . pleased?"

She looked hard at the desk in front of her, thinking again, seemingly trying to find a way to put things, wondering if she should speak at all.

"I don't know what she's told you. She should have come herself. I know why . . ." She looked up at him intently, decision made, then hesitated. "Maybe not . . . Tell her . . . I don't have it here. I've moved to . . . the white part of the map . . . Now, I'd like you to take this and leave, please."

He looked at her blankly, whatever he had expected to happen, this had not been on the spectrum. "But it's a Brancusi . . ."

She cut him off. "No, Mr Milo, it isn't. And even if it was, we've never had this in our collection. If you don't leave now, I'll have you thrown out."

"The woman who . . ."

She cut him off again. "Tell her she's . . . not here . . . There's . . . I've gone another way."

She stared at him, willing him out of the room. She seemed to be trying to impart something he couldn't understand. She jabbed at an old-fashioned button on her desk.

"But . . ."

"Goodbye Milo."

The door opened and her assistant stood, waiting. He took the bag and closed it up, silently turning for the door. His head was running through a hundred different possibilities, but first and foremost he was making an enquiry to Beijing, getting background on the woman and cursing himself for not beginning there.

Back on the street, he stood looking at the building, replaying Julia on his neural net. He reviewed her face, her voice, looking for his error, the street address. Had she been lying? If so, why?

Ms Dawson seemed to know everything about it and know nothing about it. He walked away, heading for the lunch date he had made with Julia. Not wanting to, but having to be there now, either with a lump of rock or with millions of dollars' worth of art that no one seemed to want or own.

CHAPTER TWO

Milo didn't expect her to be there as he made his way to the little cafe. No good deed ever goes unpunished, they say . . . Was this a good deed? He wasn't sure. In his head, it had just been a little romantic, chivalrous thing but now it was morphing into a mess.

Getting out of his cab, his account docked as he stepped through the door. He looked down the street to the corner and . . . nothing. He had hoped she might be there, sipping her water, reading the menu, enjoying the sunshine, defying his expectations, but she wasn't. He walked up to the cafe, looking around him.

Something had happened to him. He was sure he had been . . . something . . . But what? The cafe was old-school: food cooked on the spot, waiters with white aprons and a bad attitude, sweet wine and bitter coffee. It was all the things he loved about Paris, all the things he expected. He stared inside, still hoping. What the hell was going on?

He walked up and gestured to the waiter to get him an inside table, which wasn't difficult as few other customers wanted to be inside on a day like this. He sat at a spot just back from the door and away from the bar. One of the guys at the bar had noticed the bag, and Milo had noticed him noticing. He put his back to the bar and the bag on the chair to his right, on the side near the street, with the table between it and Mr Curiosity. There were only two other people at the bar: a woman, nervous, checking and rechecking the time, and a man, nicely dressed, reading a paper and not reading a paper, eyeing up the nervous woman.

He ordered an omelette, mushroom and ham, with garlic. He was running through what he found out from Beijing, which was exactly in line with what Julia told him, to a disturbing degree. He sat staring out at the street, at people passing, and he realised what most shocked him was that he had got it, got *her*, so wrong.

The waiter brought bread and water. Milo thanked him and returned to his internal search. He read, listened to the reports, went over the record from last night. It reminded him of his headache, so strongly, in fact, that he got it again. Not as badly, but still. He was rubbing his temples when the waiter slammed open the kitchen door. Milo jumped and his head throbbed.

Lunch arrived. He ordered a beer from the waiter and took a long drink of water, then glared at the glass as though he had expected it to be the beer. He sat, balefully eyeing the bag in front of him. Silence. Finally he asked himself, "What do I do now?" He could just shrug, pay the bill, know he was still a good guy and walk away, but he was never going to do that. Call it chivalry, call it professional pride, call it whatever you like, it irritated him that the world had refused to conform to what he thought was its proper course. He wasn't going to walk away until either it did or it gave him a pretty good explanation for why it was behaving the way it was.

Just then, two things happened at once. The waiter arrived with the beer and Milo, jarred out of his thoughts, turned to see who it was. Instead, he saw the man from the bar dive for the bag, snagging one of the handles and making a dash for the open front of the restaurant.

Milo was a careful man. He never just sat with luggage of any kind in a position where it could be snatched, so the shoulder strap was wrapped loosely round his ankle, though the thief would have been unable to see this. As a result, the attempt to take the bag meant Milo was coming along for the ride. He was pulled forward and smashed into the table. The bag swung out, knocking over a couple of chairs. Milo's leg was thrown into the air and he followed the momentum toward the would-be millionaire. His foot slamming to the ground allowed him to bring his fist crashing down onto the man's hand.

The crunch as the hand was caught between Milo's fist and the elevated chair back was followed by a grunt from the man. That and a surprised look was all the encouragement Milo needed. His other fist swung at the man's head. Ducking and heading for the door, the bag snatcher was saved by the growing mass of tables and upturned chairs between him and Milo and he was gone. Without the bag.

It happened so fast that the pair beside him were still turning from the now-empty bar, their mouths open. They looked down at the nicely distributed meal on the floor in front of them. Jolting into action, the waiter started to apologise. He insisted that the lunch was on the house and that he would bring Milo a new meal if he would wait.

Milo started to untangle himself from the table, the chairs and the bag. Lifting the bag onto his shoulder, he turned to the waiter, "Thank you, I know it wasn't your fault. I'll have to go."

He aimed for the door, scanning the sidewalk and street for the next threat. Happy everything was clear, he made a sharp left, then left again down the next street, checking behind and ahead to see if he was being physically followed. He was, of course, being followed in any number of other ways.

Standing to one side, he called Beijing. "This just happened".

They watched the playback he sent them. "You're being followed."

"I thought so too, I'm going off-grid. If I am being tracked, I'm pretty certain we're right."

"Do you think they have Ms Church?"

He shrugged. "I'm the one who broke cover in the gallery. They may be onto her, but maybe not."

"They?"

"Whoever is so damn keen to own and not own this head"

"Why not a common thief?"

"He was too well dressed, and too poor a thief"

"Oh."

"Find me somewhere discreet to take a breath while we go over this, would you?"

An hour later, sitting in his hotel room with a new lunch in front of him, idly shovelling down the occasional mouthful, Milo looked out of the window, trying to figure out what was going on. The hotel was in a back street in the north of Paris, near the Gare du Nord. The kind of place that used to be ubiquitous in the city but had mostly been replaced by those identikit automated jobs, no people running them and no character at all. The rooms here were low-end, but they were clean and the linen was changed daily. There wasn't even a printer for cups or any of the small extras preprogrammed in, like buttons and spoons.

'The Room' in Beijing was busy looking for answers. The Room was the name given to the virtual round table of the China12. Milo had reviewed the footage of the street outside the gallery and the cafe. He had seen the would-be thief arrive just as he was making up his mind to sit down. Then later he had watched him run away. He had also seen the gallery director leave the gallery in a hurry about ten minutes after he had left, but she had gone off-grid after that. She was clearly no ordinary gallery owner.

He had exhausted all his options for the moment and was waiting for The Room to come back to him. As he was off-grid, they had to use secure channels, but that wasn't unusual for Milo. Still, they were taking their sweet time getting back to him with anything concrete.

The advent of 'face recog' systems earlier in the century had been a boon for the statutory authorities hunting criminals and terrorists, but, like all systems, it had only been useful for so long. By that time, however, police forces and intelligence agencies had grown to depend on it. The evolution of better cameras and better algorithms had put them back on track, but again the bad guys adapted. Computing power had come to the rescue. By knowing where everyone else was, the system had been able to develop filters that allowed it to find those who were hiding or using other means to obscure their features. After that, probability narrowed the search down to find particular targets. Since policing had changed to be about enforcement rather than detection, the latter becoming a commercial venture, the sophistication had jumped and it had become almost impossible to hide. Almost.

The China12 needed, at times, to be very discreet. They got round the possibility of being found or followed by supplying the system with more, not less, information, all of it false and confusing. Then whoever was looking would actually find out less. Even if they could filter it, the China 12 operative would be gone by the time they did. The opportunity this opened up for criminality was catered for in the protocols surrounding the crime group system. If necessary, the group's anonymity could be lifted and their records seized by an investigating group.

Beijing came back online. Dr Zhang Xin, a gifted statistician and analyst, was chair of The Room, and the 'first speaker'. Most but not all of the non-operatives, were in Beijing, as it was convenient to use the staggered clock to their advantage.

Milo got straight to the point: "Who are they? It's beginning to look like a conspiracy theory sort of gig."

"We don't know yet," she replied. "Whoever it is, they have high-level access. They probably tagged Julia from her insurance scan, and face recog will have picked her out with you. Some gangs have regular little deals with the insurance groups, or with the recog system . . . They must be very well connected, but it's not unheard of."

"So the chances are they won't take too long to trace back and run me to ground here?"

Xin nodded.

"So why did the gallery owner deny she knew about the Brancusi? Is it real? Obviously, the snatch in the cafe was connected."

"It *was* connected. As you saw, they were watching the gallery, though we believe they were at first looking out for Ms Church. That doesn't mean the gallery owner, Ms Dawson, had anything to do with it . . . unless . . ."

"Unless she did?"

"We've checked her out and she had no reason to be. She's financially secure. *Very* financially secure."

"Blackmail?"

"We would suggest not. The chances are only about thirteen percent. But . . . blackmail . . . perhaps."

"You think she knew they were out there?"

"She knew something . . . She's clearly connected. But then why not just say 'Thank you' and then place it back in storage as though it never went missing?"

"I'm China12, not a witness you can just blow off".

"You had offered her reassurance on that front. There's no point in going back to the gallery now. She's the only person who would know anything about it."

Milo agreed and went over what he knew. Ms Dawson going off-grid like that suggested she was well connected, and either she was *in* trouble or she *was* trouble. But what trouble? How could the return of a piece stolen years earlier be trouble?

Milo turned round to Xin, "We're looking for the threads and at the moment we have just about nothing and everything. There are too many threads and none of them from the same cloth. How long before you'll be able to run down her likely location?"

"One of her previous addresses is showing up as unoccupied. Also it's off-grid. She may not be going there, but it's a lead. There's a thirty-eight percent chance that she's there or has just been there. I'm sending it to you now."

"Thirty-eight percent? So, I shouldn't bet my house on it?"

"Given the near certainty of being found here if you stay, and the absolute certainty of not finding her if you don't try, I think you could do worse . . . Saying that, I think you may have company."

Milo walked to the window and looked out. The narrow side street was quiet apart from two men in a nondescript Samsung E47sd, who had rolled up to the pavement and stopped. They were not so well dressed as the mugger in the cafe and their faces showed signs of wear and tear. A brief conversation, then one of them got out and walked back to the cafe on the corner, his green jacket flapping in the wind. The second dragged out an old game pad and began to amuse himself, keeping the door of the

24

hotel in camera. The image formed a window-in-window so that his motion detector would flash up any activity.

Milo could just make out the screen from the street cameras. These were no high-end thugs, they had little internal bio-tech.

A few minutes later, Milo walked through the quiet reception area, populated only by the desk clerk, who was taken up with his latest comic-vid, staring into the middle distance in a way that would have caused previous generations to shiver. Milo didn't even notice. Slowing down as he got to the door, Milo's own eyes drifted to the middle distance as he looked at the internal images supplied by his system. He watched as the men in the car shared out coffee and buns from the bakery on the corner. He knew their presence might be entirely innocent, two ugly-looking men in a quiet car sharing a strictly non-romantic coffee in the middle of the day on a quiet street in Paris. But he was willing to bet it wasn't. If it wasn't, it meant their bosses were well-resourced to have traced him so quickly.

He scanned the room and spotted the entrance to the kitchens. If he was very lucky or wrong, they weren't following him, they were just what they wanted to be seen as and wouldn't have someone out the back. That way he could use the old alley to get to the main street. He shrugged. They could be lazy, not expecting their mark to be aware he was being followed, or able to spot who they were if he did think of it. Maybe he had caught them on the hop.

"Lot of 'ifs' in that, but I don't have many options" he muttered to himself.

Milo headed for the back door. The clerk didn't look up from his show for an instant. He walked along the passage to the kitchens confidently but was ready for an assailant to jump out at any second. The kitchens were dark, mid-afternoon, just a few commis chefs and some cleaners preparing for the evening. The smell was typical of kitchens across the centuries, all steel surfaces and scrubbed tiles.

Milo was self-assured so even when they looked up the staff assumed that he was supposed to be there. The back door was open, jammed that way against the automatic spring by a box.

Milo stopped, his eyes going into the now-familiar middle distance. "Shit." No working camera. He shook his head and edged out. No one in sight. He walked smartly along the back of the hotel, by the edge and into the alley that ran away from the staff entrance and allowed for deliveries and rubbish collections. The smell there was not so savoury.

He reached the edge of the alley and stopped to talk to The Room. "Ok, silent protocol, I'll contact you from the apartment."

The covert link to Beijing was broken and Milo was on his own. He walked out into the street. If he could avoid line-of-sight contact with anybody for a few minutes, he should have bought himself some breathing space by the time he got to the Metro.

Down the crowded street. Milo stepped lightly, weaving between the shoppers. His body relaxed, his movements calibrated to those around him, not faster than them, not slower. He didn't look back. He paid attention to the odd item in the shop windows, using the street furniture to mask him in as natural a way as possible. It gave him a sense of being back thirty years, when he couldn't simply access the public surveillance system to watch the street around him. Being 'off' made him invisible to technology, but it also made him blind.

The Metro. Plunging down the steps, he passed the cameras. The itch in his back made him long to access their gaze to check behind him. Through the barrier and down towards the platforms. Once there and waiting, he could look around. If they hadn't followed him in, and it looked like they hadn't, he'd got his opening. Time to find Ms Dawson and see if he couldn't get to the bottom of this.

CHAPTER THREE

He emerged from the Metro at Port-Royal and walked up towards the Luxembourg Gardens, turning off the main drag into the side streets of the continuingly smart 5th. The streets still bore the unmistakable imprint of the Hausmann makeover, supposed to make Paris less likely to be the centre of revolution, though the 'Commune' had put paid to that idea within thirty years.

Prosperity was what stopped the common folk rioting. Food on plates and roofs over heads and people just want to get on getting on with life. Not that this part of town had ever seen or was ever likely to see much rioting. The people who could afford to live round the 5th had very full plates and their roofs cost a pretty penny. As for the rest, when the rich had finally been persuaded the only way they were going to keep their heads and lifestyles was a minimum 'basic wage', they had given in with bad grace and then gone on to work out how the change could increase their profits.

Milo was running through the intel fed to him on the property before he left the hotel. No images of the inside of the place, no surprise there, but Ms Dawson wasn't listed as the owner. In fact they couldn't find a listing for the owner, just a management company, 'Three Heads, Inc.'.

Turning this way and that, he came to the Rue de l'Abbé-de-l'Épée, at Saint-Jacques-du-Haut-Pas and went down looking for number 2-6. The building was smart, discreet and secure with an old wood door and very modern locks. Of course, given that it was China12 who had come knocking, they would have been better off with the less modern, a solid, medieval, thirty-centimetre-key-requiring lock would have stopped him dead in his tracks. As it was, Milo examined the entry system and took out what appeared to be a short pen. Pointing it at the door, he stabbed a button on one side several times and the door opened. It was an arrangement with the manufacturer in that nice grey area somewhere between legal and illegal.

The lobby was discreetly fashionable and painted in a way that said 'money', even though it was flat white. He walked swiftly through the lobby and round to the stairwell, ignoring the rather beautiful lift. He clambered up the stairs, which were still the original marble and stone flooring worn by thousands of cleaners and those few who were afraid of lifts. It had the air of a place not used in many years, but it was still clean.

He stepped out into a corridor that made the silent, empty stairwell seem noisy. Not that he'd expected an empty corridor to be anything other than quiet, but this place seemed to suck the noise out of the air. It made him want to whisper not that he was planning any speeches just then. It was the kind of place the rich have to intimidate the less rich into believing themselves less powerful.

Milo remained untouched. The atmosphere just seemed to roll off him. He walked smartly to a door about twenty metres to the right and to the back of the building. The door, heavy, blank, white, brass numbers, 18. He rang. Nothing. Knocked. Nothing. He rang again, then smiled tightly. Taking out his pen, he jabbed it again and the door popped open.

He pressed on it gently and looked inside. The hallway was large and quiet. A raincoat and a pair of shoes were on an old stand beside a full-length mirror. Milo checked as far as he could without walking in, running his eye over the ceilings and corners. No cameras, not to normal eye-sight, but there wouldn't be. He didn't look with his eyes alone, but even his scanner picked up nothing. The walls were lined with some expensive-looking paintings right to the room at the end from which light flooded through the door. Pushing the hall door open wide, Milo surveyed the rest of the hall, two more doors, both closed and a corridor that ran away to the left and then turned. The place was huge.

Milo breathed a slight laugh: what else would the rich spend their money on?

He moved into the hall and, again scanned the ceiling and the corners. This time the whole hall, including the floor.

He shrugged. "No security, just like the gallery used to be."

He eased the door closed behind him and put the bag with the head by the door. He breathed in the place, picked a side, and walked down to the open door. He entered a large lounge, again he scanned. A single window, floor to ceiling, running along one side opened onto internal gardens, clearly shared by the complex's occupants. A comfortable and worn couch, an occasional table and a small and very old harpsichord.

Milo walked to the window and took in the view, trying to measure the events he had just gone through, against people who could own a place like this. He crossed the room and began to go through the items on the antique sideboard. He was thorough, yet seemed to disturb nothing. He noted their record collection. He hadn't seen many of those in the last ten years. They had every kind of recorded music ever developed, and the means to play it. A turntable and more modern amplifier below it, a gramophone and a pianola roll, an old CD player and a couple of digital systems, though no cloud player and no wi-fi connection were apparent. Even the screen in the corner was a modest 180cm, and not new either.

He picked through the apartment and it was the same story all over. The kitchen was clearly used by people who liked their food, but there was no food, though plenty of wine. The equipment was from a bygone age, even her recipe books were classics and they were actual books. In fact, there were books everywhere, many leather-bound, many, on close inspection, first editions. Eighteenth-century first editions.

There was also a large collection of science fiction works, again first editions. HG Wells, Aldous Huxley, Jules Verne, Edgar Rice Burroughs, Philip K Dick, Robert Heinlein,

29

Moorcock, Clarke, Hamilton and Asimov and more. There were sections on philosophy, in particular Hume, Reid and Chomsky, and theology, at least one very early printed Bible and editions of the Koran, the Bhagavad Gita separately, the Mahabharata in several volumes, bound Chinese copies of the works of Confucius and on and on. Not complete, but pretty interesting for a woman who ran an art gallery.

Despite all the opulence, the place also didn't look lived-in. It felt just like the gallery. Sure there were some clothes in the drawers and the wardrobes, but not many and they were for both genders. He already knew this was a bolthole of some sort for Dawson, but who else was it for? A lover? A friend? And if it was for more than one person, how come no one appeared to come here very often? The questions piled up, the more rooms he went into, the less sense it made. Were these part of the tapestry he was trying to piece together, or just random passing images?

Finally back in the hall, using the building wi-fi, Milo called The Room. The connection was poor. In spite of the late hour in Beijing, Xin was waiting. The connection downloaded Milo's scans of the artwork on the walls and the first editions. As the estimated prices came up, it was clear that Ms Dawson wouldn't need financial support any time soon.

Xin turned to him "These are only estimates based on our own figures. A more accurate scan would light the place up and bring your friends calling. I'd say we're certainly into the millions anyway, hundreds of millions, I'd guess."

Milo was unsurprised "And no alarms, no cameras. The lock company will know I've been in, but that's about it. All this money on the walls and more in the gallery . . . Why'd she have such a fit when I tried to return one piece?"

"Maybe she's become allergic."

To her horror, Milo seemed to consider it.

"That was a joke," she said.

He gave a tight smile. "Was she afraid it was some sort of scam? *Was* it some sort of scam?"

Xin's head leant to one side, "Scam?"

"Sorry, a trick, an old-fashioned word for a confidence trick."

Milo's eyes narrowed. "What was all the babble about telling Julia Church things? And another thing, if these criminals have been watching Dawson, why haven't they raided this place?"

Xin considered this. "Even if it's not secured, I'd imagine it has been insurance scanned. The head may be a commissioned theft, someone rich, with no intention of selling or displaying it."

"I didn't think people did that any more."

"Some things never go out of fashion. I imagine wanting things that don't belong to you will be around for a while."

He looked at her and jerked his head in agreement. "It's still surprising that no one's paid them a visit."

"It's very down and low. You'd have to know what was here and where it was before you came knocking."

He looked round the hall as if sizing up the place, "I'm going to use this as a base."

"What if Dawson comes back?"

"Then I'll get to find out what's going on, but like you said this place is on the down-low."

Milo shifted his position, trying to increase the signal strength without opening the door. "So, what else have we found out?"

Several other members of the China12 appeared. Dr Himura Hoshika, an expert in probability, Dr Wolfgang Schultz, a forensic archaeologist, and Ms Koura Arippe, a designer and ergonomist.

This being closest to her field, Ms. Koura took the lead. "What we know so far is that the head was acquired by Dawson Senior, in 1953, directly from the artist. While unique, it is one of several similar heads done by him in different sizes and with slight variations. Ms Church's assessment of its value was approximately correct. Stealing it however, even to keep it in a dark basement, would be risky, as the provenance is undoubted and the slightest sniff on a scanner would throw up some difficult questions, as Ms Church has found out."

Milo moved uneasily and leaned in, "Except that the gallery has denied ever owning it and run away from having it back . . ."

Dr Himura nodded, "Ms Dawson does appear to have done so, yes. We have examined why . . ."

"She seemed frightened by something," he said. "There was something else going on."

"Yes, we picked up on that, but it seemed to us that she wasn't frightened by the immediate circumstance, but rather what it represented."

"You mean it was the something else, not my powerful physique and dominant character that scared her?"

"Yes, we would agree with that assessment." This was said without any humour, and with no sense that Ms Koura thought Milo might be joking.

He smiled to himself.

"Her leaving shortly after you and going off-grid suggested to us that she was afraid of something or someone else."

Milo frowned. "Given her resources and connections, who could possibly . . .?"

"We ran the numbers on that and the results were inconclusive."

"Government, corporate or gang . . ."

Himura nodded "In that order, though all low probabilities. They all came out based, not on the art work, but on whom she could possibly fear. Why any of them would want such a piece did not become apparent."

Milo paced, the images flickered and he pushed back against the outer wall again "So far, so unhelpful."

"I regret we clearly lack data," said Dr Himura.

Dr Schultz spoke up. A tall, spare, rather intense man, he looked like what he was, an archaeologist. "One newish thing you should know is that we've observed reports that her apartment in London, Ms Church's that is, has been broken into."

"Have you told her?"

"If she is where her co-ordinates say she is, she'll get a standard notification, and a report from us with some extra background," Xin interjected.

"Is she in danger?"

"The criminals don't appear to have taken anything, so we presume they were searching for the head. If they believe she has it, there is an eighty-three point three-six percent probability that she is. If they realise that she does not, it falls to about two point eight percent probability"

"Should we, perhaps, let it slip that she doesn't have the thing?"

"We agree, though it puts you in an exposed position."

He smiled. "I think I'm comfortable with that."

"At present, those pursuing the head do not appear to be violent."

"At present . . . That still leaves us nowhere with regard to why any of them want this, or who it is that's chasing me."

"That is correct."

"Why would anyone want to have it or, as in the case of Ms Dawson, not want to?"

"If this was a normal situation we would, of course, point to financial reward as the prime motive, and indeed this still figures as fifty-six percent probable. High, but not very high," said Xin.

"So is there something else about it?"

"Looking at the insurance scan from Ms Church's apartment, it appears to be normal. The head is solid limestone, made in about 1910. Brancusi seems to have liked it, as he only sold it to Dawson in the early fifties, shortly before his death. Dawson, it would appear, was a frequent visitor to the artist's home around that period. They shared a certain mystical spirituality."

Milo felt they were getting nowhere fast. He was running through the bits and pieces they had, but none of it made sense. "Is there any political angle on this? How about his East European roots? Julia said he was Bulgarian?"

Ms Koura spoke again. "Romanian. We can go there, but it would seem tenuous at best. There's no chatter, either pan-Slavic or nationalist. Whoever these people are they seem to have been waiting for this to turn up."

Milo tutted irritably. "Best look anyway. Hold on. This 'spiritual bond' Dawson and Brancusi had, could this be religious?

You said they were 'waiting for it to turn up'. Is this just a work of art or something completely different?"

Silence at the other end as the four looked at their screens, checking data, religious theories and history. Finally, Dr Schultz, "It could be."

Xin frowned. "It doesn't make any sense. It's definitely an objet d'art, created by Brancusi."

Milo interjected. "You're expecting sense from any of the people who have been dogging us, and now you're expecting it from religious people?"

Schultz chipped in. "It fits with millenarian movements. They may believe it to be 'inspired by God' or a harbinger of something or other."

Milo knew they had a thread of something. Belief, blind and often senseless, would tie in with most angles, even with Ms Dawson's desire not to be associated with the thing. "Ok, without ignoring other angles, let's work this one, see how far we get."

They signed off and he was alone.

He pushed himself off the wall and paced the room. This was annoying and beginning to be time-consuming. He hadn't heard from Anna, his friend who had stood him up, though, with his being off, he couldn't really have expected to. He wasn't sure which annoyed him more, that he hadn't heard or that, with all the running around, he hadn't noticed.

His com lit up. Dr Lopez-Real.

"Yes?" His impatience showed.

A pause, as she gauged his response, which was difficult with the reduced signal. Of all of those in China12, he had known Dr Lopez-Real, a forensic pathologist and biochemist, the longest and was closest to her. In the early days she had backed him up, made sure the brainiacs didn't lose the run of themselves.

He sighed to himself. "Sorry. What can I do?"

"Is everything ok?"

"Yeah, just getting a little frustrated with this"

"I was really calling about that. There doesn't need to be a 'this'."

"In principle, I know that, but with what little we know, I wouldn't want just to abandon it. These people are too desperate to get hold of the thing. That can't be healthy, especially when its proper owners are so desperate not to own it. They could just hand it over or have me do it."

"Ok, that's fine. I just wanted to be sure you remembered we could simply walk away from this one. No one even knows we're working on it."

"How long would that last?"

"We can make it last as long as you like."

"The road to hell, my dear, is paved with *hidden* intentions."

She broke the connection with a smile, he liked that they didn't need more. Milo sometimes wondered why there hadn't been a more, but there hadn't and they were both comfortable with that.

The silence of the room dived in on him. Outside the huge windows, the world played out like a silent movie, kids running and screaming in the park, the trains in the distance, the traffic's rumble, all absent from the cocoon provided by the room. He could remember back when traffic was very noisy and trains really rumbled. The fact that this kind of noise had ceased, making rooms like this possible, did not make its silence less unnerving.

He looked for an ambience track. The room controls hadn't connected automatically with his net which was odd. The panel laid in between the door and the first bookcase was a bit 'olde worlde', a bit 'iPad', but it lit up at his touch, and he ran through the usual options, temperature, humidity . . . There: AIS, ambient image and sound.

The selections offered were unusually broad and particular, everything from birdsong, 'South Ireland' to New York, '2023, spring', even, Skagen, 'the sea', whatever that was. There was music too, Gregorian chant and Bach cantatas, but he wasn't in the mood for so much God. He picked 'mountains, Tibet', and the volume level. At his touch, the walls had transformed, there was a live feed from a Tibetan mountainside. So there *was* some connection to the world, probably hardwired and through the building's system. The view was limitless and bright. It was early morning in Tibet and the ceiling was a little cloudy, but it was going to be a nice day.

The effect was familiar to Milo, but it was nonetheless impressive and he shivered slightly at the cold conveyed by the image. The paint, laced with nanoparticles that picked up the signal from the system, could be anything from the current panorama to the sedate eighteenth-century wallpaper that had been there before. This was the best paint on the market. Well, it would be. The effect was odd, slightly vertiginous at first, but it was a more familiar sound and settled his nerves.

He stood still, just breathing for a short while then he said "Food" out loud. He knew he couldn't order electronically, as that would light up his presence or, at very least, the presence of someone in the apartment, so he would go on foot. He wondered yet again at the fact it was easier to cover his physical tracks than his electronic ones, and the way it might have seemed to people in his youth. He checked the time. 18.51.

"What was happening in Paris in 1851?" he wondered. Coup d'état, not a great omen. He took the head out of the bag. They looked at each other and he considered what to do with it. He didn't want another 'incident' like the one that morning. He went down to the bedroom, rummaged through the wardrobes, found a coat with outsized pockets and dropped it in. Risk a shower first? He wouldn't be gone for long, anyway. He walked to the door, switched his clothing to a warmer setting, then left.

For a while, about twenty years earlier, he had lived in Paris and he knew of a small Turkish place, just off the main drag. He wondered if it was still there, and the thought brought on a pang for the stuffed vine leaves and lamb meatballs they had served. Traffic was light and the noise of the delivery drones overhead was the loudest sound.

People were out after work, browsing the food emporia and service joints along Boulevard St-Michel. So few actual goods were sold through physical shops that they had all but disappeared, leaving 'display' shops, where you could see and touch the more expensive type of handmade merchandise, always assuming you had a lot of money and the desire for something bespoke. There was another end of the market of course, an actual market with stalls and displayed merchandise and bustle, but not in this part of Paris. Milo imagined it must have been like this in the ancient world and that, for all it had seemed like normality, the era of the big high street shop had actually been the anomaly.

The sound of an enforcement drone, its heavy motor breaking in on the light buzz of the commercial traffic, Milo barely noticed. Up ahead he had seen a familiar sign and he felt a sense of pleasure at realising that some things change only slowly. He hoped that he was like that.

The restaurant was half full in the early evening, clearly as popular as ever. Good job he had felt hungry early or they might not have had room. He took a table in the corner. From there, he could see the old place unfold in the way he remembered it had.

A waiter came across and offered a menu. Milo appraised him, wondering what age he would have been when Milo had visited last, thinking about how much had changed in his view of life since then. That was before and just about everything was different for him now.

He ordered a meze and a glass of Retsina. He also asked for some garlic-stuffed olives immediately. He wasn't seeing anyone he wanted to impress or feel close to. The clientele was young and hip and before his meal arrived, there was a short queue at the door. This was the kind of meal Milo liked, no large main dishes but food that left you satisfied and was assembled in a way that left you thinking you'd done at least some of the work.

Milo might have been born in the north of Europe, but his heart was in that band across the world following the ancient trade routes, from Seoul through China and Persia to the Mediterranean. Merchants, he decided, knew what it was that made up the elements of good living. He was just letting the warmth of the room and the meal wash over him, cleansing the frustrations of the day from him, when the day bit back. His com fired up, China12 broke into his 'off' status, an official communication.

"Yes?"

Xin. "Hi. Sorry about this, something's come up."

"I presumed it had."

"You were in Paris to see . . .?"

"Anna, from the law firm we dealt with in Brazil."

"Yes. They have just asked us to investigate the suspected murder of someone from the firm in London."

"What does the official posting say?"

"That's just it, there *is* no official posting. This is an unofficial priority commission."

Milo considered this. Commissions like this were rare and could get messy.

He looked at Xin. "You think we should take it?"

"Yes."

"Why?"

"There is a certain congruity with the events of the last twelve hours."

"As in?"

"As in, the commission coming from the company whose staff member you were going to meet."

He turned his head to one side, his eyes running over the crowd, watching them eating, enjoying an intimate moment, realising he was on the outside.

"I'll go right away. I'll be a couple of hours."

"Sure, they'll meet you in the station in London."

She snapped off the com, he called for the bill and for remains of the meal to be wrapped. Obviously the gods didn't want him to have that baklava and sweet coffee. This day was never going to end.

He walked out smartly and began to think of what he might do with the head. In the old days, he could have left it in the lock-up at any of the main stations, but passive scanning had put paid to that after the bombing in Berlin. Mostly he agreed, but today it was a pain in the . . . The apartment? It might be found and targeted by the people oh so anxious to find the head . . . Except that they would know now he still had it, but wouldn't know he had been to the apartment yet. How long would that last? Depended on how good they were. They seemed good, but not amazing, which might mean a several days. He had few options in any case.

He quickened his step. What the hell was going on? Xin said the victim was someone at Anna's firm. Why? Was this connected to Brazil? The fuzz of not knowing was depressingly familiar. Was the Brazil mess going to come to Europe? There was always that religious connection to consider . . . The enforcement agencies knew, of course, that their traffic was monitored, so any time they wanted to keep things to themselves it was dropped out of official coms, but why would this one not be on the boards yet if it even sniffed of murder? A sudden realisation now, he was back on grid. He stopped. He couldn't go back to the apartment. The head would have to look after itself.

He used his link to bring a taxi over to the curb and climbed in. "Gare du Nord" he told it, and it slid away.

Where was Anna? Xin hadn't said Anna, just someone from the firm. He quickly tried her number but it bounced him to messaging. Milo had an uncomfortable feeling and he didn't like uncomfortable feelings.

CHAPTER FOUR

Gare du Nord was still resplendent in its nineteenth-century glory, having just received one of its periodic polishes. As a bonus, since the end of the last century, the train he was going to catch went to an equally great station. Milo loved trains and train stations in a way that he never would airports. He wasn't sure if it was the proximity to the vehicles or the intimacy of the place, but he had always found airports more impersonal, more lonely. He had grown up in an age when trains appeared to be dying out and then suddenly they weren't. To him, they held on to the last of the romance of travel, without spending a fortune on a synthetic version of 'the good old days'.

Milo was well and truly 'on' now. The public web that allowed him high-band contact with The Room was too traceable to be anything else. England and France might have sorted out their political differences, but the unstable political situation that had come with the early twenty-first century had thrown up strengthened borders, creating pinch points that made tracing people easy. He had approached the station via a contoured route to make tracing his point of origin difficult.

He entered the station and bought his ticket, first class for a change. It wasn't his usual style but Milo thought it would make anyone following easier to spot. Anyway, if they wanted to follow him he may as well make them pay for the privilege. It also allowed him the luxury of a good coffee and that dessert, though he knew it wouldn't live up to prospective one he'd missed. "Untasted delights are sweeter still", as a friend of his had been in the habit of saying.

The journey would have nothing but darkness to offer through the windows and this seemed to be reflected in his review of the facts. No matter which way he turned it, it made no sense, unless it was something religious. That would be weird, but at least it would tie into its own sense of logic. On the other hand, it could simply be the Brazil hangover which he couldn't shake. Like the headache he had had all day, which seemed to get worse when he travelled.

He picked through the news but saw nothing there – not that he had been expecting anything – and The Room were as quiet as . . . He had to resist calling them. He knew he would know as soon as they did if anything turned up. He pressed himself back into his seat, angled himself outward, set his personal zone alarm and closed his eyes.

An announcement woke Milo as the train approached London. It broke in over the ghostly sound of plainchant – he'd always liked Hildegard of Bingen – that was still going at the quiet level he had set before he went to sleep. Opposite him, but across the gangway, a young woman was now seated. She looked up as he stirred and smiled. He smiled back and felt better about himself. He took a long drink of water from one of the complimentary bottles on the table and liberated a biscuit from its packet.

The train hissed to a stop without a jerk. Though manned, it was almost certainly automatically controlled and that made for a much smoother journey. The doors opened and people filed out, many into the arms of people waiting for them, some rushed away to a busy appointment, or simply to get home. That was something else he liked about train stations, the immediacy of the experience.

And there was Anna. Whatever had happened, she clearly wasn't the missing colleague. She was standing, anxiously scanning the faces, and when their eyes met she seemed relieved rather than pleased. Medium height, smartly dressed, her hair cut to a short bob, her face stressed and tired. Things were obviously less than optimal.

They hugged, Anna holding Milo a little more tightly than he would have expected, and when they broke apart her eyes were red-rimmed.

He looked at her quizzically. "Not sleeping?"

"It's late."

"Not in Beijing."

"If only I were there."

"Why do you think it's murder?"

"You'll see."

"Who is it?"

"You don't know her. She wasn't part of the company when we employed you in Brazil ... We don't really know what to make of it."

"At your offices?"

"No. Come on, you'll see."

They headed out into the street, where the air was thick with the hum of drones. Unlike Paris, London had at first allowed unregulated drone traffic, including taxi drones, fulfilling science fiction's long-awaited 'flying car' prophecy. The processor and guidance chips were very good and the scanners and mapping software, excellent. What they hadn't counted on was the noise. Singly they were quiet enough, but the swarms of them that quickly appeared had been overwhelming. They had since limited their hours over most of the city and set a floor altitude.

King's Cross, however, was in a main exchange depot and they could barely think, much less hear themselves think. Thankfully, the soundproofing in the automatic taxi brought peace. Anna told the system the address and off they went. Heading down to the river, they were going to one of the more sought-after city locations, with access to the new marinas and bans on drone traffic, which made for a quiet life. Even amidst economic turmoil and the breaking up of the European Union, parts of London had prospered.

"We've commissioned you to rep us on this, by the way."

"I was told. It hasn't gone out to the public groups."

"No."

"Do you want to talk to me about it?"

"I'd rather you saw what the situation is first and then go through the last day or two. It really is the damnedest thing."

"You said she was new."

"Yeah . . ."

"What . . .?"

"I don't know, I only have the strangest message and . . . I don't know . . . I haven't been to the apartment yet."

Traffic was light at that time of the morning and they were soon outside, looking up at the early nineteenth-century warehouse exterior, the cast-iron lintels and pillars round the windows dripping from the moisture in the air and glistening in the sharp LED streetlight, an ambulance and a police car at the door, and, just a little way off, the staff of a forensic lab, who, like Milo and China12, were freelance.

He flashed his ID and wrist-chip at the cop, who passed it through to his superior upstairs. As the ok came down, Milo got a message from base.

"Bad news."

He was surprised. What were they doing?

He was about to read it when the forensic team met them at the door and they dragged on protective clothes and those funny little hats and walked through the vacuum portal, feet being sucked to the floor, making it awkward to walk. He made for the lift, but the cop held the main door open again and led them away, round the side of the building, on the forensics' pathway.

As they rounded the corner, the empty calm of the front of the building disappeared. Forensics were gathering material and taking photos. On the far side of the scene there were two patrol cars and a perimeter had been set up, with a couple of cops on either side. The laser line glowed dimly in the darkness. It was too late at night, too early in the morning for there to be any people around – not that there would have been in this neighbourhood anyway – but one or two peeped through their windows, wondering what the commotion was about. An ambulance crew waited patiently at the corner. They approached the

43

cops, who opened the line, and a senior cop came over, arm out in front of her,

"District Superintendent James. We've been waiting for you. You took your time."

"I was in Paris, on a job."

"Right ... Even forensics have had all the time they want, which makes a change. We've had complaints."

She jerked her head at the building, meaning the well-heeled inhabitants, who didn't like having their beauty sleep disturbed. She stepped back from in front of them, and Julia Church's body came into view.

Milo's stomach lurched. He was expecting it, but his stomach wasn't.

He watched the copper as they walked to the body "What's your take, superintendent?"

She eyed him critically "You know we aren't allowed to have a 'take'. That kind of thinking isn't police business. We leave that to you clever chaps and execute the orders of the court."

"But you must have formed an opinion, an instinct."

"Strictly off the record, it wouldn't surprise me at all if you were to come back to me and say it was a robbery that went wrong, but then nothing else would surprise me either."

And she turned away, ending the exchange.

Cops were in a difficult position. Inevitably, experience gave them a feel for a crime scene, but the changes brought into the system had placed them in a position where that feeling wasn't welcome. What had previously been an internal game of one-upmanship, had become a feud of sorts with the crime forums.

And then, there she was in front of him, when just a few hours earlier they had been romantic collaborators in Paris. They had faced a problem, yes, but hadn't been in peril, or so they had thought.

She was face down and there was little blood. The place she had landed was a small garden. She had clipped some shrubs and ended up in a bed of roses, apparently not as great as folks might have been led to believe. Milo kept telling himself he had been

44

expecting it, but it was still a blow. She was in the same clothes she'd been in when Milo left her in Paris. Suppressing his more human instincts, he moved forward and crouched at her head.

One of the forensic guys turned and said, "Third floor, she jumped."

"You were there?"

"No, I . . . never mind."

Milo surveyed the scene, recording the whole thing for modelling and examination later. Noticing something odd about her head he bent down to look closer. The hair on one side, matted, or . . . burned? He focused on it and made a side note to cross-check it with the forensics report.

He made a circuit round the body, then nodded to the superintendent. Anna had just stopped at the line and stared at the body. Milo noticed her as a grieving friend for the first time and he made his way over to her.

"She wouldn't have felt anything."

Anna looked up "Really? Isn't that what they always say?"

"Yeah, I guess."

The super came over. "Sorry, who are you?" she asked Anna.

Anna held out her hand. "Anna May, she was a colleague."

"Are you the people who put the suppression notice on this? I have to tell you, it makes me very uncomfortable."

"Yes, we're the people."

Milo stepped forward. "Superintendent, can you take us to the apartment?"

That bought him a quizzical look.

"The one from which she fell. I presume there is one and that she didn't just materialise here?" he continued.

"Can they move the body now?"

Milo looked to Anna and she sighed her agreement.

The cop held out her arm. "This way."

As they walked to the apartment, Milo ran through a series of commands to activate a search for Julia's last movements. The operation, using mental commands via his neural net, was discreet. Shocked, pale and close to tears, Anna said nothing.

The super flicked her head towards the lift. "Third floor. One of my guys is up there."

They went up and, when the door opened, a young woman, not more than twenty, at the entrance to the apartment, snapped a smart salute. She looked sharp and wiry, her hair tied back beneath her cap.

Anna jumped, but Milo simply looked at her, surprised but amused.

"New in the job?" he asked.

"First week, sir."

"Keep up the good work."

"Yes sir, try to sir."

Anna was still looking at her as they went into the room. "What was that about?"

"You heard the woman. First week on the job, probably her first stiff."

Like the rest of the apartment, the room was beautifully decorated. Everything was understated, but just so. The whole place had an eerie familiarity, as though it were an annex to the apartment he had just left in Paris. On the walls and in occasional corners, paintings and pieces of art, all twentieth or twenty-first-century, but nothing appeared disturbed or taken. Several science fiction magazines from the 1950s in frames, sealed and mint condition. What was the point in that? A huge and it appeared, original, poster from the film adaptation of Dick's novella, 'Blade Runner'.

He looked at it for a few moments then sighed. Milo's system scanned the room, accessed the last-known insurance scan and ran a comparison. He paused, then shrugged, grunted. He searched the survey system, triggered in the event of violent activity in the immediate surroundings and was unsurprised to find that the last few hours had been wiped.

Anna stopped looking round the room and turned to him. "Something?"

"Maybe, maybe not."

They walked to the window and looked out. Below, the ambulance was just being closed up while the forensic team examined the ground under Julia's body. They had all the appearance of being thorough. He scanned the window frame and, taking out a biometric glove, he ran his finger round the edge and then round the window itself.

He looked back at the room, raised his voice "Officer?"

In she came. "Yes sir?"

"I take it forensics have finished in here?"

"So I understand, sir."

"Ok."

She hovered about the doorway for a moment and then left.

Milo looked at the space she had left. Something was odd, wrong, he couldn't quite . . . Perhaps it was just her manner, first week and all.

He turned back to the window. Forensics hadn't done as thorough a job as they ought. Several fibres, probably from her clothes. Some blood, not Julia's. His system couldn't isolate blood types but could pick up differences.

Anna was looking through the apartment. She had stopped at the desk and was pushing papers round using the end of her pen.

"Find anything?" Milo asked.

"Eh? No, not really."

She continued looking through the papers but didn't appear to be paying a lot of notice to them, almost as though . . .

"Why the suppression notice?"

"It's standard protocol for anyone at her level in the partnership, in case they have left anything behind."

"This isn't your first time here this evening?"

She stopped and looked up at him, weighing her answer. "It is."

"You don't seem too worried about what you might find on the desk."

She looked at him again, picking her words. "A team came earlier, tidied up. I know what they took and what they left."

"How come the cop didn't know you or your company?"

"When they were here earlier it was with her boss, had to be. There was no sign of her then."

"You people aren't responsible for this by any chance?"

Her head snapped up "No! What kind of a question is that?"

"A necessary one."

His system threw up a range of figures, raised temperature, pupils contracting, slight watering of the eyes ... Could have been guilt, surprise, anger ...

"There are lots of less messy ways of controlling senior staff available to the firm. We would never ..." Anna shook the idea out of her head and looked back at the desk, but she wasn't pushing paper round any more.

He took that in and turned back to the window. "You guys didn't call in this forensic mob?"

She looked up, trying to gauge the question, "No, why?"

"Because they are very sloppy."

"They looked pretty good downstairs."

"*Looked.*"

"Perhaps they have enough evidence."

"There's never enough evidence, and it's not like they can take a second 'first look'. Mind you, if you've been in here before ..." He shrugged.

"We weren't. I told you they were with a senior officer. Anything else would have been illegal."

"And you can't afford to do that."

"No. We can't."

"So what did they take away?"

"Not much. Some papers related to a client in the Gulf and some correspondence to do with her appointment and remuneration. It's logged."

"Was anything missing?"

"What do you mean?"

"Anything that you expected to find that wasn't here?"

"No, but she'd just been to Paris, which was a surprise."

He smiled tightly. "I'd like to do a level-three scan before we leave, would you mind stepping out? I'll meet you downstairs. Can you tell the young cop what I'm doing so she doesn't blunder in?"

"Ok."

"Thanks. Then we have to talk."

She gave him a funny look, lips pressed together firmly before walking out the door.

Milo ignored it and called up his scan system. He made a connection to the server in Beijing. "Level three."

In his eye, the signal offered him 'ready' and began to scope the apartment. It did this as he moved through the rooms, making a preliminary assessment of the scan's parameters and the available equipment there to make it. The system used all of the resident scanning and surveillance resources and supplemented this with recordings from the operative's own system. Milo was looking for places she might have hidden material related to the head, but saw nothing.

He found a spot suitably out of the way of anything he might be interested in, but comfortable enough for him to keep relatively still while the scan happened. His, or anyone else's, presence would not be a major issue except for the time it took, with the need for whoever was moving about to be discounted on an ongoing basis. There were systems that could do this quickly, but this one was two years old and had some modifications which caused it to slow down. It was also dependent on the connection with Beijing.

Milo was tired. He sat in a corner, folded his legs up into the lotus position and relaxed. He triggered the scan and began to review where he was.

So Julia worked for Anna's company and not the one she told him. Odd. Perhaps she hadn't wanted to draw attention to her new company, so maybe that bit tallied. Anna didn't seem to know her all that well yet. He would ask about that later.

The apartment showed no sign of having been tossed to find the head, so whoever had done this either knew nothing, wasn't interested in the head, or knew it wasn't here. Perhaps they had been here when she came back.

The first scan was a bit too clean, almost as if the insurance scan had been used to fix up the place, so it might have been tossed. And then there was the little matter of Anna's firm having given the place the once-over. This was all too open-ended.

He checked the scan to see how far it had got. A little over halfway through. He looked at the scanned rooms and was happy enough. He was always impressed at the detail.

He stopped. A small utility room off the kitchen. He had given it a look himself earlier, but he hadn't noticed the panel on the back wall. It was slightly out of alignment, as though it had been removed and put back. Could be maintenance, but this was an expensive place. Perhaps Julia had hidden something there after all.

"Moving," he said.

Standing, he walked to the kitchen past the open front door. The rookie appeared to have taken a break. He stood at the kitchen door and looked round the room. Very neat, preternaturally neat. Something was off. Perhaps she had a cleaner. Unlikely, given the company's paranoia about security. Perhaps the company had contract cleaners. He would check.

He stepped across the kitchen to the utility room and pushed the door forward with a finger. It drifted open and stopped against the wall with a soft bump. He looked in at the room and round it. To his left, the panel and the misalignment, though slight, was noticeable. Irritated he had missed it the first time, Milo walked over to it, reminding himself that he was tired and that travel takes it out of a man of his years, whatever he looked like.

He reached up to the panel's corner. Pulling gently, he wasn't surprised that the first thing to come into view was the kitchen plumbing pipework. He was just thinking how out of place that word, 'plumbing' was now that all the pipework was graphene, when something came into view that did surprise him. First the blonde hair, then the clear face of a young woman, similar in size to the young cop at the door of the apartment. As he pulled back the panel, it also became apparent that she wasn't moving and was in her underwear. He had just dropped the panel to the floor when the lights went out.

Downstairs, all the cops' radios went off at once. Straight away they began to head for the door of the apartment and were met by the superintendent coming out.

"We got a call, the 'tec upstairs, something's wrong" the first cop said.

"I know, sergeant, I have the same radio, remember? Set a perimeter round the building, cover the back door. You two check the woman who came with him is ok and stay with her. I'll check that everything's ok upstairs. I don't want you lot mucking up a crime scene until I've had the okie-dokie from forensics."

Without waiting for an answer, she turned and the door was already closing before anyone moved.

"You heard the woman, let's go!" the sergeant shouted.

Inside, the super headed for the lift and punched in a security code that accelerated its speed to the third floor. When the door opened, another code kept it open, blocking access. She took out her side arm, noticed the young cop at the doorway was gone, moved to the stairwell door, swiped the lock with her badge and engaged the deadlock. Eyeing the open apartment door, she rounded the jamb, covering the open space with her gun. The hallway was empty.

She waited, listened, touched her glasses and tried for a connection with the house scanner, but it had gone dead. A slight noise, maybe a groan, from the sitting room and she was all attention. Watching the other doors that opened into the hall, she made for the sitting room and, barrel first, she stepped in.

She relaxed, holstered her weapon and tilted her head to one side. "Just the way I like my men, tied up and helpless."

The young cop snorted.

"What happened?"

"The level three, it switched him onto the panel my 'friend' was sleeping behind, so I slugged him."

"That's not helpful. They'll know. We practically had the whole response squad up here and they'll send along another team in a few minutes."

"I didn't think there were lots of options or the time to talk it out."

"Pity."

Milo was slumped on the couch, his right wrist cuffed to his left ankle with a pair of mag-cuffs. He groaned. The women turned and waited.

The younger one hissed, "He must have an adrenaline pod."

"Or you didn't hit him very hard."

Milo snapped alert, moved his head gingerly.

"Adrenaline."

The super nodded.

Milo eyed them both, tried to get his bearings. He looked at the cuffs then at the two watching him.

"You've done it now. Who are you?"

The super eyed him. She didn't like that he wasn't intimidated.

"We're two people considering what to do with you, so, unless you're answering our questions, shut up," she said.

Milo nodded, "You're official, which is bad for you. Which branch?"

The younger woman was more amused than her boss, "People's Invest. Corp."

Milo made a face. "The pixies! Which state, or are you city?"

"We could be corporate. Consider all the options!"

"My colleagues are, I promise. We're very good that way."

The boss, having been ignored, was tired of being ignored. "Enough of that. Who brought you in on this?"

"You were told, Ms May's firm."

"You've been on this longer than that."

Milo looked at her, considered. Then spat out, "Why'd you kill her?"

"Kill her? She's alive! Oh, her? We didn't, but we were trying to find her for a little chat. Seems someone else was quicker."

Milo shook his head and sighed. He looked at the cuffs and they sprang open. China12 access codes had their advantages.

The pixies snapped out their guns. Looking at them, he smiled. He began to rub his ankle, then touched the back of his head. He winced and smiled at the young woman, who grinned.

Shaking his head again, he said: "You're stupid. As soon as you realised I was doing a level three, you should have left. Now I know who you are."

"You're arguing yourself into an early grave, I'd say" the younger woman observed.

"That won't do you any good. As soon as I went down my colleagues knew and will have captured the images of everything that happened. Including your faces."

"We have a suppression field."

"Not before I began the scan. The system would have picked it up, like it did when I began the scan. You have about a minute and a half before the early response team gets here."

The super stepped in again. "Look, we're not going to touch you and the cop is fine, just out of it. But we need to know who you're working for and if you have *it*. Oh, and you need to know you should back the hell off."

"Well, in the first place, screw you it's none of your business. I don't know what 'it' is but if I did, screw you. And lastly, screw you. I'll do whatever I please, so long as it's within the law." He gave her a broad and savage grin.

She looked him over then turned to the younger woman, "Come on."

"But what about . . .?"

"Him? Like I said, we're not going to touch him. Not yet, anyway." Turning to Milo, "You've been warned."

She marched out followed by the junior operative who flashed him a look that could have been attraction, could have been her noting him down on the list of people she was going to kill. Then she pointed a finger gun at him, "Pam, Pam, Pam" she breathed, and was gone.

CHAPTER FIVE

Two minutes later, the rapid response team spilled through the door, pointing short-range charge guns at no one and everyone. Milo had used his best endeavours and some drugs to revive the cop from behind the panel. He had also offered her a jacket from one of Julia's wardrobes to give her a little dignity on what it turned out really was her first day on the job. It was a tough break and a rough lesson in where being keen can land a newbie. Along with the coat, he had given her enough of a steer on what had happened to pull the day round.

The bozo now in charge was very officious, not a little suspicious, and frankly didn't believe that two pixies had slipped through his fingers. He hadn't been impressed either, at Milo's quip that 'pixies do that'. It took bozo fifty-five minutes, give or take, as well as a careful review of the arrival logs, the say so of what seemed like most of the cops there, and a dire threat from a tired and on-the-edge Anna, for him to let them go. Milo couldn't resist pointing out to the man that he was "the reason thinking had been outsourced", several times. This might or might not have increased the wait.

In Anna's taxi again, a snap message from base.

"What was that about?"

"Later."

Anna folded herself into the back of the taxi and he sat beside her. They fell quiet. It had been a long day and not one that ended well, no matter how he looked at it. They headed for Anna's flat in Islington, a quiet square that had probably looked the same since the day the last builder left, apart from the large graceful trees in the gardens at its centre.

Once off the commercial drag, the street lights flicked on and then faded as they passed, a moving pool of light in the sleeping city. Milo tried to remember the noise of the old petrol engines as they screamed and fumed their way round the country, but he couldn't. It was like looking at the lights and trying to see the amber-coloured streets and starless skies of his youth. LEDs and light-absorbing street surfaces had changed everything so much, it seemed almost alien. Not everywhere was like this. In the badlands of southern Europe and the eastern Med it was like stepping back a hundred years or more. They even smoked tobacco, for God's sake, leaving Milo's clothes fit only for the recycler, which had largely replaced dry cleaning.

The taxi rolled away, having docked Anna's account as she left, and they walked through the opening front door. She had suggested staying at hers and he thought it would help so hadn't argued. Anna had dialled ahead and a local tapas bar sent over a drone with a light meal, which was waiting on the kitchen table. Not everyone lived like this, but the upper crust, those not on state 'allowance', had automated entry systems that allowed the delivery of items below a certain size through a system not unlike old air-conditioning ducts or large cat flaps, depending on the building. Milo poured out some wine while Anna changed out of the clothes she had been in for the last twenty four hours and took a quick shower.

Milo tapped into his com system. "Hi."

Xin shimmered into view "Hi, what was that about?"

"Pixies."

"Really? Not many of those about."

"Can you run IDs on the cop at the door of the apartment and the superintendent downstairs?"

"It was them?"

"The very same."

"How deep? It will flag up if we chase their IDs."

"Only enough to confirm they are what they say they are."

"Ok. Anything else?"

"There will be, but I need . . ."

". . . Need?"

"Sorry, yeah. I need to work out what the hell's going on. I'll talk to Ms May and then get back to you with what might be a long list."

"We await your pleasure." Xin smiled and the com was cut.

Anna walked into the room.

"Hello again!"

She smiled back weakly. "Hi."

"Feeling better?"

"A bit."

"Food?"

"A bit, then sleep I'm all in."

"I need to ask few questions first."

He could see she was on edge and held up his hand.

"Not lots, just a couple for tonight, but I will have more."

She nodded and they sat down. They sipped on the earthy white wine and Anna played with her food while she watched Milo eat.

"You said Julia was a colleague, as in she worked for your partnership?"

"Yes, she'd just been promoted. She'd been with us for about eighteen months, very very bright."

He looked puzzled, perplexed.

"What's wrong, I mean aside from . . .?" She trailed off.

He looked up, took a drink. "Tonight wasn't the first time I'd seen her."

"Oh?"

"Yesterday. I met her in Paris, just bumped into her. I tried to help her out. She had a problem with an expensive work of art."

"In Paris?"

"Yeah, you remember, where I was meeting you."

"Yeah, sorry about that . . . Actually I stood you up because we couldn't find Julia."

"Did she know we knew each other?"

"I don't know. I guess. It's not a secret, the whole firm was aware of Brazil and what happened, but it isn't the first thing I bring up in a conversation either. Why?"

He sat back, put his hands behind his head and thought. Anna waited.

He picked up his glass again and drank. "There's a chance that I've been set up."

"What? How? Why?"

"I would like to know the answer to both of those questions."

"Milo, what went on in the apartment?"

"Pixies."

"What?"

"Pixies. Government-employed surveillance and detection operatives."

"Are they those kids they take in at what, fifteen? That's not allowed."

"It's not and they don't, officially, exist. So . . . 'pixies'. And yes, she was young."

Anna shook her head.

"It disgusts me. They're kids! What did they want? Did they kill . . .?"

"No, they didn't. But they wanted me to go away for a start."

"Not surprising."

"They also asked about the same thing that had got Julia all worked up, though not in so many words."

"You've lost me."

"Julia wanted to give back a work of art to a gallery. She said she'd stolen it years ago."

"Stolen?"

"Yeah, but that was all baloney, 'cause when I tried to give it back, the gallery owner talked a lot of mumbo jumbo, tossed me out and then ran for it."

"What? You're not serious! That makes no sense."

"No? Whether it makes sense or not it's plenty serious. It cost Julia everything she had."

Anna looked puzzled and sat thinking, probably trying to remember every conversation she ever had with Julia, he thought. She picked at the food idly and took a drink before looking at Milo and shaking her head.

"I've got nothing. I don't remember talking about you, although you might have come up in passing. She had reviewed the case in Brazil. I remember she was impressed by your notes, I might have said something then."

"Lawyers! You're so discreet."

"But she's never asked about you particularly."

"Did she know you were meeting me in Paris?"

"I don't know, maybe. You know what offices are."

"I'd appreciate it if you could ask around, see if anyone else remembers mentioning it."

"Ok."

She yawned and stretched and he grinned.

"Yeah, me too. Go to bed. I'll head that way in a minute. Where's the spare room?"

"Across from mine."

"Thanks, I have to have a chat with Beijing."

She got up and smiled at him. Whatever Paris had been going to be, it wasn't now.

"Thanks for this evening," she said.

"Anytime."

Then she wandered off and he watched her go.

Sitting still at the table, he brooded. The simple job of helping out a damsel in distress had turned nasty and mysterious when they, whoever they were, tried to steal the head. At that moment it seemed simple enough – bad people wanted valuable item – but only if you forget the 'good' people not wanting it. It had become more complicated with the appearance of pixies. He didn't like that. They would be difficult to get a handle on and probably impossible to control. More important at the moment, why they were there at all. They seemed to know a lot, too much about his involvement. What did Ms Dawson know? What had she been on about and why had she run off?

He sighed. He could hear Anna washing, getting ready for bed, and suddenly realised how tired he was.

He opened a com. "Hi."

"Hi, we have nothing yet," said Xin

"No, I'm not in any shape to deal with it if you had. I just want to add a few things onto the end of the list."

"Ok, shoot."

"We need to find the connection between Church and Dawson."

"There's a connection?"

"There has to be, I think . . . I hope. The way Dawson talked implied there was and we need to know if Julia targeted me in Paris. If these guys in London were pixies, who were the bunch of thugs in Paris and is there more than one bunch of them?"

"We have the surveillance record for the hour before Ms Church was murdered, they tried to suppress it, but they're either not very clever or they're not very connected."

"Or they were in a hurry and didn't care if they were fingered, if they thought they'd get what they were looking for."

"The scan of the apartment at this point suggests Ms Church may have been trying to get away, but the forensic report isn't in yet and the scan is incomplete because of the partial suppression."

"Meaning?"

"Meaning we can't see who it is she was running way from when she hit the window or what it was that threw her against it."

"Right. Oh, one other person I'd like to talk with, whoever it was who was with her when she stole the head."

"You think there was someone?"

"No, but if there wasn't, she didn't steal it."

"You don't think she stole the head?"

"No I don't, and if she didn't, I want to know how she had it."

"Right."

"And . . . that's it for tonight."

"For this afternoon."

That threw him for a moment, and then he smiled. "Just have it for me when I wake up."

The com closed and he got up, already dragging his clothes off before he left the room.

In her bedroom, Anna was already asleep. He looked at the bed in the spare room and considered falling onto it and forgetting everything else, but he didn't. He walked to the bathroom and took out a small phial. He poured the contents into a tumbler, added some water and drank it down. He followed that with a short series of exercises, ending with a truncated Tai Chi routine. All together, it took about ten minutes.

In a slightly more centred state he walked to the bed and sat, just sat. He didn't move or stretch or anything at all and then, at the end of another five minutes, he lay down, turned on his side facing the door and closed his eyes.

He woke after a short four hours and could hear vague noises from the rest of the apartment. The sound of the shower was the key to what woke him and he pushed himself off the bed, wondering why the sound of the shower should be so like the sound of a jackhammer.

Milo didn't like missing his sleep, he never had. He rarely managed to get the regular seven-point-three-five hours his DNA suggested he should be taking. So, like most people, he managed the rest with drugs. They were good, he really didn't notice, and that probably annoyed him more than anything. They had evolved from the chemico-herbal tablets of his youth into tailored, personal, DNA-based enhancers, along with some genetic alterations that made their effects invisible, mostly. He was still sitting on the bed holding his head when Anna breezed in from the shower, all towel and wet hair.

"You're up! Any word from your colleagues?"

He shook his head, wished he hadn't and hoped that the answer to his next question would be positive. "Any food? Coffee?"

"Of course, I'm a lawyer, coffee *is* food. But I've also been out and got some stuff. It's in the kitchen."

She smiled and walked across to her room, then turned to a silently opening mirror door beside her, revealing her extensive wardrobe. He watched the splendour exposed and thought this was how Ali Baba must have felt. Then he thought that Ali Baba wouldn't have had much use for all those suits, pushed himself to his feet and headed for the food.

By the time Anna joined him, he had fresh crusty bread buttered and coated in honey, coffee poured out in mugs and was looking through some of the information from Beijing. Information that disturbed him, wrong-footed him. He waited for her to get some food inside her and a couple of mouthfuls of the black magic, but she knew it was coming.

She put down her cup and looked straight at him.

"Out with it."

"How well did you know Julia Church?"

"Like I said, she'd been with us about eighteen months. I met her when she joined. She seemed quite driven, but in a nice way. She was very brilliant when she put her mind to it, which she generally did. I didn't socialise with her outside of the office. Maybe a couple of trips to clients abroad."

"So it would be a surprise to find out that she wasn't Julia Church?"

"What? More than a surprise, it isn't possible. Our system checked her out and she was clean, or she wouldn't have been working with us. Unless . . ."

"Unless someone on the inside of your firm knew and covered it up."

She really was shocked by this and his monitoring of her system confirmed it.

"Did they? Who?"

"Relax. So far as we can tell, they checked her out and she checked out. Hell, we checked her out and our system's a lot better than any I know."

"So why do you think . . .?"

"We don't *think*, we *know* she isn't, wasn't, Julia Church."

"So who was she?"

"That we don't know. The top probability is a Jane Cruikshank, but she's only a ninety-three percent probability."

"That sounds pretty good to me."

"Yeah? It's not. Your last five cases were convicted. We had them at between a ninety-six percent and ninety-eight percent probability and one of them still beat the rap on appeal, so ninety-three percent ain't all that great. But it's a lead. Did she ever mention her school days or college?"

"Like I said, we didn't have that much time together. I sort of got the impression that she was Oxbridge, but they usually tell you and her profile says Bristol. A lot of those guys get the patter off, specially in firms like ours."

"Ever mention a teacher, or friends?"

"Mmm, Julia used to like the work of one Mathmo, though she'd never been to Cambridge."

"Mathmo?"

"Cambridge slang, mathematician."

"And she called him that? The slang thing I mean."

"Uh, well that could just as easily be me projecting, so I'm not sure."

"What was his name?"

"His?"

He sighed. "Her name. His or her name."

"*Her* name was Gog."

"Gog? Gog, wasn't she a biologist?"

"Top of the class, sparky! But no, she was a mathematician who won the Nobel for medicine, because of her work in modelling the spread of pathogens. It changed the way we looked at all sorts of things and not just in epidemiology."

"So Julia liked her."

"No, the one she admired was Gog's niece. She won the Field's Medal about twelve years ago."

"Ok, don't know what that is, but let it slide."

"It's a big prize."

"Check. And this Gog, the niece, she's in Bristol?"

"No, Cambridge."

He looked at her, working the pieces together. "So all roads lead to Cambridge."

"Apart from the ones that lead to Bristol." She smiled.

"Jane Cruickshank went to Cambridge."

"Well, Julia seemed to have an extensive knowledge of the bars round Bristol."

"Ok, that does suggest student life. Was she a drinker?"

Anna thought, then looked up at Milo. "She liked whiskey, but otherwise, not so much."

"One other really odd thing."

"Another one?"

"Perhaps the same one. Her apartment had a lot of really nice things and at least part of the reasoning around this art work she'd been trying to get rid of was its value. We couldn't discount plain robbery as a motive."

"So what's changed?"

"Like I said, her apartment had a lot of nice things and all of them are still there. Not one thing moved or removed."

She frowned. "Perhaps it's a commissioned theft?"

"It could be, but thieves are not that particular even when looking for something specific. A little bit extra is a little bit extra."

*

As he walked away from the station in Cambridge, on what had turned out to be a bright sunny day, Milo reflected on how the new and the old were constantly mixed up, rubbing up against each other. The wonder of a morning shower and fresh socks, a constant simple pleasure. He looked around at Cambridge, one of the centres in the world for cutting-edge science and technological advance but the transport he had just stepped off was forty years old, the system more than two hundred years old. It was more appropriate for the old classic 'Harry Potter' books, while those medieval spires he saw poking their heads above the tree line could be the old school from those books. He imagined it wasn't too unrealistic at that. The characters in the book dealt in magic and the gals and guys who worked here did too, as far as most people were concerned.

Jane Cruikshank had pulled some kind of magic trick of her own if the guys in Beijing and his reading of what he had been told by Anna were right. It wasn't easy to hide in the modern world, but she seemed to have done just that. He had asked Beijing to try to make sure that whoever was hunting for the head didn't find out what China12 had just found out, but it was foolish to imagine they would be able to keep them away forever. Still, long enough was long enough. With all of the 'impossible' things happening, he was beginning to hope that Gog wouldn't turn into a bat and fly away, although at this stage it wouldn't have surprised him. He'd be happy enough if he could shake the headache that had hung around since he woke up and was getting worse.

Milo and Gog had exchanged pleasantries by text and arranged to meet in her rooms at about four. Never mind forty years ago, he felt he was drifting back to the nineteen thirties. He walked past a scriptorium, a shop where graduates could, through the college, get their degree written up on parchment or, if they were of a theatrical mind, could have their will drawn up in similar fashion, replete with thick sealing wax. The accountants and lawyers loved it, it looked very snazzy framed on their walls.

It was funny, all through his life he had been listening to 'experts' telling anyone who would listen how it was the end of this or that, and the next era would usher in the end of people's minds, morals or souls. But it never quite did, nothing ever quite went away. Often there were fewer of whatever was being left behind, but people could still see the plays of Aeschylus in recently reconstructed amphitheatres, hear the compositions of thirteenth-century Chinese masters on authentic instruments, watch silent movies in cinemas with live organ or piano music. Little parcels of the past and the future all mixed up together.

Knocking on her door produced the same emotions as being sent to the dean of discipline when he was thirteen, and he hadn't been thirteen for a long time. He tried to suppress the butterflies as he waited an age for her to answer. He raised his hand to knock a second time but was blinded by the flood of light that poured into the dark corridor as the door opened.

She looked a lot younger than he was expecting, such that his next words were a question not a greeting. "Dr Gog?"

"You were hoping to meet someone else?"

"Uh, no, I'm sorry. Milo Talbot." He thrust out his hand.

He never introduced himself using his last name, not since . . . and her hand was taking his. "Gog, pleased to meet you."

She swung the door back and he walked in.

"You'll take tea?"

"Um, thank you."

She looked young, but her manner was bicycles, baskets and college gowns flying in the wind.

The room was lined with books. It had one clear desk with a computer terminal and a very large screen. A tablet and stylus were on the side table near a large armchair, which sat beside a large window that looked out over the internal courtyard. The building he was in was only about eighty or ninety years old, but the buildings that surrounded it were hundreds of years old and had students wandering about between them.

"Nice place you have here."

Gog looked out the window at the unchanging picture. She smiled and nodded. "Yes, this life has its compensations."

"You were here as an undergraduate?"

"Was that a question, Mr Talbot, or a statement?"

He smiled. "A question."

"Yes, yes I was, at this very college actually, though I escaped to Princeton and then to that little place you're from."

"Dublin?"

"Eh no, I meant Beijing. You hail from Dublin? Funny little backwater."

"Yeah, we'll come back one day. We've made good from being a 'funny little backwater' in the past."

"It wasn't meant unkindly. On the contrary, this is a funny little backwater, and I wouldn't change it for the world."

"And I wasn't being touchy. Even Beijing has had a time as a funny little backwater. It gives you a chance to find out who you are."

"Sit."

This was a command, Milo sat. The 'tea' was set out on the smallish table in the middle of the window and was ample. The kind of tea that if you'd packed it in a basket in the back of your car, it would be called 'lunch'. Presumably one of the compensations.

Milo resurrected his teenage appetite. It seemed to fit with the room anyway. Gog poured.

"Afternoon tea is a habit I picked up as an undergraduate. My DoS took it every day with several students. I think she found it a way of squeezing in an extra informal supervision. It wasn't usual, and it made us feel special. Help yourself to sugar."

"Thank you. Um . . . DoS?"

"Director of studies." Gog smiled, in the way professors smile when imparting information they felt that perhaps their students should know.

Milo began to feel he was in an old movie. He half expected the world around him to drain of colour.

There was safety in action. "Dr Gog, I want to ask you about a former student."

"Righto."

She had poured herself a cup and dropped in a slice of lemon, which was being gently pressed with a spoon. She looked up at his silence. Milo had become mesmerised by the precision of her actions and he stopped, just stopped.

He jumped and forced a smile. "Sorry. Her name is Cruikshank, Jane Cruikshank."

Gog looked at him and thought about it. She put down her tea, and walked over to the tablet and called up a file as she returned. A sea of young faces filled the screen. Touching the screen replaced it with files.

Gog looked up, "Graduation pictures. Which year?"

"'Twenty-nine"

She flicked through the files then picked one, it filled the screen. Neat rows of graduates, she moved along the rows. Milo thought it odd that, here he was sitting with a woman whose daily life was dealing in concepts so far in the future it made his head spin, yet she was still using tech decades and more out of date. But then his eye flicked to the desk and he noticed a pad of paper and a pencil.

"Ah, here, yes, a quiet young woman. Very serious. A good mind without being someone who would light up the world."

She had stopped the picture in a row of students and Milo could easily recognise 'Julia's' face smiling out at him. Beside her was another young face he thought he knew.

"What has she been up to Mr. Talbot? I hope she's not in any trouble?"

"Sorry, before we get to that, do you remember the girl beside her?"

Gog looked down and then up, looking for a little more guidance.

"The one on her right," he pointed.

Gog's eyebrows rose with understanding, "Not immediately to her right then. Yes she is an altogether . . ."

"No, I mean on *her* right. Standing directly beside her, there." He touched the screen directly.

Gog looked up at him and narrowed her eyes. "I know the woman you have pointed at Mr Talbot, but the woman immediately on her left is not Jane Cruikshank."

Now Milo was confused. He looked from the screen to the professor and back, he slowly placed his finger on "Julia's" face which jumped in size.

"Her?"

Gog nodded just as slowly and her tone was frosty. "Yes Mr. Talbot, *her*. She is not Jane Cruikshank."

"Then who is she?"

"She is Elspeth Martin, and the woman beside her is her half-sister. Why do you wish to know about these particular women?"

Milo was stunned, both by the news and by the change in tone. Elspeth Martin wasn't even on the list.

"I . . . Dr Gog, I'm sorry to have to tell you that Elspeth Martin, this woman, was killed last night."

Now Gog was silent. She lifted a hand to her mouth.

"How?"

"She was murdered, I believe, but the exact circumstances are confused."

"You said in your message that you were from China12?"

"I did."

"I'm sorry, Mr. Talbot, you'll have to leave. We should not have met."

Milo stood, but not to leave. "Doctor, I really must insist. I am an agent from one of the statutory organisations, licensed to investigate crime and we are the appointed agents for this incident."

"I cannot tell you more than I have. This is a protected institution as you well know . . ."

"Not for this kind of thing."

"Oh yes, for this kind of thing. You have asked me, are asking me about students who are not involved in . . ."

"And you know this how?"

That brought her to a stop and she was clearly not used to being stopped.

"Dr Gog, I don't know what is going on in this instance. I came to find background on someone who turned out to be neither who she claimed to be nor who we believed her to be. Your reaction is extreme, to say the least, given the mild enquiry."

"Mild? Perhaps, but the situation is anything but mild, Mr Talbot. You said a young woman, a brilliant young woman, has been killed. Murdered!"

"What did she study here?"

"She read mathematics. I really cannot say any more. If you insist, you'll have to come with the full array of the powers at your disposal."

He looked at her, and at what looked like it would have been a very nice tea and considered.

"Look, Dr Gog, I met Julia, – she was calling herself Julia Church – and she asked me for help. I have nothing but her welfare at heart."

"You've certainly failed in that regard haven't you?"

He turned to the window and looked out at several students lying on the lawn, laughing and joking and he imagined Julia-Jane-Elspeth doing just that.

He sighed. "Yes, doctor, I did, but it would appear she is not the only one who may be in danger and I still have no idea why she was killed, beyond the fact that some people want to get hold of a work of art that she had in her possession."

The good doctor now looked at him again, appraising him and considering. "I have already told you far more than I should, however, China12 have a good reputation and that is not nothing. I am not going to tell you any more . . ."

She raised a hand to still his immediate objections. ". . . I will put someone in touch with you who *may*, and I emphasise *may*, wish to help you. Whether they do or not will be up to them entirely."

"Look, Doctor, if you know something that could . . ."

"You will have to be happy with that!"

She marched over to the door and opened it, and waited without looking at him. He looked at the empty space and thought of the things he could do, some of which were legal. Then he walked out and the light dropped as the door shut behind him.

*

He was at the station, just walking into the main hall when his com system snapped into life.

"There you are!"

Milo was puzzled.

"We've being trying to get hold of you."

"How hard can it be?"

He started a validity check to ensure that his system was as it should have been, that it was in contact with valid com systems and that he was available. It was. He was.

"About as hard as it gets."

"What?"

"Your system has been, we're not sure, 'fed' perhaps a stream of data that has no relation to reality and it has put out a superb stream of fake data and images designed to make us believe you were simply having a nice afternoon tea."

"I should have been."

"Were you?"

"No."

"We have footage of you having a lovely time. Very polite, very uneventful."

"Well that part's right."

"What's going on?"

"First things first, Julia Church aka Jane Cruikshank, is in fact Elspeth Martin."

"Who?"

"Elspeth Martin."

And Milo knew that at least two people were flying though search systems and running probability algorithms against that name.

"Milo, is this who you're talking about?"

An image flashed in front of him. He was half expecting to see Jane Cruikshank, but he didn't recognise whoever this was.

"No."

"Elspeth Martin, first class degree from Cambridge, forth wrangler in her year, M. Math, PhD from MIT and now in Singapore teaching and producing some very interesting papers on topography."

"Fourth what?"

"Fourth wrangler. It means she was fourth in her year in maths at Cambridge."

"No horses then?"

"None."

"The first part about her degree seems to fit, but not the bit about Singapore nor the picture. Gog was adamant right before she clammed up."

"Ok, we'll stretch the parameters. How do you know you were talking about our Julia/Jane?"

"She showed me a picture. A graduation photo."

"Ok, that's a start."

"There's more. She let it slip out and then tried to cover it up by getting all huffy, but Elspeth is Dawson's sister, no, half-sister."

"Wow, right, that's a connection. We were looking for connections."

"It is, we were. But what are two bright Maths students . . ."

"Dawson studied Maths as well?"

"Oh, I assumed, as Gog knew her. Let's go with that anyway. What are they doing in the law and running art galleries?"

"And teaching in Singapore? The law and the galleries, they could be making money or looking after daddy's bequest."

"They wouldn't be the first bright sparks who cared more for gold than for greatness, but that didn't fit with Julia so much. And why all the names, and the hiding?"

"And *how*? We haven't figured that out yet."

Seated in the seats across from where Milo was standing he saw a face he knew and not trying to hide either. Their eyes met and held.

"Right, let's wind back a bit. Why were you trying to get hold of me and why couldn't you?"

"Cambridge has a suppression system as a protected institution. Your safety is assured by their own internal system and we aren't allowed to beak into it. Not formally anyway."

"But?"

"Most crime groups have their own collection systems and take it badly if even protected institutions decide to get in the way, and we're no different. Everything was as normal until you went into Gog's office."

"And then I went out?"

"That's just it. If you had, your alarm would have alerted you and us. No, we just kept getting our normal feed, except it wasn't. It was made up. I doubt any other group would have detected it. They might have put down the lack of coms to interference from the university system."

"So there's some strong tech involved. Figures, she's pretty important."

Milo's mind went back to the image of the old-style tech Gog was using and he began to think it wasn't just a case of an ivory tower academic not wanting to let go of the 'old ways'.

"Yes, but we don't think it's the university's."

"Ok, but then why were you so anxious to talk to me?"

"Oh, that. We think that young Pixie is following you. You should probably watch out."

"Oh, is that all? Do you know if she's trying to kill me?"

"Probably."

"I think you guys have enough work to do." He snapped off the com.

In China12, there had been only three field operatives, the others were boffins. The fact that the field operatives were all a little different was what gave the group part of its special character. That and the fact that their boffins were the very best in the world, bar none.

Milo pushed himself away from the wall he was leaning against and wandered over to the young woman who had decided to sit opposite him. In the busy station there was little possibility that she would do anything that would threaten him, although when you're dealing with killers who don't exist, there is no guarantee of anything.

He stopped in front of her. "Hello. I didn't think we'd be seeing each other so soon."

"The higher-ups thought it would be an idea to keep an eye on you."

"They're probably right."

"No knowing what you'll get up to and we presumed you'd ignore our warning."

"I did tell you I would, so bravo on the detective work there. I think your 'higher-ups', are more interested in the notion I might find out something they'd like to find out. It's a cheap way of doing detective work."

"I guess that played its part."

"So they told you not to kill me."

"They might have mentioned that."

"You should just go ahead and hire us. We're very good, you know."

"I have heard. You keep telling me."

"For instance, I could tail someone without letting them know I'm tailing them."

She shrugged. "Yeah, but it's such a fag, all that dark doorway stuff. I know I'm good enough to track you and I know you're just about clever enough to know that you're being tracked. Everything else is a waste of time."

He agreed.

"If my orders change, I'll give you a ten-minute head start, I usually track ten minutes away from my target."

"That is uncommonly civil of you."

"Hey, just because I'm going to be lazy about tracking you, doesn't mean I should take the fun out of killing you."

"And you think it will come to that?"

"It usually does."

Her voice and attitude were simple, flat, matter of fact, in a way that sent chills down Milo's spine. He had no doubt that she was as good as she said she was or that her list of kills was long enough to forget some of them.

The train pulled in and she got up and headed for it with Milo. He reflected on whether it was a good idea to accept her as a travelling companion, but then her reasoning had been solid. She could track him and he would have known and it would have been irritating. Going off-grid was straightforward enough, but she had access to government systems and dodging that was more difficult. They found seats and sat across from one another.

Milo leaned back and looked at the neat woman opposite. She was taut. Yes, that was what sprang to mind. Her clothes would pass inspection at most of the 'good' restaurants but wouldn't get her into the high-fash joints. They hid a body that would have turned heads but could just as easily break necks. The equivalent male body would have possessed the easy grace of a top sportsman. It was funny, he thought, that the equivalent male operative would have had more bulk and less agility than he supposed she possessed.

He didn't think she would but, "You want to tell me why you were so interested in Ms Church?"

"I think you know that she wasn't Ms Church. Would you like to tell me why you were at Ms Cruikshank's place?"

"I was called in by my friend, Ms May, and I had already met Julia or Jane, in Paris, so I was naturally interested. Now you?"

"When did you find out that she wasn't really Ms Church?"

"Probably just a little before you."

She grinned at that, but he could see it rankled. "That 'little' is probably the reason you're still able to talk to me."

He nodded. "Not in a sharing mood?"

"I don't know all that much, too far down the food chain. But I know she was mixed up in something and that this is a cross-agency affair. When I said I would probably get the order, I probably will. This is messy whatever it is and messy things mostly need cleaning up."

"And you're a cleaner."

She just smiled. She had told him a lot more than she knew but it wasn't going to make things easier, even if it made things clearer. Whatever system Julia had used to cover her tracks was very effective, effective enough that several agencies as well as his own had not been able to find a way through it. But why?

She jerked him out of his thoughts, "So are you back at the girlfriends tonight or do we have somewhere else to go?"

"I will be at my *friend's* for the moment, but don't go to sleep on me now, you never know when I'll spring into action."

"Look, I know this is a tough break, but you should just walk away from this one. The guys upstairs are pretty serious about it."

"If they are, then it's a good bet that they'll decide I'm superfluous if I'm not turning up goods they can leech off."

She considered this and nodded. "You might be right at that. Pity."

Then she went into whatever internal world was being supplied by the system she had in her and on her. Milo leant back and did likewise. Using text-speech, not always as straightforward as the manufacturers claimed, wasn't as discreet as they claimed either. First he had to put up his fences. Everything, given the proximity of a government agent, would need to be in top-level encryption. The method was a constantly changing series of codes, still based in part on the system dreamed up by the sometime actress and mathematician Hedy Lamarr. Breaking it was like trying to guess the value of several hundred coins being tossed at the same time and then milliseconds later being tossed again. The communication was, at best, staccato, made worse by the fact that Beijing could reply vocally.

"So, she killed you yet?"

"*No.*"

The synthetic voice always raised a smirk.

"Oh, is she near? . . . Right then, why don't we tell you what we've got and you listen and respond when and if. First, the Pixie, as far as we can tell, she's on observational status, so she won't kill you yet, but there is a hold on what we presume is a kill order, so watch your step. Ms Martin is proving to be . . . elusive. I think we can say there is some connection with Holland, we think parental, but they have managed to confuse the entire pattern of relationships so that each lead comes back to the impression they want us to have. Is any of this any help?"

They waited while Milo tries to put together his bits and pieces of information. It's not a long wait. "*Yes, some. Holland. A name?*"

"Yeah, we're hunting for that and will let you know in due course. How near is the Pixie?"

"*With me.*"

"With you? Right. Keeping enemies close I guess. We've been looking into the head and you'll be surprised to find out that we have nothing that you can't read in a standard art lover's guide. Apart, that is, from the obvious fact. Brancusi is a really well known artist. In the past ten years there have been three biogs and two major retrospectives. He has two heads here in Beijing and at least one student here is doing a PhD on him, so fencing the head would be impossible, even if you were to wait decades."

The Pixie looked up at him as he tried to compose a question and she grinned, kicked out at him. "Difficult composing these little speeches isn't it?"

She smiled at his irritated look. "Especially if people interrupt your train of thought. Oh, I didn't just do that did I? I hope it isn't important."

He relaxed and grinned broadly. To Beijing, "*Out.*" To the Pixie, "I don't know what you mean, I was lost in a Bach cello concerto."

"Casals?"

"No. Daisy Griffiths."

"Oh, very sophisticated."

He gave her a fake smile.

"Were base happy? Tell you more interesting things about Ms Cruikshank?"

"They did. How about you? Time to give me my ten minutes? Or have you been redeployed?"

"Neither nor. They're so pleased with the job I'm doing they want me to keep right on doing it!"

"Oh joy."

CHAPTER SIX

Later that evening and Milo was pacing the floor of Anna's apartment. She wasn't home yet and the table was untidily strewn with snacks of various kinds and an empty coffee pot, which looked like it had recently been full. The snacks were high sugar and high salt, all the things he was under strictest orders not to go near, but his head hurt, he was stressed and had always reacted to stress this way. Even fifteen minutes under the hot shower hadn't proved to be the tonic it usually was.

A brush of the carpet and he'd snapped round, pistol pointing at the door ready for whoever it was had come through it.

Anna stopped and then stepped back.

He relaxed. "Sorry."

She put her head round the door and eyed him over, gun at his side.

"Sorry, I'm on edge"

She looked over the table and then at him. "I'm not surprised. Rough day?"

"Perplexing."

"Oh, how so?"

"Take a seat."

"Let me just, um, get into something more comfortable." She gave him a weak smile and trotted off to her bedroom.

Ten minutes, well, fifteen minutes later she was sitting on the couch in a thick towelling bathrobe, beside her on a clear table a freshly brewed cup of coffee, all ears.

Milo, still pacing, was working up to telling her something and she couldn't figure out if he was upset, angry or just tired.

He stopped and smiled. "I don't know where this is leading. I meet a woman in Paris who tells me about an extremely valuable artwork she's stolen and wants to give back. She's a lawyer and we meet by accident. Then it turns out the gallery doesn't want the work of art and says it isn't stolen or if it is, not from them as they've never owned it. The lawyer, who is a lawyer but doesn't work for who she says she works for, turns out to be a colleague of a woman I know well, very possibly meaning that meeting her was no accident, especially in the context that I meet her instead of her colleague who had to stay in London because she, the woman I met in Paris, wasn't in London.

"She then turns up dead, in a clumsy fake suicide and the forensics are coming back looking like someone has an agenda. There are at least two, if not three, different sets of people trying to get hold of this artwork or of this same unfortunate young woman or possibly both. Oh, and no one can ever sell or exhibit the art as it has such strong provenance, and was, in fact, owned by the gallery, in case you were wondering. The gallery owner has disappeared, having run away from this valuable sculpture. Still with me?"

Anna nods.

"Then it turns out that not only does she work for someone else, but she's not who she says she is and she isn't even who we *think* she is. She's someone else entirely, who turns up on no one's list. Asking about her gets me thrown out of her old university, which was Cambridge by the way. She was a top maths grad, but when with me she talked as though she knew nothing about the tech of surveillance to the point where I almost had to explain what an algorithm was and my group – the best at what we do in the world – is stumped. Yes, and the gallery owner is her half-sister, of course, but never hinted at that, and when I check out her sister in Paris, she's nowhere to be found. Not a photo, not a name. To cap it all off, I get accompanied by an operative for an agency that doesn't exist and who is quite open that she 'may have to kill me'."

Anna sits up on hearing that. "What?"

"Yeah, the Pixie from the apartment. Apparently there is a 'kill note' out on me, but it's on hold as long as I'm turning up interesting stuff."

"Do they know all that?"

"All that confusing stuff, mostly about things we don't know or are wrong about? About two-thirds of it, which is why I have a complete block on communications here."

"So they won't kill you yet?"

He looked at her, understanding but a little shocked by the directness of the question. "No, not yet."

"That's something anyway."

"Not much, but don't worry about me I don't think she's as tough as I'm afraid she might be."

Anna seemed half-convinced, but it had been a long day and Milo had a confusing way of speaking, even if she'd figured out he wasn't joking. Or possibly was. With a concerned look on her face, she asked, "So who is she . . . was she?"

"Elspeth Martin."

Anna looked blankly at Milo and he thought something surprising was about to pop out when "Never heard of her" came out instead.

"Right, join the gang."

He sighed and sank down beside her, his head in his hands. "What the hell is going on? Oh, and her professor, Doctor Gog, said I'd be contacted by someone or other before she threw me out."

"That's hopeful."

"That's nothing. Unless, that is, they appear with all the answers in a neat package, but the way this is going, that ain't gonna to happen."

She sighed. "Let's eat."

They ordered an Indian takeaway and sorted out the elements of the meal onto plates. Milo normally had an antipathy for hot foods, but unaccountably had to fight the urge to order several of the spicier dishes. They settled down and Anna added a nice white wine, strong enough to cope with the highly flavoured meal.

They ate in silence, Anna brooding, seemingly trying to match up what Milo had told her about her workmate. While Milo was feeling decidedly odd, at least his headache was beginning to fade. They got through the meal and settled back to consider the options.

Anna was the first to voice what was on her mind. "How real is the threat to you?"

"Pretty real, but I'm not without resources. The Pixie said she'd give me ten minutes' head start and I won't need that long."

"You believe her?"

He thought about it. "Yeah. Doesn't mean it'll happen, but she thinks she means it. Anyway, I have no way of testing it."

She nodded. "I just can't match your portrait of Julia with the woman I know . . . knew. God, this is hard to get used to."

"I know." He winced, the room went spinning and he reached for his head.

"Are you alright?"

"I don't know, probably these stupid drugs that mean you don't have to sleep."

"They usually work. You didn't have a problem before."

"No one ever does, until they do."

She looked worried. "Do you want to go to sleep? I'm tired, but after this I might have to take something. I do know what you mean, I don't like them either."

"If you don't mind, I'm going to sit a while, run over things. I don't really feel tired, but I think a few minutes' downtime will do me no harm."

"Sure, I'll watch some news, quietly. There's a livecast from the Met I'd like to see. It's probably as good as the drugs."

The end wall turned into a huge screen, as though the room had grown into the theatre. The lights sank to a suitable level of illumination and Anna's com system picked up the sound.

Milo could see the screen if he looked but he didn't want to hear, so he didn't. He lay back and closed his eyes.

He wasn't sleeping, but just having his eyes closed was restful. In spite of this, he could still see as though he had his eyes open, in fact, it was slightly clearer than that. If he wanted, he could actually see into the room using his link to the scanning system and even choose in which wavelength to see the room. In a room that had a scanning system, he need never be blind. But, on this occasion, he didn't want. He flipped though the items he'd noted, from his first encounter through to the meeting with Gog, not once but several times.

Disturbed, he opened his eyes and picked up a movement to his left. He noticed Anna had joined the livecast, Delibes' '*Lakmé*' if he wasn't mistaken, but that wasn't the movement and Anna had fallen asleep.

He froze and waved his hand in front of his eyes, but it didn't go away. He closed his eyes, it still didn't go away. He asked the system to do a recheck.

"System, level five diagnostic."

It flickered and the OKs appeared one by one on the ocular display. He shook his head, rubbed his eyes. He could still see it, her, it. Now it was smiling, causing a really cold shiver to run down his back.

"No hello?"

He blinked. "What?"

"Aren't you going to say hello?"

"Um, hello."

Milo was confused. He rubbed his head feeling for the bump the Pixie had given him the night before, which was was still there, still hurt, though where it was shouldn't give rise to this kind of illusion.

"No, it's not your bump, although, can I say, ouch!"

"Then what *are* you?"

"Don't you recognise me? It can't have been, no, it isn't that long, not long at all, perhaps it is the bump, but where it is shouldn't give you memory loss . . ."

"I recognise you alright, but you, you're . . ."

"Dead?" She stopped to think about that. "I was rather afraid of that and to be frank it's a little disturbing."

"Julia, I . . ."

Anna stirred, opened her eyes and looked at Milo. He was sitting upright and staring into space. "What did you say?"

His head snapped round and his eyes creased up. "Can you see her?"

Julia started to laugh as Anna looked confusedly round the room.

"Who?"

"Julia."

"Julia?"

Julia smiled smugly. "If you guys keep this up, I'll start putting it to music."

Milo made a face and Anna sat up, reaching out to him with growing concern.

"Do we need to get you scanned?"

"I . . . I don't know. I don't think so."

"You don't," said Julia. "I'm surprised you haven't cottoned on to what I am."

"Julia did something?"

Anna, confused, still not knowing who he was talking to. "What did she do?"

Milo turned to look at her and talked to Anna directly. "I can see Julia, more, talk to her."

"Milo, she's dead"

He gave her a 'Don't you think I know that?' look. "She must have put something in my head. In the electronics"

"Oh, when? Um . . . Wouldn't you call that a conflict of interest?"

"I was off-duty, and alone, and she wasn't a client, remember?"

Milo made a face at Julia.

Julia smiled, "Childish."

Anna smiled at the face, "Childish!"

Milo closed his eyes, "Jesus, you too!"

"Well you clearly weren't careful. You've picked something up now. Didn't Mother Talbot warn you?"

"No she didn't, but I can't see how she could have done it. Julia, I mean. We have really complex systems protecting us from this kind of hack. If not, anyone could find out lots of things we don't want them to."

Julia smirked. Whatever she was, she was clearly growing more embedded into his system as she was using the access to the room scanning. She walked around before she leant against one of the walls.

"So what do you think she is?"

"I might ask The Room to do a diagnostic, but when I did one earlier everything came up roses."

"And it will if they do one, Milo. I'm getting more settled." Julia frowned. "Although I appear not to be complete. When Elspeth put me in here she had a purpose, and I'm not able to see all of it yet. It's either time-locked or event-locked, I'm not sure which. What I am is an Artificial Intelligence, based on her personality and character. And, obviously, her appearance. What I can tell you is that I, she, became spooked at some point in the night and uploaded me."

Milo nodded. "Ok, that makes sense. You're a ghost."

Julia thought about this and Milo had the eerie sensation of knowing she was thinking.

She brightened. "I guess I am, yes."

Anna was watching Milo becoming increasingly disturbed. "What? What's going on?"

Milo focused on Anna. "Right, she's explaining what is going on, she still seems to be coming online. Obviously she's not working . . . wasn't working alone, because something told her things were not what they should have been and she did this. Whoever she's with might be Gog's mysterious 'you will be contacted by' person."

He pointed at his head, "It's an AI, based – and I don't know how far this holds – on herself. It must be projecting into my ocular system as an interface, but I don't know how she did it."

Turning back to Julia. "Can you be deleted?"

She thought about it. "Not by you, certainly, The system seems to be embedding into yours. It'll processor hop, use whatever you're not using, but I'm guessing you should get an upgrade soonish if you don't want to go mad." She grinned broadly.

Anna leant back. It was clear to her Milo was having a conversation with this thing.

"This is seriously weird, you look like you're talking to the air. It's not at all like a com link either. You'll have to do something about that."

"I'm sorry, you're right. And she's warned me that I'm going to need an upgrade to my systems. Hold on. Julia, can you link? Like when people share a file?"

"Yes, I think so."

Anna sat bolt upright. "Holy shit!"

"Impressive isn't it?" said Milo.

"Julia?"

"Anna."

"I am really weirded out by this."

"Imagine how I feel!"

"Can you? Feel, I mean?"

Julia checked. "Umm, yes, but I'm a bit confused, Milo's feelings are getting in the way."

Anna looked seriously concerned. "Do you know what happened on Sunday?"

There was a pause while Julia checked, "I . . . I don't have access to that. Sunday happened after I was uploaded. It may be on the system, but I seem to be a bit compartmentalised. Clearly I'm cautious as well as talented." She smirked again.

Anna and Milo looked at each other, caught between amazement, shock at Julia rising from the dead, slight irritation at the intrusion and the desire to know more.

Milo asked "Why did, um, Elspeth do this? And why are you Julia, and not Elspeth?"

"Elspeth wanted to help and she was worried something would happen to prevent that. As for who I am, this is how you'd met me and she couldn't have known you'd see Gog before I came online."

"You know I've seen Gog?"

"I know, what you know, Milo."

"Oh."

Anna perked up. "That's handy. We should talk sometime."

Julia gave her a conspiratorial grin.

Milo changed the subject. "Why did you come online now?"

Julia thought about that. "I seem to be set to come live in the event that there is no contact between Elspeth's com and yours for thirty-six hours. She evidently expected to be in touch quite regularly."

"And how long are you supposed to be around?"

"I can't see a term for the system, so maybe a while." She grinned brightly again.

Anna turned to him, "It might be very useful."

Julia looked put out. "Might be? It?"

"Even you don't know the extent of what Elspeth installed, why, or for how long, so I think 'might' is fair and . . . sorry."

"I guess . . . Accepted."

Milo's com lit up and Xin appeared. "Milo?"

"Here."

"Hi Anna . . ."

Then silence.

To Beijing, Julia appeared as real as the other two, not even the faintest hint that she might not actually be there.

Julia broke the ice. "Hi . . . Xin? is it?"

". . . It is. Julia? Milo?"

"It seems that before she left me, Elspeth installed an AI system into my net."

"Right. Um . . . How?"

Milo explained the back and forth of the last few minutes to Xin. She was more perturbed at the breach of his implant security than anything else. She wasn't quite sure whether to include Julia in the conversation.

"So what now?" Xin asked.

Julia had decided she was going to add her twopence worth. "Milo has to wait until he's contacted, but I can act as liaison with you guys in Beijing. It means we can work while he's still asleep."

Anna frowned. "Won't that keep him awake?"

"No, I can be discreet, certainly enough for coms. And as for surveillance, I can watch that Pixie who has your best interests not at heart."

Anna nodded. "Are you going to be 'on' all the time?"

Julia smiled. "I can be invisible, unless you don't want me to be . . ."

"This could get very . . . intrusive," said Milo.

"Right, I get that, I do."

Xin coughed. "This is an unhelpful conversation. You say he has to wait for someone to contact him. Who?"

"Sorry, I'm locked out of that piece of information."

Xin concluded, "Excellent! Milo you're going to have to let us check this out while you're asleep. You'll need to be asleep while we do it, because we're doing a thorough system check. It might take a few hours."

"Ok. That seems a bit extreme," he replied.

"Not really. Your secure system has been compromised. The AI says Julia did it but you were out of com and unconscious in her flat for long enough for the Pixies to have done something. You were then brazenly approached by the junior on your way back from Cambridge. Suddenly, 'Julia' appears. It's all a bit . . . odd."

"Ok you're right."

And that was where they left things, with Beijing pretty sore that somehow someone had skipped round their systems and Milo annoyed that things couldn't be resolved quickly.

Julia was being understanding, but Milo could feel that she resented the distrust, which was weird.

Anna didn't know what to think. She offered that she really was too tired to think and thought bed a good idea. Outside, wherever she was, the Pixie's thoughts were going to remain all her own, if she had any on this subject, and that was moot.

Anna was already in bed and asleep, or seemingly so, by the time Milo did his night-time routine, triggered a drug and climbed into his own bed. He lay on his back staring at the ceiling. Julia had disappeared since the conversation with Beijing, which showed that she could do it, and Milo wondered what Beijing would turn up.

He was worried, she felt 'right'. He hadn't known her all that long and he knew people were prone to all sorts of weird ways of thinking about one another, but still, there was a something he didn't think would be there if she had been installed by people who didn't know her.

Somewhere in the middle of all of this speculation, sleep took him. Not the kind of deep, restful sleep that's supposed to be the privilege of the innocent, but not filled with dreams either. Just chemically induced dark.

When he woke, he felt better without feeling refreshed. He wasn't sure why but he wasn't worried about the 'Julia' situation.

Milo and Anna were eating breakfast when almost the full set of 'desks' from The Room came online. It was mid-afternoon in Beijing and the conference-room appeared to be full of people, seated around a long table.

"Hi," said Xin

"Whoa!" Milo replied, startled.

"Hi, sorry, we thought we should all be in on this. Cathy and Erasto, won't be here because of time differences, and Cathy's exhausted after her last week."

"So, seven of you . . . Did you all work on it?"

"No, three of us investigated and the other four reviewed the data. It's taken a while."

"And?"

They looked at one another but, as usual, Xin spoke first. "We can find nothing that would suggest Julia is not what she says she is, but we can also find nothing to confirm she is what she says she is."

"Can you remove the program?"

"No. We're not sure where it is. There's an overlay, but it's very unusual. It's almost as though your system was causing this."

"Is it?"

"We don't see how it could."

"Anna would like to join the conversation."

Up until then, Anna couldn't see The Room.

"Sure."

"Hi Xin, wow! Lots of you here! I wanted to know, is Julia a threat to Milo? Could she do something … something independent?"

"We're unclear as to what her capabilities are just yet."

And the conversation went on like that. Beijing still very uneasy, particularly about where Julia had sprung from, and Milo pushing them for something concrete either way and pressing them to find a way to extract the program from his system.

After much talk, they came to the conclusion there really was nothing to be done. The coding was unlike anything they had come across before. If what they were discovering about Elspeth was right, there was a possibility that she was the source, but it was all ifs and maybes.

Milo finally came out with his feelings about the situation, only to be told by The Room that his feelings on the subject were, if anything, to be ignored, if not outright distrusted. It came down to this. Given they could not get rid of the AI, as it appeared to be deeply embedded in his net, they could either trust it, in as guarded a way as possible, or, pull Milo from the case. The reality was they were two people short and Milo was already familiar with the situation, so they decided to take the chance and watch the AI as closely as they could. Beijing's system security had already been enhanced and they had people working on improvements, but no one was comfortable with the situation except perhaps, Julia. Milo wasn't uncomfortable but couldn't work out why. Not very comforting.

Moving to the case, The Room had put a trace on the Pixie, but couldn't be certain it would stick, and they could find so many lines to the various men in Paris they presumed most of them had to be wild goose chases. The probability was still that these people were after the head for its financial value. No credible alternative had been shown to have a very high probable value.

Then Beijing closed the com and, on the instant, Julia appeared. She sat across from Anna and Milo. "So, do you want to tell me?"

Anna straightened. "Don't you know already?"

"Yes, but, I thought you might like to tell me."

"Oh."

Milo was getting used to Julia's sense of humour, "They've given you a clean sheet."

"Until I screw up."

"Until you show you don't have my best interests at heart"

A message came through to Milo, in text, but it was garbled. Showing it to Anna got them no further, so Milo turned to Julia and asked her if she could make something of it. It wasn't encrypted, or at least that wasn't the problem specifically. It appeared, rather, that it was incomplete. Then the house com lit up and Anna answered. It was the Pixie.

Anna was about to let her in when Milo stopped her, not out of fear of what she might do, but because, with recent experience in mind, he was worried that the com system might be compromised. Julia assured Milo the Pixie was in more danger than the apartment.

In she came. She looked round and shook her head. "Nice! This cost you a bit."

Anna smiled, not taking the compliment kindly. "Thanks."

"So this is what a dishonest living can get you?"

"You should see the summer house."

Milo intervened in the exchange of thoughts on a life badly lived. "You wanted something?"

"How do you know I'm not just trying to get in from the cold?"

"It's not cold."

"Good point." She looked around again. "I just received word."

"You're going to kill me?"

"Not yet, but there's a lot of chatter around Amsterdam. The people who pay me wondered if you'd like to check it out."

Julia, who was now only visible to Milo, and who had been circling the Pixie as she checked out the apartment, nodded. "There is a lot of chatter about Amsterdam, but they want you to draw it out not check it out, a lightening rod."

Milo smiled. "Are you putting me on the payroll?" he asked the Pixie.

Anna frowned. "How do we know it's not a trap?"

"Trap China12? I think that would be a serious challenge to their professional bona fides, eh Milo?"

Milo considered the position. "It's probably a trap, but it's not set. Not yet anyway."

Julia spoke again, "I have a bit more on that message. Whoever sent it, either sent it via Amsterdam, or it was intercepted and resent from Amsterdam, which would account for the distressed nature of the message."

Milo, who had already begun to relate to Julia as though she were real and present, asked: "Distressed?"

The Pixie looked confused. "Eh?"

Anna realised what was going on. "Oh, that confuses me too. He talks to base all the time."

The Pixie frowned at that.

Julia's eyes flicked over to the nervous agent. "She is thinking that her disruption field should have stopped any external coms."

"Your mother was from Amsterdam. Is this Gog's mysterious contact?" asked Milo.

"My mother was Elspeth. I wouldn't know about Gog's contact, but distressed? The mangled way the message came in."

Milo stood and looked at the others. "Right, we're going to Amsterdam."

CHAPTER SEVEN

Easily said. The one constant in being a hired hand, even one from the lofty China12, is that you have a budget. Anna's company was rich, but she was accountable for how money could be spent.

"Not so fast, Milo." Anna said.

He turned and the Pixie turned and Julia grinned.

"This sounds like a trap."

"It is a trap."

"What?"

Milo turned to the Pixie. "It's a trap, isn't it?"

"That would be my guess."

"You guys in on it?"

"I haven't been told we are, but then I haven't been told we aren't. If it is, it's not for my benefit."

"Either way, it's a trap."

Anna was open-mouthed. She coloured a little, annoyed. "Then why in the world are you going?!"

Milo scratched his forehead with his thumb, and his lips flattened together, as though he was trying not to say something he shouldn't say.

He nodded at the Pixie. "We know there is, more than one group interested in this . . . case. This is a chance to get a close-up look at one of the others at least. It might be uncomfortable for a minute or two, but I'll find out more this way than chasing random, hopeful fag-ends."

"But you might get killed."

"Unlikely. They know who I work for and we're not the kind of people you want to get the wrong side of."

"I think you're depending a bit too much on your reputation. They've killed once, or someone has, and whatever they're after just might be worth ignoring your reputation. Remember Brazil, not everyone plays by the rules."

She had a point and Milo knew it. The Pixie watched the tennis, unused to seeing orders debated or ideas talked out.

"Look, this is a lead, and we've had precious few of those so far. I want to know who killed Julia and why. I want to know why it suddenly became so goddamned important and who else is in on it. If it is this important, there's no guarantee that we won't be tidied away as 'loose ends' no matter who we are."

"Oh, you think you, or . . . I . . ."

He nodded. "If people like this one," he jerked a thumb at the Pixie, "are involved, it goes high up and those that high up don't like to have too many people knowing what they know."

Anna turned to the Pixie, "Are we? Are we something to be tidied up?"

The Pixie swivelled her head, considered and then smiled in that way she had and shrugged. "I have no orders in that area at the moment. I don't know if I ever will have. I don't know if they will order me to do something before they order me to do something. I do know that if they do I will carry out that order."

The Pixie was completely dispassionate. Anna looked at her. She looked slight, vulnerable even, attractive, pleasant enough company and probably a psychopath. Anna knew from her work that the 'official' bodies had programs for finding and then training certain personality types for specific roles. She had come across one or two in court but hadn't had much experience with the raw end.

As she turned back to Milo she looked like she felt sick.

The Pixie was impatient. "Are we going?"

Milo turned his head to look at Anna. She nodded. Milo and the Pixie headed for the door, but Anna didn't move.

As they walked out, Milo held back. "You ok?"

She forced a smile. "I'm going to go into the office, tell them what we know and make sure they're happy to extend you the resources you'll need."

He held her gaze and they understood what else she would have to do.

"Your area, I guess, and this is mine"

She nodded and he was gone.

By the time he was on the street, the Pixie had a car waiting and was already inside. Climbing in, he could see she was communicating with base.

Julia had 'seated' herself in the back of the car. She smiled at Milo.

"I can tap her end of the signal without her noticing," she said. "If I take the whole thing, the system will pick me up."

Milo looked dumbly at her, he couldn't talk. He called up the non-verbal system.

"Just think it, I'll hear."

So he did. "*You can hear my thoughts?*"

"I can hear coherent thoughts, directed in the same way you would if you were trying to use the non-verbal system, but you don't have to make such an effort."

"*Because they pass through my implant?*"

"Exactly. I'm not sure how much I'll grow into your organic system and not sure, if I do, what I'll understand or know. This is new."

"*Ok, I am freaked out all over again.*"

"She's dangerous" Julia said.

"*The Pixie? All believers are and she seems to run her life to order.*"

"Hmm. Whatever the other end's saying, it isn't to do you any harm at present."

"Thanks."

The Pixie turned sharply to look at Milo. "What?"

Realising he had spoken out loud, he said: "For the car."

She frowned. "How else are we going to get to the station?"

"Right." He nodded, trying not to look at the grinning Julia.

The car had been rolling along the side streets towards the main motorway. Once there, it pulled straight out into traffic, having synchronised its speed in the last fifty meters of the side street. Transponders on all cars ensured they were aware of the taxi. A gap was allowed for and the heavy rush hour press was undisturbed. Since the automated systems had arrived in all of the big cities and on all of the major trunk roads across the five mayoralties, traffic had taken its first significant rise in average speed since the nineteenth century. Accidents had plummeted, particularly those related to excessive alcohol or drug consumption.

It still amused Milo that when it had been introduced and made mandatory there had been many voices raised against it on the basis it might be dangerous. Between the end of the second war and the start of the war of economic collapse, more than half a million people had been killed on the roads every decade in the European area. Since the introduction of automated traffic systems, that number had fallen to a few thousands and the traffic flowed smoothly, quickly, without jams and with few reasons for executive intervention.

Only the movies and criminals disliked it, as it meant the enforcement authorities could pluck out a single car at any point, and no more car chases. The movies solved their problem with a rash of historical dramas set in the bad old days. The criminals found other ways round it, as they always do.

Just over fifteen minutes later, they were walking into St Pancras and to the Amsterdam train. The Pixie was on a budget too, so they headed for the cheap seats and grabbed a coffee on the way. The carriage was about half full, people going on business mainly, with one or two day trippers. They found seats alone easily enough.

"So what did your bosses tell you about this?"

"Not as much as I'd like." She stopped to consider how much she would share. "Whatever the chatter is, it's . . . semi-official, mayoral maybe."

Milo gave her a long look, "Meaning you're not mayoral?"

"Not meaning anything, one way or another."

"Are you working for an extra-territorial group?"

"Asks the man working for China12."

"We're a crime group. We have recognised status across all legit authorities, and the ones who aren't legit . . . aren't legit. Answer my question."

"No. Could be the people I'm working for are not part of the petty squabbles your mayors are interested in. And before you ask, I don't work for any corp either. And I didn't get a chance to have breakfast served to me by my girlfriend, so I'm hungry. Want anything?"

She climbed out of the seat and paused long enough for, "Whatever looks good"

"That won't be much," and she stalked away.

Julia popped into the seat opposite and Milo jumped. "Do you have to?"

"There's another way?"

"I don't know."

"Sorry, but I would have thought fading up slowly would be infinitely creepier. You got her goat."

"She gave away more than she meant to."

"She gave away a lot."

"Yeah, but I don't know exactly what. Do you know?"

"No. What she said makes sense of this fishing trip though. Her bosses don't know who intercepted that message you got and they're keen to find out, I'd say, and they may find out who sent it as well."

"But if she's not working for the mayors and not the corps, then who? The states? I didn't think they had the money."

"Could be a new grouping, transregional?"

He shrugged and asked, as much to himself as to Julia, "What are we heading into in Amsterdam?"

"Don't worry, I'll keep you safe."

"Thanks."

"Looking out for number one. If you go I go too and I'm beginning to like this."

"So what about this communication? Was it Gog's person?"

Julia thought, eyes up and to the right. Then she faced him again. "No . . . Yes . . . it might be. I don't know who Gog was thinking of. But I thought it was to you as it came in on your com. It wasn't."

"Oh?"

"It was sent to me."

Milo, eyebrows raised in surprise, "By someone who thinks you're alive? Or by someone who knows you are . . . like this?"

"Right now I have too little data to answer that."

"Why'd it come to me?"

"I seem to have diverted all of Julia's communications to me, here."

"You mean to me."

"No, I don't, but I didn't realise it until a short time ago. Look, I'm still growing into this."

Milo narrowed his eyes. He was not a happy man and now they both knew it . . . "I suppose I can get used to it," he said.

"Anyway, the message is too garbled to make a lot of sense of. I'm trying to put it together, but it's not cooperating."

"Can you ident the originator? Or where they are?"

"All of that's been stripped out, whoever sent it is being careful, it's quite cryptic. They may just be checking if I'm alive. The relayers, on the other hand, were a bit clumsy."

"That's probably deliberate"

"Whether or not, *they* are showing up as being in central Amsterdam and they look mayoral."

The Pixie appeared in the carriage, arms filled with whatever they were selling, which she dumped on the table.

"Your brains trust come up with anything?"

"Welcome back." He eyed the assorted packages warily "This looks good to you?"

She was still none too happy with him. "It's what they had. No one has a gun to your head . . . yet."

"In answer to your question, I have an address, but no clue as to who it's from. The intercept was by "something mayoral", but they're the reason your bosses suggested going to Amsterdam. Very naughty, you guys really have to learn to leave things to the professionals."

The Pixie bit into something soft and Milo wondered which bit of him it was a substitute for.

By the time they were slowing down into Amsterdam, the table was a mess of discarded cellulose wrapping and cups, from the protein and carbs the Pixie had brought back. Describing them in more detail would go back to a set of chemical formulas because whatever it had started out as, it probably wasn't in any place you would call a farm. The 'sandwiches' bore no relation to anything that most people would have had in their normal lexicon. Milo was left pondering. He had both seen and consumed them, the joy of nutritional printing. He hoped at least it had been hygienic. He thought he knew it was that, at best.

Amsterdam was the usual bustle of bicycles and beer shops. The collapse of the Belgian and northern French beer industry had seen the ever-enterprising Dutch step up and a thousand small breweries had sprung up, almost all of which had been around since the late nineteenth century, or so they said. Whatever the truth, the resulting industry had given the place a nice, faintly festival atmosphere and the addition of low-alcohol regs and compensatory drugs made the place moderately safe. If you were a civilian.

A cab drew up in front of them, its info-panel flashing 'Mr Talbot', and the door slid open. In the days when cars with blacked out windows stopped beside you and two guys with dark glasses hopped out to 'invite' you to join them for a ride, it was considered foolish to turn down the opportunity and terrifying to accept. Having an empty cab do the same to you was no less insistent and no less terrifying.

The Pixie waved him in with a smile but stood back.

"Not curious to see what's at the other end?"

"I wasn't invited. It would be rude."

The door slid shut and the cab moved round the circulation ring and out into traffic.

Milo sat back. "Is she in on the pinch?"

Julia, sitting beside him, said: "Don't think so. The cab's instruction came from a source associated with the interceptors of the message this morning."

Milo looked back through the rear window, though spotting if he was being followed would have been near-impossible.

He shrugged. "We'll find out soon enough anyhow."

They were moving into a less connected part of town. It seemed, on the face of it, a little odd to have parts of a big city that were only lightly connected into the central network, it wasn't. There are times, most of the time, when it is in the interests of the authorities to be able to see, record and to connect with its populace, but sometimes more discretion is required. Sometimes it pays to be blind.

The cab rolled along an empty street full of warehouses, full of nothing. The aftermath of war can leave a lot of people very broke. They stopped and the door slid open.

Milo didn't exactly jump out but, as soon as he was out, the cab closed up and slid away. It hadn't taken any money. They were in a narrow side street. The warehouses were uniform and had been built to supply ships heading to resupply Baltic troops. Since the war, they were a resource looking for a problem in a world that solved its problems in another way.

The bricks were red, the roofs grey and the doors a cheap anti-rust red-brown, but, as they weren't made of metal, that was just for old times' sake. In front of them were large double doors with locks at either end in case anyone felt like stealing the air inside. The watchman's entrance was ajar.

Milo eyed it and looked at Julia. Her eyebrow lifted a centimetre. "It doesn't say 'Eat me' . . ."

"No, it says, 'Come into my parlour . . .' Shall we?" he replied

The warehouse was huge and dim, though not completely dark. An intense, old-style LED lit up a pair of chairs at the far end. Milo could see no one.

He walked in a few feet, "Hello?"

Silence.

Milo turned to Julia who shrugged. "I can't find any signal here. We are very much on our own."

A noise from the farthest end of the space and a door closed.

Clipped footsteps then a man appeared, dressed very smartly: white shirt, black tie, top pocket handkerchief – you don't see that too often – and a grey suit, a Kevlar-graphene mix given away by the sheen from the LED. In more modern lighting it would look like a silk job. Either way it looked smooth, sharp and comfortable, it just showed up he expected to be shot at, but he didn't care. Whoever paid for the suit cared, though, and wanted him smart and wanted him alive.

He gestured Milo forward, "Come Mr.Talbot, join me."

Milo thought about it but ambled forward. Only way to find out, was to find out.

The man sat and took out a vape, which he lit with a click. Milo wondered if it was nicotine or if the substance had some purpose other than recreation. He was about ten feet away.

"Mr. Talbot, we are honoured!" He had a slight Dutch accent, which meant he was speaking English.

"Milo, please."

"Very genial of you. I am Errol."

As Milo got closer he guessed Errol was in his mid-thirties. Though he wore a suit, the bulges at his shoulders and the taut fabric of his shirt spoke of a well-kept body.

"Errol?"

"Yes, very good. We saw you were coming and sent a cab. Save you a lot of running around looking for us."

"I was looking for you?"

"Come now, we are both grown-ups. You must have been monitoring the communications of the sadly lamented Ms Cruickshank."

Milo looked at him with a practised puzzlement.

"That's right, we know her real name. Or did you think you could keep that one to yourself?"

"As part of an ongoing investigation, I had and have no notion of keeping anything to myself. I know your name, but you haven't told me who you work for."

"No I haven't, have I? Discretion, as they say Milo . . ."

"The only reason to be discreet, Errol, is for you to hide, and you would only hide if you shouldn't be doing something but you're doing it all the same."

"Just because the law has told the authorities they shouldn't do something, Milo, it does not follow that they should do nothing."

"No, but you are prohibited from – as the minister so delicately put it all those years ago – 'thinking'."

"I assure you, Milo, I barely ever think."

"I can well believe it. Tell me something, was it your guys who threw Julia through the window, without thinking?"

Errol didn't pay the slightest attention to the question. "Do you have it Milo?"

Milo looked blank. "*It*?"

"The item Ms Cruickshank removed from her apartment earlier this week."

"Not that I know what you're talking about, but do I look like I have anything with me, unless the item is very small?"

Errol put a finger to his ear. Julia, who had been circling him as he spoke, gave Milo a sharp look and then disappeared.

Errol turned back, "There is no reason to be obtuse, Milo. We are on the same side."

"I doubt that."

"That's a pity. Either way, I can tell you, in the event you don't already know, which it is my turn to doubt, the item we are seeking to find is an objet d'art, and a very valuable one at that. We would rather it does not fall into non-European hands. The artist was Romanian. We know that certain museums in other parts of the world would like to, 'fill out' their collections."

"So you are European?"

Errol looked at Milo and then smiled, "Mayoral"

"Good. But there's a problem with your, 'they're trying to get our stuff' idea. It would mean they would have to own up to stealing it."

"Yes, but it is easier to apologise, and keep the item, than to ask for it and be refused."

"Still, killing someone seems a little desperate, no?"

"Our guess is a clumsy accident. Perhaps they were not expecting to see the lady there."

Milo shifted at that. There was something in the way Errol said it that gave the impression he might have been there or have been watching on vid . . . or was he reading too much into it?

The mayors were a complicated bunch. Their growth from the loose organisation before the war to being major power brokers centred on their capacity to generate and need to consume actual power had been swift, and people were grateful and resentful in equal measure. 'The Five Mayors' – Paris, London, Berlin, Milan and Barcelona – were transnational and had added to their number. The title a nod to their beginnings.

Errol touched his ear again and the light flashed against the hard edge of the device he was using, very old fashioned.

Milo took a quick survey of his surroundings. Still no sign of anyone else, still no sign of Julia. He probed inside his own systems but came up empty. Errol had come back to the room and was eyeing him up. Milo looked quizzical.

"Sorry we are in such a dead spot, the city still hasn't recovered. The war, you know."

Milo nodded, "Why did you want to see me way out here if you're just looking for some . . . art junk?"

"Not junk, Milo, and the people who we fear may be looking to take it away could be watching you. If we know you are connected with it they might too, and they don't seem to be too particular."

"Or capable."

Errol's lips pressed together in a way that made Milo feel his professional reputation had been stained.

"You met Ms Cruickshank in Paris. She didn't give you the work then?"

"Is all of that a question? Or are you telling me you've been following me, which would also be illegal?"

"I'm asking you a question and I really must insist you begin to answer."

"Insist away. I don't have to answer anything and you know it. I'm protected under section 38 of the European penal code, as well as under international treaties."

"Yes, all true, but you are out of communication and all on your own. I am neither." Errol lifted his chin.

A shuffling from behind. They must have followed him in, it's why you normally have back up. The three men came forward: two away to Milo's sides, the third just behind his right shoulder.

They had a different tailor from Errol and they didn't look as though they were the talkative kind. Each was dressed in a different kind of rough clothing, but all of it was the kind you burn when you get blood on it. From the scars and the rings on their fingers they looked low-grade – strictly plumbers' mates, not plumbers – but they looked like they knew their business and their business was often 'clumsy'.

One of them stood out, Milo speculated he was the ranking thug, at a guess an old army corporal. He weighed up his options.

"Do you want answers or to eliminate competition?"

"I suppose a bit of both."

"We've been brought in on this officially. If you wanted us out, you should have jumped me yesterday, or were you too busy being 'clumsy' in London?"

Milo wasn't sure he'd seen the flick of the eyes that gave the order or if he had imagined it, later, you've always seen it, but the train hitting the back of his head definitely happened at the same time as the lights went out and the floor got tough.

Everything was blurred as well as dim when he came to and he felt a little sick, but Errol seemed very concerned about him. Touching. Errol, that is. He was touching Milo's jacket, putting things back having searched him. The 'boys' were either side of him, the ranking thug to Errol's right, and Errol's chair was a lot closer than is usual in polite society.

"Wow, that was quick. You guys take the best drugs."

"Mmhuh." None too coherent, but in the circumstances Milo thought it was a pretty witty reply.

"Now, are you feeling more talkative?"

Milo shook his head, more to get the cobwebs and the ringing out, than in reply.

Errol was seeming patient. "I do hate unpleasantness, Milo, so it would be better all round if you just answered up. As you might have guessed, we will be tidying away loose ends, but we can be more or less nasty in that regard. While I don't like it, per se, there are some who positively enjoy it."

"Yeah, I guess. Trouble is, I don't have all that much to say. I mean I could make things up, and if it comes to it I probably will, but it won't be any more . . ."

He stopped speaking when the Pixie just appeared to Errol's right, smiling as ever.

"How did you get here?" asked Milo.

Errol was surprised and looked to his side. He did a double take and pulled out a gun.

He shouted. "Watch out!"

The Pixie grinned maliciously.

The heavy mob had no idea what was going on but looked around in confusion. The corporal took a step toward Errol. Mistake. Errol fired and managed to wing him, as the bullet passed right through the Pixie. Milo realised what she was.

The corporal fell down, surprised, and the gun he was holding skittered off into the darkness. The other two turned their guns on Errol who was amazed at what was happening. He reached out with his arm and waved it through the Pixie and as he did so she reached out to his earpiece, touched it.

Errol jerked as the charge went through him. He collapsed in a heap, unconscious. The thug on the floor writhed away and the others stepped up to Errol. One prodded him with a foot.

Out of nowhere, the Pixie was in the middle of them. This time, not as an ethereal vision, but as a lethal machine. She slammed her foot into the face of the first man, snapping his head back. He wouldn't be getting up again. The second man, more alive, was in the process of stepping back, fists up, when Milo threw himself at the man's legs causing him to fall over onto his back.

The Pixie stepped forward and smashed him with her elbow on the junction between his nose and his forehead. He couldn't see, but it didn't matter. She reached round and jerked his neck upward and back onto her knee, and there was a loud crack.

The corporal with the gunshot wound had struggled to his feet but kept slipping in his own blood, she calmly walked over to him.

"Don't!" Milo called out as he clambered to his feet.

The Pixie just punched him in the jaw and he was out cold.

Errol stirred as Milo stood and, with surprising speed, spun, turning on his back, and took Milo's feet from under him. In one movement he was upright and heading for the door.

The Pixie vaulted over Milo and was reaching for him as he got to the door when Milo called out again. "Leave him."

The Pixie stopped and spun round. "Why?"

Milo got up awkwardly, leaning on his knees.

"He's not going to tell us anything."

"He might have been the one who killed your friend."

"It won't bring her back."

Julia appeared. Milo looked her over.

"Was that you, being her?" He jerked his thumb in the Pixie's direction. Julia smiled and slowly moved her head to confirm it.

"Neat trick."

"I needed her help, so I borrowed her hollow projection."

The Pixie came across and looked Julia up and down. "I would have thought she'd want closure."

"I am right here, you know."

"Not really. You're not the same!"

"Still, you could ask."

Milo looked at them, "So you two became acquainted."

Julia smiled. "She nearly shat herself!"

"I'm not used to seeing ghosts. I thought there was a problem with my implant. Turns out there was."

Milo looked puzzled. "I don't understand though, if you are in my implant, how did you manage to contact the Pixie?"

"The earpiece Errol was using, is old-fashioned, radio. I was able to . . . hack isn't the right word . . . piggyback on his signal long enough to get our friend's attention."

"Right, and you thought she was a ghost?" he said to the Pixie.

"No! Not really."

Milo prodded the injured thug with his foot.

"Anyway, I saved your ass, didn't I?" said the Pixie

"You sure did."

Julia bent down and touched the thug's head. This time it had the opposite effect from the time she had touched Errol and he stirred.

She looked up. "Helped his drug recovery system a little bit, you'll be pleased to know it's not much good. Cheap."

Milo hunkered down, reached forward to support the man as he pushed himself up. The thug ran his tongue round his mouth several times. The Pixie held out a bottle of something. The thug's head jerked back and he looked up at the Pixie, wondering who exactly she was.

Milo answered. "The seventh Cavalry."

"What?"

Milo looked at Julia. "Can he see you?"

She shook her head.

Milo and the Pixie helped him up onto a chair. Then she wandered away to the wall near the door and watched. Julia stood closer to Milo, but also just watched.

The thug glared at the Pixie. "I don't know anything you know."

"None of us do, but you might add to our file of nothing, just a bit."

"How?"

"Who are you working for, corporal? Can I call you that?"

He shrugged and then remembered his shoulder. He looked away as though that would mean no one would know he had talked.

"The guy who just left. Who do you think?"

"This is one of the Free Cities, but I guess he's not working for one of them."

"Why not?"

"They wouldn't care about the 'objet d'art'. They have too many other problems. And it probably isn't the states"

"Why not them? I could be a G-man!"

The Pixie snorted and pushed away from the wall a little. "No you couldn't."

Milo looked across with a grin. "That position is all filled up, so that leaves the Five Mayors."

He said nothing this time, but turned and stared back.

"Do you know what it is, this, piece of art?"

"I was just here to help."

"With what?"

"Search me pal. All I know is that they wanted to ask you a few friendly questions. I was to told to bring a unit down and do what the higher-up told us to."

"You hadn't met Errol before?"

"No, and we weren't told something like her would be involved."

The Pixie took a few menacing steps toward him and he winced.

"Look, they think you have something, or had it or know where it is, or who has it. And they want it bad!"

"What?"

"They didn't tell me. That's all I heard."

"So it might be about money?"

"I guess, it usually is. All I know is I'm in way over my head if she's involved. I think you are too."

He swung a slow look at the Pixie, who smiled. Milo was puzzled and scratched his head.

He looked from Julia to the Pixie, "Any ideas folks?" Julia shook her head but stepped nearer.

The Pixie walked toward them, "We should off him and leave."

The thug looked alarmed and his head snapped round to Milo.

The Pixie stopped about eight feet away. "He's seen me. That's too many people seeing me."

Julia stepped in. "Don't worry, I can sort that. He won't remember a thing."

Milo and the Pixie looked surprised. The man, looking from one to the other and wondering who they were talking to, looked frightened.

"You can do that?" the Pixie asked.

"Yeah, simple, we haven't been talking long, I can block it, he won't remember you." She nodded to the Pixie. To Milo she said: "I think he will remember you, can't stop that, not without damage."

The Pixie perked up. "I don't mind damage."

The thug heard that and was getting desperate. "What are you going to do?"

Julia stepped to his left side. Milo smiled at him and said. "Give you a hangover."

Julia reached out and touched his head again. This time he jerked and went out like a light, slid onto the floor.

"You're sure he won't remember me?"

"I'm sure."

Milo shrugged. "Hidden talents."

"I didn't know about it until I needed to. Stuff keeps coming up like that."

The Pixie gave her a look and headed for the door.

In a cafe in central Amsterdam two of the three were eating. Julia was watching, mesmerised by how much the Pixie could put away. In front of her was enough food to feed a small family and she was devouring it as though she was half starved.

Becoming self-conscious, the Pixie looked up, "What?"

Julia looked away. Milo speculated as to whether an AI could become embarrassed, but he felt embarrassed and even coloured. Julia was aware of it and a faint smile drifted across her face.

The Pixie shifted her attention. "Can the two of you have conversations without my seeing it? I mean can you . . . are you having a conversation right now and all I see is Julia sitting there staring at me, while you stuff your face?"

Milo looked speculatively at Julia, who shrugged.

He turned to the Pixie, "I would think it rude to do that, but I have no idea if we could. Anyway, it might fry my tiny brain."

The Pixie turned to Julia. "I have to eat, the drugs and the system processor consume energy at very high rates, especially if I have to . . . take care of business."

Julia shifted. "All right, I was just surprised. You're very . . . trim."

"Goes with the territory."

Milo took a mouthful of beer and leant back. "I thought that went well."

Julia's eyebrows rose. "Really? What does it look like when things go badly?"

The Pixie snorted. "It doesn't. If you walk away from it, it went well. If you learned something or found something out, it went very well."

"So did it go well or very well?"

Milo considered Julia's question. "I would say we learned something."

The Pixie stopped eating for a moment. "Apart from discovering you need to be looked after, what exactly did we learn?"

"I'm guessing *you* learned a lot. What it is you're dealing with just for a start. We know that there are at least three sets of people looking for this thing and that it may or may not be for its value on the art market, which might explain certain events."

The Pixie was now curious, "Such as?"

"Such as, if you don't know already, you are behind the curve and that explains why you're hanging on my coattails instead of checking them in."

She nodded and went back to her meal. "Our friend was more forthcoming than I expected, I wonder why that was?"

Julia leant in. "He'd just seen his colleagues butchered. That could have something to do with it."

The Pixie stopped, shook her head, "No, those guys were just muscle, low-level, badly trained. Whatever he said about a 'unit', I doubt he ever saw those guys before today. I know he didn't care, and he knew things. Things he shouldn't have."

Julia smiled. "He didn't get a lot of opportunity."

Milo smiled indulgently. "He didn't put up any resistance to my questions, he just answered up. He wasn't high up, but his sort, ex-army, they have a certain pride and they're trained. Whatever he told us he wanted us to know."

Julia, irritated by the attitude of the others, "Being in peril for your life does concentrate the mind you know, resets your priorities."

"It didn't yours now did it?" Milo shot back.

"That's different."

The Pixie took Milo's part, "Not really, people like Errol and the Corporal are just as strong believers in their 'side' as any of us."

Milo looked at the other two. "China12 doesn't have a side"

The others simultaneously, "Everyone has a side!"

They were surprised at the shared reaction and would have high-fived if they could.

Milo smiled, "Not in the sense you two mean."

Julia sniffed. "Smug much?"

The Pixie grunted. "The Crime groups? They're the worst bunch of smug . . . *people* on the planet."

"Aside from academics and people who think that because they operate outside of the law, they are also above it."

The Pixie stiffened and her head spun round to stare at Milo. "Are you getting this?"

Milo sat up to answer but Julia interrupted, "Oh! . . ."

Milo looked at the Pixie, "Did you?"

"No! How would I? I was with you."

"Your people?"

She shook her head. "Who would want to kill Errol?"

Julia frowned. "Hold on, look at the time stamp."

"The real Errol was already dead. So who did we just meet?"

Silence descended and Milo sipped at his beer. "We were given a message today by someone. They either want us to find it and hand it over, or back the hell off."

Julia looked at the Pixie who was still munching. "Which?"

"The fact we don't know says they aren't sure which they'd rather themselves, both have their advantages and drawbacks from their point of view."

The Pixie wiped her mouth. "And who are they? I should have stopped him."

"I guess they'll tell us when they're ready," said Milo

Julia leaned back. "So what are you going to do?"

Milo smiled at her. "We'll do what we would always do, what we've contracted to do. We'll find your killer and find out what was so important that you needed to die."

CHAPTER EIGHT

Anna wasn't available for an update, wasn't even in London, just another holo-message and Julia was puzzled. She and Milo decided to finish the first conversation he had started with Gog and headed for Cambridge.

The train was the usual mix of the mid twenty-first and late twentieth centuries, causing Milo to feel conflicted. Was he at home because of the former or the latter? Looking around him, most of the other passengers seemed to have made a choice between the two. The Pixie was sulking or talking to base, or sulking and talking to base, Milo wasn't sure which. Julia had disappeared for the moment as the crowded train had left her seemingly 'in' people or in parts of the train, which was too weird even for her. A conversation with The Room had reassured Milo that this time there would be no blank space in China12's tracking and monitoring, and they would form their view of the situation afterward.

Arriving late in Cambridge, too late to meet any normal person, they checked into a hotel near the college. Cambridge hotels were an odd mix. They were either very fashionable or seriously down at heel. However even the latter could offer a reasonable and clean room, slow wi-fi and quite a good breakfast. Since the squeeze on education after the war, visiting academics were always on a budget and the upper-end establishments were strictly for the parents, friends and relations of students attending the august institution.

The Pixie had disappeared, Milo couldn't imagine where, while he and Julia took a brown room in a brown hotel, the last word in discretion.

The next morning they were enjoying breakfast on the terrace when the Pixie reappeared and joined them. It was the second cup of coffee before Milo was feeling civil enough to speak.

"You can't be there when we see Gog."

"Why?" asked the Pixie

"To begin with, she'll refuse to see you."

"You've spoken with her?"

"Not about that, but I know she won't see you and I don't want her refusing to see me because you're there."

"Why would she refuse to see me?"

"You know why."

"If, in the course of my job, I have . . ."

"Then you'll do so on your own account and not on my ticket, and I seriously doubt you can do so on your own account."

"You're running a dangerous line."

"No, I'm running a professional line. If I get anything and if I think I can, without putting anyone's life in danger, and if I think I can trust you, I'll share what I can."

A displeased look crossed the Pixie's face. "That's a lot of 'ifs' and 'thinks', Milo."

"It's the best you're going to get."

*

The corridor to Gog's office was deserted. There weren't even cameras. The Pixie was outside pacing up and down, annoyed at having been told "no" by Milo a second time, and less politely than at breakfast. Then the college porter, though more politely, had told her she couldn't go with him. The room was quiet, as it had been before, but knocking produced no reply this time.

Milo turned to Julia. "Could she be at a lecture?"

"No, I've checked her timetable. She's supposed to be here, returning work to post-grads. I put off the next two students to give us some time."

"Can you check inside?"

She shook her head. He knelt in front of the door and pulled out a pick for the old-fashioned lock. In a few seconds, a click and the handle turned. A quick look round and they were in. The

112

office, while still exhibiting the same organised chaos as last time, was empty.

Julia smiled. Milo looked at her oddly.

"What?"

She made a face. "Nostalgia."

Milo felt it, strongly, and his head throbbed.

"How can you feel that?" he asked.

"She left me with a lot of her memories, perhaps all, not sure about that yet, but this is a strong one."

"I thought you hadn't unpacked all of you?"

"I haven't. The room triggered the memory and it unpacked itself."

"Weird."

They looked around. Milo checked the desk for any sign of where Gog might be, while Julia checked her electronic records but it was clear after a moment or two that they had no clue.

"Do we look for other evidence?"

Milo wondered what she had in mind. "Such as?"

"You said she was spooked. Maybe stuff about that or about me?"

"I thought you remembered?"

"There's something in the way Elspeth put me together. Not everything is available to me right now. My feelings for this place were strong but they only triggered a sense I have about it, not information. Either it's time-locked or geographically locked or something . . ." her voice trailed away, clearly frustrated.

"We could look. Any idea what for?"

A knock on the door and they froze. Milo looked at Julia, alarmed.

"Student?" he hissed.

"Think it!"

He grimaced, thought, "*So?*"

"I don't know"

"*Can you check?*"

"How?"

113

Another knock. Milo's eyes were glued to the handle. He moved quietly behind the door and thought, "*Check on the Pixie, would you?*"

Julia disappeared and then after a moment she was back. "She's gone."

He glared at the door. Should he open it? A muffled voice from further up the corridor and the footsteps receded.

"*Check, see if that was the Pixie would you?*"

Julia disappeared again.

Milo had another quick look round the room, but found nothing and headed for the door.

Julia returned. "Not her. It was one of the post-grads I told not to come, little git! But the Pixie's gone. Totally disappeared."

Milo got on his knees again, locked the door and they walked away. He contacted The Room.

"Xin?"

"Milo."

"You get that?"

"We did."

"Could you find the Pixie for us?"

"We'll try."

"And then Gog. I get the feeling they're connected and I'm worried . . ."

"Probably, we'll find out."

By then Milo and Julia were back out in the open.

Julia looked perplexed. "That's not like her."

"No, I wouldn't have thought so."

"Where to?"

"The station, London. Hopefully we'll get some answers."

*

They could tell they were nearing London by the increasing intensity of the drone whine. Milo reflected on it as one of the reasons he didn't live in the City.

They tried to contact Anna with no luck but headed to her apartment anyway. It was a useful base and Anna had given him access. Beijing got back with essentially no news, which was big news. Both Gog and the Pixie were gone. While they were aware that the Pixie could disappear at any time, that Gog had been able to do it was very surprising. This wasn't just a case of going absent from the usual academic hotspots and social networks or even being 'out'. It was like vanishing into thin air and there were only two ways for that to happen.

Milo considered the chances of Gog being able to take herself off-grid so completely and was uncomfortably aware of how unlikely it was she could do that, which brought up possibility number two, a possibility he didn't want to confront.

He was flooded with a sense of unhappiness, which was interrupted by Julia in his ear.

"No, me neither."

"Do we have no barriers between our minds?"

"Not at the moment. We might be able to develop them over time."

"Over time. Suggesting that this is permanent?"

"Suggesting, if it is, we could find a way . . ." Her voice trailed off once again.

"Don't worry about it at the moment . . ."

"You never know. I could be like an unquiet spirit and disappear when my needs are met."

"You are certainly unquiet. I wonder what your needs are, exactly. Is it to find the people who killed you, or the person, or something else entirely?"

There was an unhappy silence. As was becoming familiar, he didn't know how but he knew it was unhappy.

"How does that work?" he asked

"What?"

"My feeling what you're feeling?"

"I'm not sure. I'm not sure how I'm feeling at all."

"We'll figure something out. Just one thing . . . Julia and I, we were intimate. Will that be a problem?"

She smiled at him amused at his discomfort. "Milo, Julia and I, we're different, like the Pixie pointed out."

He gave a sharp nod. They pulled up outside Anna's apartment. It was late evening and Milo had a new reason for discomfort. Here was another person they couldn't contact. Once inside, the place was quiet and tidy and, Milo thought, remarkable for the absence of dead bodies.

"Only one person has been killed," Julia observed in response to Milo's unexpressed thought.

"You mean apart from the Pixie's 'collateral damage' in Amsterdam? Anyway, too many people are going missing and the people we think are involved with this can make people disappear, just like that."

He began to look around. He sat opposite Anna's terminal but didn't expect to find anything of significance. At first he didn't, but a couple of searches in her diary and a holo, not sent out, snapped on.

It was Anna. "Hi, Milo, if you're seeing this it's because the system has detected you and I'm not back yet. Just after you left, I brought our London partners up to date but, as I was getting ready to join you, I got called to New York. They've taken me off-grid. I leave in about ten minutes, but I should only be there about a day. If I'm gone more than two days, come look for me, as something will have happened. Regards to Julia. I hope we'll both have answers by the time I get back."

She had obviously just been talking with her American colleagues as her accent was more pronounced than usual. The time stamp roughly matched the time he was getting hit in Amsterdam, so she wouldn't have left the meeting yet in all probability. Ok, one down.

He took a shower and a shave. An empty pot of coffee and a dirty mug beside several dirty plates suggested they had been there more than a couple of hours. Julia was sitting forward on a large, square seat, while Milo sprawled on the couch, feet on the coffee table. They were in a meeting with China12.

Xin said: ". . . and we don't know how."

Julia replied, "So she's not with the Pixie and you think she's alive?"

"Not with the Pixie, that's certain. Alive? We have no evidence to the contrary and her going off-grid was the same as anyone else. One minute she's in her office, the next she's untraceable."

"What was she doing in the hours before she went off-grid?" asked Milo.

"For the most part nothing unusual. Indeed one might say, taken as a whole, nothing unusual."

"But?"

"Indeed, but. She was examining several papers on the particle research facility."

"I thought that was what mathematicians did," he said.

"Which is why I say, 'taken as a whole', but particle research isn't in her field of mathematics."

"Your conclusion?" probed Julia.

"We have no firm conclusion. However, we hazard a possibility, no greater than thirty percent, that she may have gone to meet someone in Geneva."

Milo asked, "Why Geneva?"

"CERN, It's the nearest town. We don't think she'd go to the research facility, she has done none of the paperwork and has no immediate reason to go, beyond being a guest. As she's 'off' we believe anyone she visits will be of interest to those who killed Julia."

Milo got up and paced the room, frustration boiling over. "Do we have any clue as to why that happened or why they are looking for the head?"

"Beyond money? No."

Milo's eyes narrowed, "So you think it *is* money?"

"No. Given what's happened, that probability dropped from ninety-five percent in Paris to less than forty percent at this point. Nothing that's happened has given any support to money being the main reason for the sequence of events following your meeting Julia in Paris."

Milo grimaced, looked at Julia. "So what do we think?"

She looked down at her hands spreading her fingers as though counting them, then looked up.

"Geneva."

He agreed.

Xin added, "We would concur."

Milo took a breath. "On the basis that . . .?"

Julia brightened. "We have no other leads and it's a nice place to go?"

Again, Xin nodded. The hint of a smile ghosted across her face.

Milo shrugged. "I just don't want to be at the airport the day my ship comes in!"

The two women looked at him, surprised, puzzled.

With the advantage of the inside track, Julia laughed and turned to Xin. "It's an old joke . . . very very old."

Xin twisted her face into what she considered a polite smile. "Good luck!"

Julia replied, "Thank you," and Xin was gone.

Julia looked up at Milo. "Real misgivings?"

"I don't like going somewhere 'just because'. It seems unprofessional."

"We have a lead and Geneva brings up something."

"Something?"

"Elspeth liked you and trusted you, but only so far, and she's not the only one, *was*n't the only one, involved. I'm learning step by step."

"But you know more?"

"I don't know what I know."

*

They had just reached St. Pancras when Xin was back.

"Change in plan," she said. "Dr Himura has put some results together with some of her neat little subroutines and she says Marseille."

"Marseille? Why?"

Julia spun round. "I had a friend there, perhaps a cousin?"

"Certainly someone in your close circle, and they work at the particle accelerator. He should be there, but he went missing about two days ago. Himura speculates he is the likely identity of Gog's mysterious friend."

118

Milo gave it the run around in his head and nodded. "Marseille it is. Any word on the Pixie?"

"We can't be sure, but some activity we've picked up says she won't be too far away."

"Anything else?"

"One thing, well, two. Elspeth was murdered. Her neck was broken before she went through the window. A single blow, but she wouldn't have felt it, something burned out her implant's processor before then. It destroyed the implant memory core as well and caused severe brain damage."

This put something of a damper on things. "And the other thing?" asked Milo.

Xin frowned. "We're not sure, but we cross-referenced the materials we found in the apartments and the head and came up with this . . ."

An image appeared in Milo's system, of the head of what appeared to be a robot, he knew it. It took a few moments for him to place it though.

"From a movie?"

Xin, still frowning, nodded, "Yes, 'iRobot', rather old."

"And?"

"It was from a book by Asimov. Dawson had the first edition. We have a question for Julia. Were they working on robotics? Had they developed what Asimov called a 'positronic brain'? The reason we ask is . . ."

And the Brancusi head and the head of the robot appeared together and the similarity was striking.

Milo turned to Julia and knew she was examining the images.

"I'll try to find out, but at the moment I can't say. It would seem plausible," she said.

*

They went off-grid for the trip to Marseille and, as they were going to be outside of detection systems for the whole trip which included an international border, it would be deep cover with no contact across public networks. Milo had always found it strange that people had preferred air travel to trains. Now, of course,

119

with the increased speed of trains, it was a no-brainer for trips of less than two thousand miles. Marseille, for instance, being only a little over two hours from London, centre to centre, was just over double the time it took to get to Cambridge. Once over two thousand miles, however, the hyper-flights that passed through the lower atmosphere were, by earlier standards, extraordinarily fast.

Milo was watching his fellow passengers as they sorted themselves out and took their seats for the trip. The crowd was very different from the one on the Cambridge train.

Then he spotted him. Four seats down seated facing away. There was nothing particular about him. He didn't give himself away, his face was unseen. Milo, running through his demeanour and dress, could pick out nothing definite, and yet he knew.

Julia appeared in the seat beside him. Milo shifted. "Is that seat free?" he asked quietly.

"Yes, or at least it's not booked and the train isn't so crowded. Why the blond?"

"I don't know *why*, I just know *that*."

"Want me to check him out?"

"Discreetly."

"Is there another way?" she grinned.

She was gone. Milo wondered if she actually needed to vanish, or if that was just one of those facets of the system designed to make one's experience more 'real'.

He watched the man. There wouldn't be any stops between London and Paris and the one in Paris, would only be for a few minutes. Depending on who 'they' were, they might switch over personnel so as not to arouse suspicion. The man was facing away but would have tapped the feed from the carriage surveillance. Even if he couldn't see that his target was Milo, he could watch the person in the seat Milo occupied. The very fact that his eyes and the surveillance system showed different people would be enough to finger Milo if the man turned to look at him. Julia reappeared as the train gathered speed.

"He's not a cop, nor is he from one of the other 'crime groups'. I can't get face recall on any mayoral database and he isn't corporate."

"Are you telling me I'm wrong?"

"No, just showing off how thorough I am."

She smiled, again and he cocked his head in query. "He's an old friend," she said.

Milo looked at her quizzically, his eyes narrowing. He looked back at the man's head, running through the blonds they had met together.

Julia smiled. "He's not a blond, or he wasn't. He also called himself Errol last time."

Milo leant back in his seat, running through the connotations of being followed by this particular 'friend'.

"I was tuned into the camera when he went off-grid, that's probably why you noticed him, but I didn't see him until I went back to the recorded feed. He has an American vehicle licence, firearms licence, pilot's licence and a military record, though not all in the same name and his passport was British, in yet another name. Discounting ident hits, there are too many of him for him to be an honest man."

"That last part we knew already, but you were quick for all that."

"I cheat. Elspeth was very clever. The system is open if you're part of it. That and I'm getting better."

"You're part of it?"

"I can be."

"Ok, so we can surmise he's not on holidays and his presence in the train is not a coincidence. Strange to use the same op to track us."

"Maybe they're short-handed, but I think you can be sure it's not a holiday."

"Was he watching us for long?"

"I don't think so. Your ticket was only last minute, literally. So I guess he picked us up at the station."

"Probably watching all the stations and ports and tapping the public vehicle feed," Milo said, relaxing. "The Americas, eh? His accent was good. What do they want with a work of art?"

"Could they be working on a commission?"

"Not likely. Not impossible, but it would involve too many people. Any record of contact with Felicity ... Ms Dawson I mean?"

This time Julia flickered away and back, in a moment. "None. Or none that are available."

"How about Gog?"

She flickered again, "Nothing direct with Cambridge that isn't public and part of ongoing contact, and nothing with him as an individual under the names I have for him."

"There could be more?"

"You tell me, you're the spook. I'm only the apprentice."

"Apprentice now is it?"

She smiled.

He took a deep breath. "If they change over in Paris, we'll take out his replacement. If not, we'll stick with our boy and try to turn the tables on him in Marseille."

"Why that way round? Wouldn't it be easier to lose someone new to the game and, on that basis, shouldn't we 'take out' Errol?"

"No, if they put someone new in in Paris, it's likely they'll have someone in Marseille so we have to disrupt the watch and go a different way. If they don't, we're better off sticking with this one and not showing we know. Picking our time to disappear."

"When you say, 'take out', what do you mean?"

"What do you think I mean?"

There was a pause and Milo could feel her concern.

He grinned. "No, I don't mean that, but they won't be getting off the train when we get to Marseille. They will, however, be around to face the music back in Paris. We're not pixies. We do exist and we have to stick to the rules."

He paused.

"Hey, one thing I've been meaning to ask. Do you disappear when you're away doing something because you have to, like, really go? Or is it so I get that impression, make you more real?"

She thought about it for a moment. "I have to. You don't have the processing power to sustain my image while I'm also doing something complex. I can bleed some off other systems, but not enough without them becoming aware of something happening."

"Ok. It does make it seem more real. I'm glad it is . . . I think."

They didn't replace 'Errol' in Paris and Milo took lunch as they passed Dijon. Time was when a decent meal was difficult to get on a train, there was a sameness to the quality of food, slightly fridged and too expensive for the quality available. Some things don't change. The coffee was so-so as well.

Milo watched the watcher. He tried to distract himself with the news feed, and then the business feed, which usually sent him to sleep. He speculated that because this article was about the change in public sentiment about coffee (another plus for the Americorp), it was keeping him awake. Restless, he was tempted to ask Julia to check on the feed 'Errol' had, but didn't want to take the chance of tipping him off, though he knew Julia would be outraged at his lack of faith, but all the same . . . The man was good, clearly experienced.

Milo started to go through what it was that had triggered his internal alarm. Was it, as Julia thought, the camera feed? Could be, everything else looked right. Everything fitted right in with the surrounding people. He didn't stand out at all. Then it clicked.

Milo remembered hearing as a child how Charlie Chaplin had come third in a Chaplin lookalike competition and he had thought it bizarre. A little while later, Charlie had realised why. In the flesh, Chaplin was too real. Too exactly what he really was, too much information. His competitors had delivered the fuzziness of the 'through-the-screen' impression of Chaplin that he was unable to see or understand. The tracker had done the same. 'Errol' fitted in too well. Most people wouldn't have picked it up, but Milo was being fed too much information, being told too loudly, "Don't look at me!" so he had looked.

The countryside slipped silently past and Milo thought how, in a much-changed world, some things changed very slowly. Some things changed overnight and the feeds would be full of how the world would never be the same again. And then you passed though countryside like this and realised much of it would have been the same to the Romans as it was to him. But even the fields would change when given the right push. The crops of sunflowers and lavender had given way to vines and then to wheat and back to sunflowers. With the crop, the field size changed. The farmers just needed the right push.

Marseille slid into the picture windows, pretty as a postcard, blue sky, fluffy clouds, old roofs. Milo waited. The American seemed to hesitate only a heartbeat, but then pulled himself together, chatted idly to the person in the seat ahead of his, made his way to the door. Milo followed standard protocol, as he would be expected to, and walked to the door on the tail of the crowd of people.

Julia was on the platform and walked beside him.

"*Did you get a look at him?*"

"Yes, I tried, but he was still off-grid so we'll need your eyes."

"*There's no danger the systems here will pick you up, or on the train, he couldn't have seen you?*"

"Oh my God!! I never . . ."

Milo looked at her aware he was being mocked.

"Bit late to ask that one, Milo. No, I can choose what video systems I trigger and it would begin to overextend your system if I was on too many other links without having their actual or tacit acceptance."

"*Just checking.*"

She smiled. As she did, Milo became aware of the phrase 'very proud of my algorithms' and smiled. She disappeared.

*

They were at the back of the usual scrum round the exits. There were never enough eye scanners and these ones seemed to be working on an old image-scan system. Since doing away with ticketing in the old sense of that word, passage was granted and tied to payment which, in turn, was tied to a DNA-based scanning system of one kind or another. This one was old, a retinal scan. Being off-grid should cause problems for travellers, but China12's system detection avoidance enabled the simple matching of retinas without needing those pieces of data to be tied to an individual. This allowed their operatives to pass freely when necessary, but could be checked at a later date to prove presence in a particular place. It also meant that they could – with quite a bit of work – be found or followed, however, the chase would be several hours behind them, at best. Agencies, such as the one the Pixie worked for or the group the man ahead of them probably worked with, had similar systems.

As Milo came to the barrier, he could see the man heading for a cafe and nodded to himself. Usual tracking protocol, do something that legitimately allows you to give your target a chance to get out ahead of you. It came as something of a shock when he was brought to a halt at the barrier and a red light glared at him. The options ran through his head as to what had caused this when a guard approached eyes fixed on his inspection pad.

"Mr . . . Jones?"

Milo had no idea who the system had told them he was, it wouldn't have mattered in the usual run of things.

"Yes, is there some problem?"

"Not really, it's just you have a joint ticket and your companion . . . Ms O'Neill . . .?"

Milo looked around. He was the last passenger. Who was O'Neill?

"I think . . ."

He was about to say that there must have been an error when the guard gave his pad a shake. Why, was anyone's guess, as there was nothing in the machine that would respond to shaking, good or bad.

"Oh, she's gone through already, the system didn't register her at first. My apologies. They're going to replace the whole lot next year. They should have done it five years ago, so we get the occasional error, although this is a new one on me!"

Milo nodded. He walked through and acknowledged the guard's smart salute with a smile. He walked away heading for the cafe. Julia appeared.

He looked at her and in a very hushed voice. "What was that? Do you think the Americans are trying to get us picked up?"

"No, it appears that your colleagues bought us a ticket each. Their honesty should be congratulated, their discretion, not so much. Plus, they do know I'm dead?"

"Our ticketing system must not have gotten the memo. To it, your virtual presence is as real as mine."

"To him."

"Him?"

"Him."

"Right . . . to him . . ."

"Anyway, I corrected the situation. It was a bit clumsy, but I gave it an error code and everything."

Again a smile that could bring warring nations to the negotiating table. They reached the cafe and Milo had his 'just about to buy a coffee and nothing else' face on. He risked a quick look round. Then he ordered and, leaning against the counter, took a longer look.

"Shit."

Julia mirrored his alarm. "What?"

"He's gone. Can you take a quick look through the station system?"

She disappeared as the coffee arrived and Milo took it over to an outward-facing seat. He scanned the station but the crowds were too dense to be certain of anything.

Julia was back. "It's not possible to tell if he's here or he's gone. Why would he go if he's following us?"

Milo stood and surveyed the station. He shook his head. "He's very clever, very discreet. He's out there somewhere, watching us, laughing his socks off, I bet. There's nothing for it but to go. Keep an eye out."

They pulled themselves together and moved to the front of the station.

And then Marseille hit them. Or rather, the Mistral hit them. Harsh and dry and one of those things that doesn't change over the decades and the centuries. That is, its blowing hadn't changed. The strength of the wind however had increased as the planet warmed and what had been a harsh fact of life along the swathe of land where it blew was now occasionally very dangerous indeed.

They were out into the hubbub of the streets. Walking the broad sweep round the Gare-St Charles and then tiny alleyways and old streets that had probably been there since the Greeks founded the place two-and-a-half millennia earlier. In Marseille, the transport systems were a little different, and while the taxis were automated, they operated more like buses, with a fixed route and a fixed fare. They went to the places the tramways didn't and the metro didn't, and there had been a hell of a row when they were introduced. Apart from transfers, most people travelled by tram, which married well the old city and the more modern suburb. The taxis themselves were pared back, very simple, but very efficient.

They walked past the cab rank and into one of the side streets. Julia disappeared as she checked out the local cameras and Milo continued down to his hotel, but their friend didn't reappear.

They reached the hotel in the old town, near the old harbour, the early evening sun chasing Milo in through the door. The intense colours of the sky and sea, the sharp tan and ochre of the cliffs and buildings contrasted vividly with the vague mist of unknowing they were in. The hotel was one used for generations by visiting writers or artists looking for inspiration, but without the money to spring for much beyond the basics. It was old, comfortable, discreet and fitted within an artist's budget.

Milo walked in and got a room, and by the time they got to it Julia had already invaded the surveillance system and the hotel records.

"Alright, there is no sign of our tail, so far as I could make out. There is no definite indication that Gog has stayed at this hotel, but then it's more likely that she would be with friends. She would have a few here."

"In short, you have nothing to tell me."

"It's a lovely evening outside, the city is looking every bit as beautiful as I remembered. The forecast is good too. Things could be a lot worse."

He looked at her and grinned, eyebrows raised in question.

She smiled. "You know, you're going to have to get over the me-being-dead thing. As far as I'm concerned, I'm a week old, as well as being in my thirties. I can think, smell, feel, see. As long as I keep you safe, there's no reason I can't have a very interesting life, and even then, who knows?"

He nodded, still smiling, and turned to the window. "It's certainly a nice city. Now let's find out about the inhabitants. Where would Gog be likely to go? I mean, is there a racy hangout for visiting professors?"

"I'm pretty sure there aren't many visiting professors in this part of town. But Gog won't be visiting the university here, so come on."

CHAPTER NINE

They spent some time checking out the warren of backstreets and main streets that looked like backstreets between the old port and Notre Dame-du-Mont. As the national authorities had narrowed their focus and, consequently, their reach, older forms of authority had emerged. Further south, around the Mediterranean, life was difficult as brutality had become the currency of rule, particularly outside the cities. The underclass created by a world that had five billion more citizens than it needed had to go somewhere, and that somewhere was the out-of-control cities. A wise man once pointed out that "people with nothing to do, don't do nothing" and the dangerous, violent world of these cities had been the result.

Here in Marseille, where civic life had been the norm for hundreds of years before central control, a city-wide government had been established. The city still had strong links to Paris, but equally strong were its links with Genoa, Pisa, Venice, Barcelona and the like, which long antedated notions of central government. In the north, the Five Mayors had strong links and formal ties, borne out of the informal arrangements put in place during the early years of the century. Here, the ties were less formal and much deeper.

Marseille had a frontier town feel to it. Most things could be, and were, bought and sold here and, so long as they paid the mayor his tax people would be all right, within certain limits. The limits were somewhat elastic, though enforcement was very efficient. Despite all of that, the city was democratic, after a fashion and most citizens were as free, or freer, than almost anywhere on earth.

129

All this gave the streets and restaurants an exotic flavour, with most needs catered for pretty well. The food shops were still open-fronted, just as they were thousands of years ago. The lumps of lamb of dubious freshness turning on skewers, the old men playing dominos and drinking mint tea, looked like they hadn't moved since the city's founding. And, always emphasised by the narrowness of the streets, the mistral.

After a few hours of drawing blanks, now cold in the darkening streets, they decided to take a break and eat some of the stuff they had just been watching others eat. They headed to a place Julia said Gog used to frequent.

The restaurant was warm and away from the door the lighting was subdued. It was about half full and the clientele a mix of young, intense men and women and older, slightly more relaxed, men and women. One or two sat alone working at something important or something trivial. The work tools in front of them were ultra high spec or pencil and paper. Some were there to argue, some to celebrate, some just to have somewhere to go that wasn't that God-damned room, wherever it might be.

Milo looked around. "See anyone you recognise?"

Julia, having done a more robust search, answered: "No, not anyone we're looking for at the moment."

"What does that mean?"

"It means, not anyone we're looking for, at the moment."

He nodded and walked up to the nearest waiter. "Table for two, please. Near the front but not too near, if you don't mind."

The waiter nodded and showed him to a table near the wall at the left-hand end of the room. "Will you be eating, sir?"

"Yeah, if you'd bring a menu, thank you." As he sat, he noticed Julia was smirking.

"Expecting company?"

Milo was puzzled and then it occurred to him. "Sorry."

"Not just that old system in Beijing then? I'm flattered."

"I wouldn't get carried away, this is strictly platonic."

The waiter was back. "Sorry sir? I didn't quite catch that."

"Sorry, I was talking on my com. I've been stood up, I'm afraid, so I'll be eating alone."

"That's perfectly fine, sir." He turned to leave.

"Oh, might I ask, seeing as I'm alone ... A friend of mine might be about in Marseille. She sometimes comes in here when she is. A Professor Gog, of Cambridge University. You wouldn't know her, would you?"

"Yes, I know Dr. Gog. Let me ask my colleague." And he headed to the bar.

Milo watched as the waiter talked to the barman, who appeared to be a manager of some sort. They looked over at Milo's table and then away, less than discreet.

After the conference, the manager came over. "You asked about Dr Gog. Might I ask who you are?"

Milo thought about it and decided to risk it. "Milo Talbot. I work for a crime group called China12. You may not have heard of it."

"Yes, I know of China12, Mr Talbot. Do you have any proof?"

Milo pulled out his reg card. "You can verify that."

The manager took it and went over to the bar, and Milo watched as the man scanned the card.

Julia looked concerned. "This is a bit risky. Won't that pin you to here? If our friend is following, he'll have a verified location for you."

"I think Gog may have been expecting us. She might have left a message."

The manager came back looking more relaxed. "Mr Talbot, sorry to have to ask you in such a formal way. The professor ..."

Milo leant forward then held up his hand. "Just one moment, please."

Milo was looking round, behind the man at someone who had just walked in, someone who was standing quietly near the door and scanning the room, whose eyes finally came to rest on Milo.

She smiled broadly. "Well, well. Fancy seeing you here." And the Pixie sauntered across the room.

Milo smiled back. "The bad penny herself!"

He turned to the manager. "So that's a beer and the pâté with some fries, thanks. Are you going to have something, Penny?" he asked the Pixie.

She gave him the broadest of grins and answered: "A beer, and one of your ham and cheese rolls, thanks."

The manager had hidden his surprise at the sudden change in direction well. He gave Milo a quick look, nodded and left. The Pixie stood in front of the table, still grinning. She was dressed in pretty much the same garb as the last time they had met. It flitted through Milo's mind that she lived in these clothes and he heard a quiet "Ewwww" from Julia.

"You left without saying goodbye!"

The Pixie didn't move. "Are you alone?"

Milo looked around. "Yeah, I think so."

"I mean I can't see Julia. Has she gone?"

"Like I said, you left without saying goodbye, you can't expect a girl to hang about for you. Am I going to hear why?"

"I was called away."

"To here?"

"Evidently."

"You didn't follow us here then, or get someone else to do it?"

Her brow creased. "Someone else? For a private eye you sure do attract people's attention."

"Just some . . ."

His sentence was interrupted by Julia. "Milo! Outside!"

Rising, "Where?"

"Across the street, third door down to the right."

Milo leant forward and made no secret that he was looking. The Pixie began to turn.

Julia shouted, "He has a gun. He's raising it!"

Milo didn't wait. He threw himself across the table, into the lee of the middle pillar supporting the entrance to the restaurant, grabbing at the Pixie as he went, taking the table with him. It rolled forward and hit the still-standing Pixie, knocking her backwards onto the floor. Her head smacked the hard tiles and the lunge sent nearby tables and chairs careening out across the room and onto the pavement. As this happened, the sound of two dulled shots from across the street. A scream from one of the customers and bullets splintering the wall just above where Milo had been sitting.

Again he heard Julia's voice, "He's stopped shooting, looking around."

Milo rolled, trying to disentangle himself from the mess. The manager came across and helped him up, crouching and looking outside. The man outside couldn't be seen. Their fellow diners had scrambled to the back of the room, others in nearby restaurants were looking out. Milo and the manager slid the table off the Pixie. She had been flattened.

Julia was still watching the assailant. "He's stepped into the street and is trying to see what's going on in here. I've blocked his access to the cafe's camera. He's moving across to us, he's stopped."

Milo had a gun in his hand and the Pixie was pulling herself together, trying to get out of the tangle of tablecloth. The sound of police sirens approaching fast, and flashing lights caught in the room's mirrors.

"He's thinking about it . . . Oh! It's Errol . . . He's going, but he's not happy."

"Can you follow him?"

"I can try."

The Pixie was recovering and she shot Milo a sharp look. Milo nodded to the manager, indicating the crisis had passed. The manager turned away to the bar and their waiter began to tidy up, trying to reassure the other guests. The calm shown by the staff suggested shootings were not unknown in downtown Marseilles.

Milo was crouched down beside the Pixie and they made eye contact.

"Are you alright?"

She nodded. He pulled her up into a chair. The manager had sent out his waiters with brandies for the other customers in the restaurant, which, for the most part, were happily accepted, though some did leave.

The Manager himself returned to Milo's table with two brandies. "I'm so sorry this has happened. I assure you, we are not normally a target."

Milo smiled. "I believe you. I don't think it has anything to do with your place. You shouldn't tidy up this area or the one around the bullet impacts. It's a crime scene."

The manager smiled indulgently, "This is Marseilles Mr. Talbot. We do things our way."

The manager was about to say something else, but a warning look from Milo and a flick of his eyes to the Pixie shut him up.

"I shall be back with your order."

"Thanks."

The Pixie looked up, cradling her head. "So, Julia *is* still with you. Sneaky."

"I didn't say either way."

"Do you know what that was about?"

"That was 'Amsterdam Errol'. Remember him? But no, I don't know what it was all about, to be honest. He tailed us on the way over here but we lost track of him. Seems we just picked him up again."

The Pixie looked Milo over, then her eyes drifted to the holes in the wall. Lumps of plaster had been removed and it was all over the floor around them.

"You're sure he was following you?"

Milo followed her eyes and could see she was thinking.

"I was. Why? I just broke cover here, so he must be well connected"

"Taking a shot in the open against someone like you would be very weird. Amateurish."

The police arrived. Two cars pulled up outside the restaurant, disgorging five officers. Three spread out into the street looking for witnesses, one of them touched his com and indicated the direction the assailant had gone. The last two came into the restaurant and the manager went to talk with them.

Milo watched. "We're going to be interviewed, niece, colleague, friend?"

The Pixie grinned again, it's always a game. "Niece, Sue Scott, on your ex-wife's side. Studying art, here for a term. You?"

The police shambled over.

"I am who I am."

The cop stopped at the table. Middle-aged, thought he had seen it all, rumpled uniform, tired, and this came at the end of the shift.

"Which one of you is Mr. Talbot?"

The Pixie turned in her chair, and she and Milo stared at the man. He cracked first, looked at Milo.

"Mr. Talbot, do you have ID?"

Milo pulled out his card that showed him to be a member of China12 and offered his wrist. The cop touched it off his compac and took a retina scan at the same time with a data acquisition terminal or DAT. Milo's face flashed up along with "credentials".

The cop looked at him. "China12?"

Milo nodded.

"We're honoured."

Milo thought this might not be true.

"Why are people shooting at you, China12?"

"I don't know."

"I thought you guys were supposed to know everything."

"No."

He looked down at the Pixie. "And you are?"

"Mr Talbot's niece."

The cop looked at her for a few moments. He'd seen a lot of 'nieces' with a lot of 'uncles' over the years.

"It always amazes me to find people have such nice relatives. Not like the ones I have."

The Pixie shrugged.

"You here on holiday?"

"I'm a one-termer at the uni. He's visiting."

"Checking up on you, you mean. I'd hate to have had an uncle in China12 when I was your age. ID?"

She handed over her student card. The touch and retina scan backed up her story.

"And you've no idea why this man suddenly decides to shoot you?"

"None."

The cop nodded, he didn't seem to believe it, but he wasn't sure he didn't want to and investigating was always going to be someone else's problem.

"And you didn't shoot back?"

Milo gave him a steady look. "No."

The cop nodded again. The second man came up behind him and in a low voice told him something.

The cop looked at Milo. "We have a report that he's been spotted. You gonna take the case if we do?"

"Can't investigate myself officer."

"Oh, right, I forgot. Make sure the group that does can get hold of you."

"They'll know how, officer."

He didn't actually add, "Don't worry your little cotton socks about it", but he might as well have.

The cop turned to go, looked back at the wall. "Good job he was a lousy shot. We wouldn't take him. Forensics will be down for the slugs, don't touch them."

They left and climbed into their cars, sirens on, lights flashing.

Julia appeared to both of them. Milo turned to look at her. The Pixie smiled.

"You responsible for that report of the 'sighting'?" she asked Julia.

"You're so perceptive."

The Pixie turned her attention to the holes in the wall and the look became a stare.

Milo noticed. "What?"

"He was right though. If he was shooting at you, that's a lousy shot. Two of 'em."

Milo turned and looked at them, really looked for the first time. The Pixie stood and looked through the door. Her eye ran the line of the bullet all the way to the wall.

"What else did you find out about him? I assume you did more than a quick look-see," she asked.

Julia answered. "He's American, military background, similar to you, lots of 'skills'."

The Pixie's eyes drifted off the wall and down to Milo. "You're sure he was following you?"

"I presumed. He was in our carriage, right background, he was traveling off-grid."

"Even for close surveillance, that not strike you as a bit close?"

"Maybe. You get used to ham-fisted operatives in this profession."

"He wasn't aiming at you."

The Pixie touched her com. "Am I out?"

Whoever she was talking with was brief and, to Milo, inaudible.

"Some American just tried to take me off roster, that's why."

Again, the response was brief.

"I will."

She turned to Julia, "Did you track him?"

"I still am."

"Did you give it to the cops?"

Julia just gave her a look.

The food arrived. The Pixie's smile was gone.

The food was placed across the table and the Pixie tore into her roll. Had been a living creature, it wouldn't have suffered long.

Julia turned to Milo. "So when we lost him at the station, he really lost us."

"Yeah, standard operational procedure. He knew we were there and spotted him. I thought he was being cute."

"It's nice to know that the whole world isn't after us."

The Pixie looked up from the roll. "Don't kid yourself. The whole world is after you, but it seems some of us don't like competition. I should have finished him in Amsterdam."

Julia sat up. "Got him! Wow! You won't believe where."

The Pixie began to get ready to move. "I don't care where."

"Where?" asked Milo

"Just one street over, at the most American hotel in town. How obvious is that?"

Milo leant forward, "There's no hurry. He's not going anywhere, not at the moment. Julia, can you arrange for some police activity not too far away, just while we eat?"

She grinned.

*

It wasn't far, and Julia was right, a typical modern American chain hotel. Though it overlooked the old port, the street outside was quiet and the light rain, added to the late hour, encouraged the quiet. For all that clothes didn't become wet because of their hydrophobic coating, it still wasn't pleasant to walk in cold rain. The LED street lamps tracked walkers as they made their way home.

The introduction of the light tracking systems had not been popular at first, as people felt they were being followed, or that it made following them easier. However, the rediscovery of the night sky as a result of the reduction in light pollution and the drop in power consumption had made a big impact and people wondered at their parents' generation, with a smirk, just like every generation before them.

Julia was able to report the hotel was smart and modern on the inside, old, classy and refined on the outside. She also noted it was a grade or ten better than Milo's.

"Hey, I'm on a client budget, not some secret government or corporate expense account."

The Pixie snorted at that one. Evidently she wasn't in palatial surroundings either, and certainly not the comfortable surroundings the American was in.

They sat across and a little way down the street from the hotel, in a rather empty three-seat bar. They could just see the entrance. The owner was engrossed in a Championship decider, a gamer league clash between two of the favourites. They had to shout to get his attention and some service but he was back in the action, his body jerking, hands going, in sympathy with the action on screen.

Milo turned to Julia. "Could you check out how we can get in discreetly, find out what he's doing?"

"I can certainly find a way in. I'll just find something for the guard to do and do likewise with the security system, but I can only get to him if he's on the system. The rooms have no internal surveillance."

"Quite right too!"

The Pixie gave the pair a look at that. "Be handy if we could see what the bad guys were up to though, wouldn't it?"

"Trouble is you'd use it to look at the good guys too."

"Small price to pay."

"He'd use it too."

She thought about that one and turned back to look at the hotel. Julia disappeared.

The Pixie eyed the place where she had been. "Does she have to disappear like that when she's doing other stuff? I mean, she can be two places at once, can't she?"

"It seems I don't have enough processing power to sustain it. Even with you here."

The Pixie opened her mouth to say something.

"And yes, I think she bleeds off some of your system too. It isn't enough," he added.

"That's why I get a slight headache when I'm with you guys. Funny, I thought it was you!"

He gave her a flat, closed-mouth smile.

Julia was back, "Shit!"

"What?" said the other two in unison.

"He saw me."

Milo frowned. "How?"

"He was on his com, a holo link to his people back home. I tried a little eavesdropping, but I didn't control the connection and came up in holo."

The Pixie grinned. "That'll give them something to think about."

"It did. It was only for an instant, but I heard his base ask if I wasn't 'the dead one' and he acknowledged it looked like it, but he wasn't saying much and I could detect his shock."

The Pixie turned to the door, "Can you get rid of the guard?"

"It's done. There should be about a five minute window, an alarm on the air-con."

They stepped out onto the street, Milo and the Pixie staring up at the window Julia had identified as the American's. Staring so much as they walked that they were nearly run down by a couple of cyclists.

"Whoa, watch out! Hey, you're cute!" That last aimed at the Pixie, not Milo.

When she ignored it, it was followed up with, "I don't bite you know."

The Pixie, without looking, "I do," and she smiled.

Nothing changes? Except in the old days it would be a young or not so young man with the cat-calling and this was a young woman who, along with her companions, laughed her way into the distance. They went round to the rear of the hotel and the staff entrance. Milo pushed into the hotel and the Pixie momentarily held the door for Julia and then didn't.

"Sorry," she said

Julia smirked. "Don't be, there's a lot of that going around. Hurry up, I'm holding the lift for you."

"Can you see what he's doing?"

"He's just finishing the call to base. They were spooked by my appearance for some reason."

The Pixie grinned, "No shit."

Milo jabbed the button to the fourth floor. "Make sure he can't get off that floor."

"I'm watching on the floor cameras, no sign yet. Oh, he's trying something different. He's trying to access the system."

"Don't block him or he'll know there's something up."

"No, but I'll slow him up a bit. Hang on."

And she was gone again.

They took the lift to the fourth floor. The door slid open onto an empty corridor and they stepped out. The corridor was wide with a thick carpet, each room marked by a lighter colour bending into it. Occasional tables alternated sides of the corridor down its length. At the midpoint, there was a crossroads complete with old-fashioned signposts indicating the room numbers to be found on each corridor and the attendant facilities. They walked quickly to the crossroads and turned right. Three doors down and they were there.

Julia appeared. "Oh! That's so rude!"

Milo turned. "What now?"

"He seems to think I'm some kind of trace algorithm and tried to put a spike on me."

She regained her composure. "He's still in there, on his system interface, the shit."

They stopped outside the door, Milo looked at the lock and saw the hotel may be trying for 'olde worlde' charm, but the locks were right bang up to date.

"We'll need the NS up at high Julia."

"Yeah he has it up there already."

"Can you do the honours?" he asked, nodding at the door.

"With pleasure."

The door popped and the Pixie was through it before anyone had taken a breath. Anyone except her, at least. Milo blocked the door as it rebounded from the wall and followed her in. The crash from the room at the end of the short hall suggested the Pixie and the American had said their hellos once more. He couldn't see the American but he saw the Pixie aim a flying kick at something out of sight and then duck as cups, a glass and a table came her way.

Milo got to the edge of the room in time to see the Pixie sailing through the air backwards. Her attack had been met with the ferocity one would expect from a decorated marine captain who had been

141

dragged unwillingly into Special Forces and then into the American Alliance Special Operations Committee Deployment Team.

The Pixie, however, was no one's mug. Rather than hitting the wall with the force of a train she had grabbed a piece of the room divider and brought her feet down under her. It was her feet that met the wall. She dropped to the ground and they squared off. The captain pulled a knife and Milo could see he considered throwing it, but realised he had given that away and he hung on.

Julia smiled she leant into Milo and said, "Now for my next magical trick."

The Captain jerked upright. The others knew she had hacked his optic system and seemed as real as they did. The Pixie didn't even step ,but spun on one foot, bringing the other crashing into the side of the bewildered Captain's neck and head. He went down.

She was standing over him, her foot about to crush his windpipe when Milo said, "Ok, you've made your point."

She looked at him like a puppy when the boss decides she doesn't want to play fetch anymore.

They dragged the American up onto the bed. The Pixie emptied his bags and sifted from the mess on the floor, dog tags on a chain with a cross. She chucked them at Milo and took out a couple of belts, using them to secure the man's upper arms in a way that he wouldn't like when he knew what he liked or didn't again. His ankles were tied with a sliced-up pillowcase which, she noted, could go on his expense account.

Once he was secure, Milo turned to Julia. "What can you find out?"

He showed her the dog tags, which confirmed he had been a captain in the marines, his number and not much else.

"As much as he knows, or at least as much as he's been told in the last twelve hours."

"Do your stuff."

The Pixie frowned, "Won't he be encrypted? You couldn't just lift things from my system."

Julia smiled, "Did you read my dossier, or just the paragraph headings?" She faded.

The Pixie looked at Milo accusingly.

He held out his hands, "Don't look at me like that, I didn't design her. I don't know what she does until she does it, and if that sounds strange where you are, it's weirder from in here!"

It took a few minutes. Milo and the Pixie closed the door, then went through the captain's luggage and effects. The noise suppression system, the "NS", in the hotel had allowed their intervention to remain private, just as it allowed other activities in other rooms to remain the business of those involved. To call the captain's property 'effects' was perhaps overplaying it a bit, or a lot. Of that, not much gave any indication of what he was doing there, though his intent became clear when the Pixie opened his weapons cache. She even whistled. She lifted a bible from amid the guns. It was well thumbed. She held it out to Milo.

He looked at it then at her. "Are you saying he's religious?"

"Nah. Probably used for encryption. Old-fashioned, but that works in a pinch. But he's been busy."

She dropped it back in the case. Milo took out the captain's ID and related documents, but they didn't tell him anything Julia hadn't already found out on the train and the dog tags had already expanded on that.

The captain groaned and the Pixie sat down. Milo walked over and got some water. As the captain came to, the Pixie pulled him upright and Milo touched the glass to his lips. He sucked at the water. Milo was careful not to pour too much.

"Hello again. Those drugs sure do leave your mouth dry don't they?" he said.

The Captain nodded and his eyes came up to meet them.

The Pixie smiled, "Got a headache?"

He closed his eyes and then nodded again.

Her smiled broadened. "It's not what you think. Well, it's not *just* what you think," she said.

And then Julia was back and the captain jerked away automatically.

Milo smiled. "No you're not seeing things,. Well, you are, but we all are." He turned to Julia. "Whatcha got?"

And then the Captain jerked again, looked around.

"Where'd she go?"

The Pixie stood looked across to Milo.

Julia turned to him. "*Don't speak, just think, they can't see me, or hear me.*"

"*Ok.*"

The Pixie stared at Milo puzzled. "Something up?"

Julia looked at her. "*Tell them you don't know, I've just gone.*"

Milo frowned, but turned to the Pixie. "Not sure. She's just gone."

The Captain was looking from one to the other wondering what exactly was going on.

Julia turned back to Milo. "*I'll be brief. Our Captain here knows where Gog is, but they had something to do with my death, and maybe the attack in Paris. They think something is going on and they can't know about me . . . about what I am.*"

The "thought com" system they were using seemed, if anything, more awkward and Milo struggled to look normal while he thought his way through the conversation,

"*Ok . . . what now?*"

"*Question him, I can't know everything and he hasn't got it all in his implanted hardware.*"

"*Who are "they"?*"

She just held out her hands.

Milo shook his head, gave the Pixie a look, trying to communicate something she could understand. What? No idea. He turned to the trussed-up Captain.

"So, you're not Errol. He was found with a bullet in the back of his head. What can I call you, captain?"

"Who?"

"Captain, you're talking to China12. You know we're investigating a murder in London of a young lawyer. Were you there when she died?"

The captain looked at him as though he was crazy.

"Look, China12 or whatever, I am an American citizen. I'm here on official sanction in pursuit of a killer who with her partner, has killed several of our operatives in the last year."

He turned and gave the Pixie a long look.

"You guys broke in here. If you want my credentials, they're over there in the yellow case and there's a card in my wallet in my jacket, that *was* on the back of the chair. I gotta tell you, the French local cops are nasty and we pay them a lot for their help."

The Pixie grinned and leant into him. "Milo has one or two things he wants to know. I already know the one thing I need to know. Other people, nastier people will ask why, *if* you make it through tonight, but the way I feel, you might not."

The captain jerked round, "What's your problem?"

"I don't like people shooting at my back."

He widened his eyes in surprise, "Someone shot at your back!?"

It was doubtful the Pixie even thought about it, her fist shot out and crashed across the man's chin and he was out again.

Milo stepped over to the edge of the bed where the captain was lying, a little blood leaking from the side of his mouth. Milo knew that the 'recovery system' implanted into the captain would be pumping a carefully calibrated shot of adrenaline and other drugs into him. The system was designed not simply to have him conscious, but capable, within a few minutes of whatever it was that knocked him out. If anything seemed like it would go on too long, or if his protocol made information he carried dangerous to his employers, the drugs could take care of that too. Permanently. Milo eyed the man and then the Pixie, who reacted defensively.

"What?"

"This man has certain information that I want. You're deciding to pretend to be angry to block my access to that information isn't clever."

145

"He tried to kill me, and he thought it was cute to make fun of it. I lashed out. So sorry."

"People try to kill you twice everyday before breakfast and you never 'lash out'. I don't believe you. Now leave him alone, got it?"

The captain was coming round, he had a slight grin as he looked at Milo.

"Hey, pal, you may think you're the tits in this room, but she doesn't exist, and I don't exist, so you're the only one who's accountable for what they do."

"So we've decided to drop the 'I'm a very important, locally connected operative' bit have we?"

The captain shrugged. "It's still true but it doesn't change anything."

Milo considered this as he walked back to sit against the small chest of drawers.

"On the one hand that's true, unless I had believed your story about being connected to the locals."

"You didn't."

Milo nodded. "I didn't. What was Amsterdam all about and why are you here in Marseille?"

The captain looked at him with a wide grin.

Julia waved at Milo. "*Keep asking him about the things you want to know, especially the things you don't think he'll answer. The results are fascinating and may be helpful.*"

That put Milo off his stride a little and he tried to cover it by looking thoughtful.

Then he looked up and smiled back. "You heard what my blonde friend here said about her nastier friends?"

"Yeah? What of it? Even if I was carrying anything worth taking the trouble to find out, the system would shut me down in a heartbeat."

"So let's see. You don't know anything about Ms Julia Church?"

"Never heard of her."

"What did you want to find out from me in Amsterdam?"

"Never been to Amsterdam."

"Have you ever met Felicity Dawson?"

"Nope."

"Dr Gog?"

"Who's she, an old crush?"

"When did you arrive in Marseille?"

"You know that, same train as you. You're not very good at tailing, I'll tell you that."

"Thank you."

"Don't mention it, a freebie."

"Who do you work for?"

"The wife and kids. Who do *you* work for?" That pointedly to the Pixie, who stayed absolutely still.

"What's your mission? We know you work for an American group, Corporate or State?"

"I have a mission now? And what gave me away, my accent?"

The Pixie had begun to look at Milo in a puzzled way.

"Why are you asking him these questions. You know he won't answer them and you know you can't make him answer them."

"Let's just say he is, nevertheless, providing a path for me."

The captain frowned at that, his eyes went out of focus and they recognised that as he did an internal system check, he was slightly less chirpy.

Julia smiled. "*Great! Ask him that last one again.*"

Milo became more insistent "Do you work for the corporates or the state?"

"I work for fuck you!"

"What did you come to Marseille to do?"

"Fuck you!"

The Pixie brightened. "Well that's mostly true! But you screwed up, didn't you? You had a clear shot and you missed."

"Fuck you!"

She turned to Milo, "He's trying to fog the access to anything on his implants by concentrating on that one phrase."

147

The captain turned to the Pixie with a snarl, "Sweetie the encryption on my hardware would take you months to get through."

"He's probably right about that, we could do with Julia right now."

The captain frowned and then, without warning, he flopped back on the bed, his arms limp within his bonds. Milo and the Pixie looked at one another. The Pixie reached forward and rolled him away from her onto his front. She held his wrist, looked at Milo and shook her head.

"His interrogation protocol must have kicked in." She began to undo the belts round his arms.

Julia looked guiltily at Milo. "I was a bit too intrusive."

"Find anything out?" asked Milo

The Pixie's head whipped round. "What?"

She looked round the room, aware now he was talking to Julia, so she reappeared to the Pixie as well.

"Have you been up to something?"

Julia nodded.

"Is that why he croaked?"

Julia nodded again. "I guess so."

The Pixie looked down at the lifeless body. "Poor fucker, never knew what he was up against. Not fair."

Milo's eyebrows shot up. "He tried to shoot you in the back!"

"Yes, but that was honest-to-goodness skulduggery. We've been doing that kind of thing to each other for centuries, but you guys . . . he didn't even know he was answering the questions you were asking him and then he didn't know anything at all. Did you get any answers?"

Julia shrugged, "Some. He was right about the encryption. It was clumsy old-fashioned stuff, but it would take a long time to wade through."

"My encryption is tough too I think."

She looked at Julia expecting, wanting an affirmation of this, but Julia was thinking.

"His tech was out of date as well. I wonder if it's deliberate."

"What do you mean?"

"Makes it harder to hack if people weren't familiar with the equipment, if the protocols are out of date."

The Pixie looked outraged. "That doesn't make any sense."

Milo stood, "No? During the Cold War in the middle of last century the Americans were given a plane, by a defector, belonging to the other side. They had to give it back of course, but not before they'd had a good look. To their amazement, the internal circuitry still used valves and relays, not transistors or what, in those days, passed for microchips. Oh they had a laugh about that one ... until someone realised that it made the plane less vulnerable to the EMP that would follow a nuclear strike. Then they stopped laughing."

The Pixie finished tidying up the captain and moved to begin to do the same to the room. It looked well-practised.

"So do we know anything?"

Julia watched her idly. "A bit."

"Like? Jesus! Do I have to drag out each word?"

"I know why he was here. Where he originated, geographically, who his last boss was, what he'd like to do to you. You know stuff."

"So why was he here?"

"To kill you."

"That all?"

"More or less."

"Long way to go to take out a single operative."

"He was also supposed to find us and find out what we knew. He was trying to send back to the woman he was talking to as you introduced yourself ..."

"What?"

"Who we were, what we wanted to know and our images."

"Did he?"

"No."

Julia spoke to Milo, a voice in his head, "*She won't hear this*,"

She appeared to be standing, watching the Pixie 'clean up', silent.

"*We have to get rid of her, to find Gog. There's something I couldn't decrypt about her. I think he intended to visit her, to do her harm.*"

"*And you're . . . worried . . . about the, eh . . .?*"

"*Yes, she's like him.*"

And just then Milo caught something, he wasn't sure what, a little tear in the fabric of Julia's emotional makeup, something harder, more desperate, more ruthless, something related to the captain and the Pixie.

The Pixie looked up. "Can you get anything from him now?"

The Pixie was turning over the situation in her mind as she worked, Julia was taken by surprise.

"I . . . No I can't. As soon as the termination sub-routine kicks in it destroys all saved data."

"Destroys?" "

Literally, a small cache of corrosive fluid is released over the implants"

"Ouch, I mean, that has to hurt."

"No, too late for that. Too much else going on anyway."

Milo was in turmoil, but trying to remain calm and composed, unsure how much Julia could glean from his system. Could he keep secrets? What did it mean anyway? Was she what she seemed, or something much more sinister?

CHAPTER TEN

Another short errand for the night watchman and another loop for the surveillance system allowed them to saunter out unmolested. The delivery area was empty. This was why, strangely, human eyes were so important to modern security. Over reliance on electronics allowed the system to be subverted completely if you could do it at all. Of course, few, very very few could, but this few they moved through the world as quiet as ghosts.

Milo could feel that Julia was preoccupied with how to get rid of the Pixie, but he had own his problem to worry over. The Pixie was reporting to her boss, her forehead creasing in concentration as she got the system to translate her thoughts into words. And then, suddenly, Julia didn't seem so preoccupied any more.

"Where to?"

Milo smiled. "I think I need a moment to work that out, see what we've got here. See what she thinks we should do."

The Pixie was just finishing up and became aware she was being spoken about. Another second or two and she had replayed the last few moments of the conversation.

"I'm not sure 'we' are doing anything. You guys should take a moment to enjoy this beautiful city, shouldn't you? Why are you here, anyway?"

Milo smiled. "We were following you."

The Pixie wasn't sure how to take that. "Were you?"

"You sloped off without saying goodbye, we were worried. Anything might have happened to you."

"Aw shucks. No really, why'd you come to Marseille?"

"Why are *you* here?"

"They sent me."

"I'm sure, but why?"

"That's above your pay grade."

She put her hand up to quieten whatever was coming next, then looked at him and smiled.

"Once again, duty calls. Sorry to leave you guys. Will you be alright getting back to your hotel?"

Milo nodded and sighed tiredly. "You see, you want to know but you won't share."

"The adults don't like me sharing and they don't like me being tracked either, so don't."

Aimed at Julia as much as, if not more than, at Milo.

"Catch you later, little people."

She headed away down the street. A car came round the corner and overtook her before slowing to a stop. She got in. Milo and Julia watched silently.

As the cars pulled away, Milo asked: "Know where she's going?"

"Yes."

"Where?"

"To find Gog."

"Will she?"

"No."

"You have anything to do with that?"

"Maybe."

"You're sure you know where to find Gog?"

"I am."

"Tram or cab?"

She gestured with her chin and a cab rounded the corner, rolled up to them and stopped. The door slid open.

In most cities, as the houses get smarter the streets get wider and leafier. In Marseille it is the other way round. As the houses get nicer, often more modern and the gardens landscaped, the streets get narrower and more hostile to traffic. Trees are absent. Nowhere, though, is immune to the mistral that still blew, the dry, harsh, westerly wind of the south. These days it often took the trees with it. The cab rolled along quietly and its occupants were equally still.

They wound their way out of the city centre, then out of the city altogether. Along the coast, in a few short miles, they passed a couple of fishing villages unseeable from the road and carried on through parkland. They were not using a direct route. The street cameras were gone but there were still surveillance drones picking out movement and logging it. Like them, Milo watched, wondering if he was being led to or away from. Julia was more distanced than usual, their route was being altered by her as they travelled he realised. She was feeding the cab successive destinations, probably to avoid being tracked, but he could pick out a sense of concern, what for was unclear.

After about fifty minutes they drew into the tiny town of Cassis. Through more winding streets and down to the old harbour they went. Once a fishing port, it was now filled with the super-sleek yachts of the super-rich. The wind-driven sea pounded the old sea wall and threw huge waves up and over it. The harbour passed from sight again as they climbed the hill behind it and stopped at the rear of a grand white villa that overlooked the town, facing south-east.

The door slid open and they got out, looking at a narrow gate. The cab rolled away and left them in the very silent street. They pushed through the gate and down some uncertain steps, past the carefully manicured Mediterranean garden. Milo's eyes scanned for anything out of place, anything that might show the presence of someone who shouldn't be there.

Turning to Julia, "Anything?"

She shook her head. "There's nothing to work with. I'm blind."

They got to the door and Milo looked carefully all round it. Unlike at the hotel, this lock was as old as the door. The house was about a hundred years old, 1950s he guessed, just when this sort of place was not quite as fashionable as St. Tropez. Milo ran his finger down the jamb and just about the lock he stopped. Julia looked at him concerned.

"Problem?"

Milo nodded, put his hand flat on the door and pushed gently. The door swung forward with a metallic ring and then stopped. He looked at the jamb, which had been smashed up, forced, but not suddenly like a kick, more like the effect of a hydraulic plate. The lock dangled, useless, from the wood. Milo thought for a moment and two LEDs either side of his head lit up, throwing a full beam focused a few feet in front of him. They stepped into the house.

Whoever forced their way in had either been undetected or had tidied up. The place was as neat as you would expect a house like this, in a place like this, to be.

Milo closed the door behind them and asked quietly, "Have you been here before?"

Julia ran through her memories, "Don't know, don't think so. Might have been."

"That helps. Right or left?"

Milo could feel that she was nervous, concerned, fearful . . . or was that what she intended him to feel?

She shrugged, so he picked at random and went right. A dining room. A big old wooden table in the French style surrounded by high-backed chairs. He could remember feeling uncomfortable in chairs just like that in his childhood. A polished cabinet on one side and a door at the far end, presumably to the kitchen, although he thought ruefully of his previous presumptions. Nothing was out of place, so they turned back and went into the room on the left.

They pushed open the door into a wide sitting-room-cum-study. The room ran the length of the house, having been at one stage two rooms. The smell and appearance of old wood dominated and the far wall, from the middle of the room onward, was lined with well-used books. Mostly old reference works, as in Paris. Some looked very old. Here though mathematics dominated the selection, leather bound copies of Newton, a battered life of Dr Dee and a whole section on statistics and probability. Further along were books about design and some about Chinese, African and Pacific Island Art.

The free walls, here as in every part of the house, had works of art hanging from them, primitive, African or Pacific Island works ranging in age from the last few years to several centuries old. His implant tagged known works with provenance and value.

The room looked in good order, no sign of a struggle. Only the piles of paper on the flat surfaces suggested activity. Milo's lamps swept the room, finally coming to light on a desk at the end. A chair was in front of the old oak desk, papers again littered the surface.

They walked down to it and, as they passed the large, lumpy couch, they saw her, lying awkwardly between the chair and the desk, as if she had been in the act of standing, turning. Dr Gog, crumpled, still.

Milo didn't rush, there was no need. His beam swept the floor, looking for anything that might show them what had happened. When they got to her, he could feel Julia's distress as though it was his. He stifled a sob and pressed his lips together in irritation. Her image looking down to his right was calm, composed, no tears. And then he felt her anger rise and sweep up over him and he struggled to contain it.

He took several deep breaths. "You have to calm down. We can't do anything for her if we become overwrought."

"We can't do anything for her at all. She's dead!"

Milo bent down and looked at the body. She'd been shot in the back of the head. From the size of the wound, he guessed twice, but it might have been a hollow-point bullet designed to produce that large exit wound.

"Don't touch anything, I have to call it in," said Milo

Julia's rage was still there, but being corralled into something more potent, and forceful enough to give him a virtual stare and clip round the head.

"Sorry."

Milo contacted the local police and sent them the coordinates of the house.

"I have to do a sweep before they get here. Get it to Beijing. If the cops start walking all over it . . . or local forensics . . ."

155

"How? There's nothing in this house to use. It's totally off-grid."

"You'd know if you looked. I have my ways."

He walked to the centre of the room and called out: "Forensic sweep, level two, no extant tech."

He stood, waited, tried not to move. But the sweep didn't start. He checked his system and tried again with the same result.

"I don't think you can do it with me taking up so much of your system. Hold on, I'll close down some. It'll be like I'm asleep," said Julia.

"Do I have to wake you?"

"No, when the system shuts off the scan I'll come up again. I told you, as time goes on we'll face a decision and I'm growing faster than even I expected."

He nodded and she duly faded. He started the scan and lit up a com with Beijing at the same time.

Xin appeared in front of him, "Hi. We have some numbers for you on Gog."

"Yeah? I have one for you."

"Oh?"

"Yeah. She checked out."

"How?"

"With the help of 'Errol' from America Corp. Or at least, we think that's who he might be working for. I'm at her place now. Going to scan the room, then let the cops have it . You'll have to retrieve the forensics from whoever contracts that."

"This is getting nasty."

"*Getting*?"

He began the scan and the numbers started streaming to base.

"Do you have a lead on the troll?" Xin asked.

"Yeah."

He sent her the captain's picture and the file generated by Julia.

"Do you know where he is?"

"He's dead."

"You?"

"Julia."

"Julia?"

"She triggered his anti-interrogation protocol by mistake. Can you check out her system on me here? I felt something I can't really explain, a wrong note . . ."

"No, that was the first thing we tried when she popped up. Her source file, what we think is her source file, is pretty huge, but it's compressed and heavily encrypted."

"And you guys . . .?"

"We could get through it, but not without stopping you and spending a few days on it, maybe longer. What kind of 'wrong note'?"

"Just something that didn't chime with what I thought I knew. It's ok, I'll keep an eye on it."

"This was a pretty effective man, Captain Skolnic, if that was his name."

"Unlikely, but some of it will be true."

The scan was coming to an end. It was able to take a three-sixty from a single perspective because the scanning beam used the hard surfaces to bounce and measure distance, in the same way very early computer games had used the edges of the screen to bounce around the playing field. A beam was in play but there were two others monitoring the main beam.

Xin seemed happy with the result. "Ok, we'll analyse that and the file on your friend, the late captain."

"He tried to shoot the Pixie, too, so whoever it was doesn't want to play ball with the Euro-state guys. That's why we think its principal might be a corp."

"And the Pixie is definitely Euro-State?"

"Speculatively. She could be English."

"Ok. Try not to get killed."

"You always have my best interests at heart."

"Since Brazil we are two operatives down, Mr. Talbot. We would find getting yet another replacement challenging. That's all."

"Right."

She faded and Milo thought he should have explained his sense of humour and then thought he was right not to.

Julia appeared. They looked at each other and he could feel she was calmer than she had been.

"Again, how does that work?"

She was defensive. "What?"

"The emotion thing? How can you feel emotions? How can I feel your emotions?"

She looked at him and considered. He wondered if she was considering the question or considering giving an honest answer.

"I don't know. It's unexpected. Partly I think it's because your system is not big enough or fast enough to handle my system or memories, so I'm bleeding into your organic processes. If it's any consolation, I'm making you smarter. We're sharing the new synapses that I'm prompting your system to make, but you're reacting to my stimuli as though you were me. Something happens and whatever it is that would normally prompt a certain response in you, that's what it does. It makes for better decision-making in the long run."

"So long as it doesn't cripple me."

She looked uncertain "I don't know. I don't think it will, but a lot of this is outside the parameters of my, I mean Elspeth's, experience."

"You're a rookie."

"When it comes to what you do, yes."

"Can you limit yourself?"

"I don't understand."

"I mean, can you not be present, seeing, experiencing, knowing what I see, experience, know?"

"At the moment, probably not. I don't know everything. I can't see the elements of your organic system that aren't tied to the implants . . . at the moment."

"Meaning?"

"Meaning I don't know how much we will become entwined within your organic system. It may be limited to elements needed but not present in the implants, but it could, in theory, spread to your cognitive processes, if you're not upgraded and I remain present. She didn't realise your system was as limited as it is."

He was about to ask if she intended to remain, when the flashing blue and red lights stopped the discussion. Milo walked to the door.

The police, two cars and four officers falling over themselves to be in no hurry. Two of the officers began to tape off the scene with laser sensors and the others headed for the house. Milo held back the door and pointed them into the room. They stood at the doorway and looked down, but didn't go in.

The first cop looked at Milo and lifted his chin towards the end of the room.

"It's down there?"

He nodded.

"And you're the guy that called it in? Talbot, China12, that right?"

"That's right."

"ID?"

The cop held out his DAT and Milo slid his ID against it. The machine took a scan of his wrist ID and a retinal scan, his details came up.

The cop squinted at the terminal. "It's gone up on the crimes, I don't know who's got it. We have a closed contract on forensics here, they're on the way."

"The only thing open for investigation will be my presence here, officer. Her death is part of an ongoing contract. Forensics will be forwarded to us."

The cop looked at the file and scratched his head. "You're not doing so great. This is your second stiff."

"Nevertheless."

The cop shrugged. "I'd hate to be investigated by you."

"I'll make a note of it."

"You packing?" the Cop asked.

Milo nodded his head and, after a quick look down at his DAT, the cop sucked his teeth and turned away.

159

Fuss at the door as the forensics arrived. Milo watched them and was surprised that the lead woman's hair wasn't completely covered. Suspicious, he stopped them before they entered the room.

"Hi, China12." He held out his ID.

The woman didn't look, just flicked her head. "Right. We weren't expecting a crowd of admirers. What do you need?"

The now frowning lead cop started paying attention.

Milo held the woman's eye a beat and then, "I need you to coordinate with the forensic team of a shooting in a restaurant earlier this evening. The ballistics on the slugs need to be compared."

"If they're there."

"They're there."

The woman gave him a sharp look. "I think I'll be the judge of that, if you don't mind."

She looked across to the cop who had taken a step nearer, threw her eyes to heaven and jerked her chin.

The cop didn't respond to that. "Are you with "Abadie Forensic"?" he asked.

The woman turned and looked at him carefully.

The cop's hand slid to his weapon. "Only, I notice you didn't ask to see ID or show yours, and, you know, they're a careful company. Sticklers about protocol."

She sighed wearily "Sure. I'm late, is all. I was just going off when this came in. The boss didn't want to pass it to the juniors. Let me just get my DAT."

She bent down and reached into her bag on the floor in front of her. A flash of silver at her throat, the cop pulled his weapon and was about draw a bead on her when the woman came up with her DAT. DATs had made protocols between official bodies and across countries standard and easy. She looked at him quizzically.

The cop relaxed, but as he looked back to holster the charge gun, she dropped the DAT, revealing the small needle gun in her hand. If there had been time, he would have looked stricken, but a blur to his right and Milo, who had until then, remained still, was suddenly across the woman and she was on the floor, the gun bouncing off the wall opposite her.

Milo had the cop's gun in his hand and was already firing it when the woman's colleague came through the door, gun out, and the man dropped in a heap. The cop was still working his way round to looking stricken.

Milo stood over the woman and tossed the gun back to the cop. Julia was looking down at her and then disappeared for a couple of moments.

When she reappeared she said, "*Same tech as the Captain.*"

"*You managed to be more discreet this time?*"

Julia nodded. Milo prodded the woman with his foot, lifting her shoulder. She had a thin silver chain round her neck and a tiny cross, which caught the light. Pulling his foot away he looked back at the cop as two of his fellow officers appeared at the door, weapons in hand.

The cop wiped his mouth, pointed at the woman, "Cuff that one." He looked at Milo, "Thanks."

Milo turned to Julia, "Check him", he said, and smiled at the cop.

Thinking he was being spoken to, the cop looked slightly miffed. "We will."

Julia was back. "He's good. Well, not good, but legit."

Milo smiled stiffly, prodded the woman again with his foot. "Can you give her a jolt and then disable her drugs?"

Julia smiled, nodded, disappeared.

The cop didn't know what was going on, "You talking to your base?"

"Something like that."

The woman groaned and reached for her head as her recovery drugs kicked in. Julia reappeared. The woman checked her system, then, "What have you done?"

Milo grinned. "Stopped you hurting yourself, or your system hurting you."

"How?"

"I have my ways. Who are you with and what do you know about Skolnic?"

She started at that and began to get up, her face filled with the little red dots of laser targeting.

Milo put out a hand. "I think you should stay where you are."

She looked at the heap made by her comrade. "Is he alive?"

"Yes."

And looking to the cop, "The meds have been called?"

The cop nodded, "So have forensics."

Beijing broke in, Xin asked. "You ok? Another shooting has just come up on the crimes at your address?"

Milo was amused considering their last conversation. "Yeah just taking care like you told me. Take it, will you, and co-ordinate the forensics on these two and the earlier brush with the good captain."

"Sure."

Xin faded and the Meds could be heard drawing up to the house.

Milo turned to the woman, "I'm waiting for an answer before these gentlemen take you into custody."

The woman searched his face and shrugged. "We're independents. Got a call to clear up a mess here, came from the Americans. I was just going off."

She stopped and looked pointedly at the cop, who stared back expressionlessly, and the med team arrived.

"This came in," she said. "We were told to hurry in case forensics got here first. Evidently there was a delay in us getting the call."

"Who in America?"

"No idea. I'm too little to be told anything important, like who I'm actually working for."

Milo looked at Julia, who indicated the account tallied with information on her implant system. "It's not true, but it's true enough. Parts of her instruction are encrypted. They were sent several hours ago."

Milo considered pressing for the parts that were encrypted to be made plain but decided to let it go.

"Can you order transport?"

Julia nodded again.

Milo turned to the cops. "You can have her. She's a four four two, section eight. The paperwork will follow."

The woman looked at Milo, "Hey, I didn't know these guys were legit and I don't know now."

"They are and all that is pleading, not part of investigation. A reel of this is already on its way to the prosecuting authority, along with a report on the discharge of a weapon."

He looked at the cop and pointed to his gun and the needle gun and then the man at the door.

"Forensics will have to bag those guns," he said.

The cop looked unhappy.

The Med team was working on the downed man to stabilise him. The cop was surprised at Milo's departure.

"Are you not waiting?"

Milo, equally surprised. "No. Should I? I can't tell them anything and if I could I wouldn't unless it had been tampered with or destroyed."

The cop was cuffing the woman. "I thought you boffins always worked it up together."

Milo raised his eyebrows and left. He passed the forensic team on the way. Along the street a few curious neighbours peeked out of gates and at windows, wondering who had ruffled their moneyed serenity.

*

Fifty minutes later, Milo's cab drew up by the kerb outside of their hotel. As it slid to a halt, the Pixie stepped out from the shadows. She waited as Milo climbed out and started to walk to the door. She said nothing, but didn't look too happy.

Julia, already in sight of Milo's system, lit up on the Pixie's. Milo pointed his chin to the hotel but said nothing and they went in together and through to the lift.

All were silent until they reached the room.

Milo turned to Julia. "Can you see to it that we are as private as we'd like?"

She nodded.

The Pixie lay back on the bed. "I suppose I deserved that. 'All's fair in love and war' and all that shit, but ... was she already dead?"

Julia looked surprised. "You heard?"

"No, but I speculated that the latest flurry on the crimes might have been you and now you've confirmed it. Was she?"

Milo sighed, "She was."

"The captain?"

"I'm guessing. My people say a 'Ninety-two percent probability'."

"What does that mean?"

"Yes. It will mean yes, more than likely. Same MO, same gun, better shot."

"Poor cow."

Julia frowned and Milo could feel her hurt and resentment, but it was quickly suppressed.

The Pixie propped herself up, "What say we stop messing around and just share what we know?"

"That your bosses' idea?"

She shook her head. "My idea."

"You're a suspect in an ongoing investigation. I can't share information with you. Not to mention the fact you're a walking, talking breach of numerous laws, conventions and constitutions."

"Yeah, but besides all that."

"Ok, besides all that, your mission might be to stop our investigation, or to terminate us, or to investigate us and find out what we know."

"It isn't."

"Says you."

"You have to admit, we've both wasted a lot of our time and Gog might still be alive if we hadn't."

Julia stepped in. "I can keep her under my surveillance," then turned to the Pixie, "if you'll give me access to your systems?"

The Pixie frowned, Milo smiled. She looked up at him. "I'll have to think about this."

"Your boss will not be pleased if you really are doing this without sanction."

"My boss isn't here, and they can decide to do away with me for a change in policy. That poor bastard this evening didn't get much of a choice, did he?"

Julia looked unhappy. "That was my fault."

"Only the trigger. He was taken down by us and that activated the system. It just needed a slight push to end him. I'm sure he didn't know he had it on such a light trigger. I'm sure I have a similar system. They never asked me either."

Julia looked sympathetic. "I can check. I disabled that forensic woman's failsafe system."

"Is that what you call it?"

"That is what it was called."

Milo looked more serious, "Look, think about it. If you let Julia in she'll know pretty well everything on your system, so if this is a con . . . I don't know about the legality of it, but then Julia will be able to check you out there too and if you're hiding something we'll know that. On your system or not, it turns out. In any event, I'll ask the team to check it out."

The Pixie brightened. "Fair enough. I'm not too worried about the agency stuff. We get a wipe at the end of each job, so there is only this one, but I have other, less 'official' things on there. You'll have access to them too?"

"I would," said Julia.

She turned to Milo. "And so would you?"

"Not necessarily, but I can't promise. We're getting a bit of bleed through."

"Ok."

Milo walked away to the corner of the room, leant against the wall. He looked like he was trying to survey the field of battle, a quarterback running through his options.

"We'll have to talk to Xin."

He called up his com and Xin faded into the room.

She was looking down at a piece of paper in her hand. "Hi Milo, we have the comparative reports from the restaurant and Gog. Same gun. The clustering on the head and the wall suggest the same shooter. Your scan of the room and the forensic scan tally, so we have confidence in the report to a much higher degree than London. A ninety two percent probability of it being the captain's work, still holds."

She noticed the Pixie was part of the meet, sitting, smiling away, and Xin looked at Milo quizzically.

"We have a mutual interest. Could you check out how legal it would be for us to share what we're are doing with her and her with us?"

Xin thought about it and looked at someone outside of the com but in the room with her. She nodded. "We will."

"Also, could you find out who owns the house where we found Gog?"

"Oh, we have something on that." She reached out and was handed a piece of paper. "The house was owned by a company, based in Paris, but with holdings in London, Paris, Geneva and . . . Denmark."

She looked up at whoever was with her. "Where in Denmark? Or is it the whole country?"

She waited for the answer and was none too impressed by it.

"We can't find out any more about it than that, but this is worse, North Africa!" She glared at someone.

Milo looked at Julia and she shrugged.

"The name of the company, Xin?"

Xin looked down the page. "Three Heads, Inc."

Again Milo looked to Julia, who frowned and looked up at him. "That's something . . . Elspeth is part of that."

"And the Brancusi?"

She nodded. "But what it means I don't know, or I don't know yet."

Xin said, "You'll have to go back to the house," Xin said, "find out what Gog was doing. We'll try to find out who 'Three Heads, Inc.' is and get an answer on your Pixie friend there."

Xin faded from view.

The Pixie stirred, "What do you mean by that? 'I don't know *yet*'."

Milo came to her rescue. "It seems that, um, Jane Cruickshank, in her creation of Julia, tiered her knowledge so that she doesn't have access to everything Jane knew about herself or about this . . . Whatever this is."

"Or so she says. Just how much faith do you have in Julia? And who's Elspeth?" the Pixie pressed again.

Milo looked at Julia and wondered exactly that himself, she looked back steadily and he could feel neither fear nor concern.

He looked back at the Pixie. "Elspeth? A suspect. You'll know more if you share. Trust? A fair amount. More than in you, less than in me, but it's under consideration."

Julia sighed, unsurprised, and Milo wondered how much she knew about his doubts. The Pixie suddenly seemed to feel vulnerable. She glared at Julia and stood up,

"We just take it on the nod because she looks like Julia, that she is Julia, or *made* by Julia and we don't even know Julia that well, or Cruickshank, or whoever she was. Why'd you let her into your system?"

Milo considered this. "She was in before I knew about it. But it fitted with what I knew and didn't seem too intrusive at first. I'm not sure what I would have thought if I'd known how things would develop. In any event, as I said, it was embedded before I knew it was there."

"But you want to give her access to my system. What do I get?"

Milo looked at the Pixie and considered what exactly was eating at her. "You don't have to . . . Have you been told something by your base?"

The Pixie turned to face him looking about as angry as you can get before you're actually sitting on a person's chest, punching their face into a bloody pulp.

"No!"

The life of a Pixie was harsh, the margin they lived on extreme. They were trained to within a hair's breadth of perfection and given a leeway to operate, which those working inside the law looked at with envy. They were exceptionally well paid and had access to facilities, healthcare and luxuries denied to most outside of the richest in society.

On the downside, they were in constant danger, were never acknowledged for their successes and rarely lived into their thirties, which, given they had been around in this incarnation for nineteen years, was telling. They were subject to violent attack at any moment, on duty or not, and they could be eliminated by their enemies or by their own side with impunity. Most carried a lethal cocktail of drugs in their systems, designed to be triggered if they looked like they would jump ship, or were about to be put under pressure to do so. Most were unaware of the failsafe system. The slapping up on the table in front of all of them, of the captain's failsafe, seemed to have gotten to her, just a little.

"Julia can shut it off, you know."

The Pixie looked at him, angry, resentful, vulnerable and hating that he could, was, seeing that. "And how do you know she's doing that? She didn't shut off the captain's system, did she?"

"I didn't know they existed until I triggered his," Julia shouted. "After I've shut yours down I can give you access to the allocation table."

"Why not before?"

"If it's the same as the captain's, it'll trigger if you examine the system. It doesn't seem to see me, or I mimic the system itself. Actually, I don't know in what way it sees me."

"What happens if you trigger the system? What happens if you get detected by my boss?"

Milo tried to calm things down. "This thing with the captain has you spooked, but you don't have to share with us."

"You're wrong. They put me on this, 'cause I'm their 'top guy'. They expect results. The last 'top guy' fell off his perch and they said he died on assignment, but I looked into it and I couldn't see how. But then, they said the same about the one before him, and I know they had her eliminated."

"How?"

"Drugs. They triggered her failsafe."

"No, how do you know?"

The Pixie looked at him, still angry but mostly hurt and her gaze dropped to the floor. "We were friends."

The silence was palpable. After about a minute, "I got a friend, he worked forensics for the agency, to do a blood test.

He said she didn't feel a thing, said he thought it would have been quite nice really . . . not so much for me."

"I can go in switch it off, get out."

"But once you're in you're in, right?"

Julia nodded. "I think I can give you an organic switch, it's like a light-up part of you, so you can control the failsafe."

"They'll spot it."

"Not if it's organic."

"You can do that?"

Julia nodded again. The Pixie chewed her lip, then agreed. Julia immediately faded. The Pixie looked over at Milo by which time Julia had been in and out.

"It's done," said Julia

The Pixie looked at her and tried to work out if there was anything different. "The switch?"

"It'll grow over the next few days. Just think of it, of switching it on or off. The failsafe, I mean." The Pixie nodded.

Milo shook himself. "Right, we have to check out whatever Gog was doing."

The Pixie grabbed her bag and Milo looked at her. "You should sit this one out until I have clearance from Beijing."

She smiled, sat back down. "I have a bit of a headache, anyway. How long will you be?"

"Give us a few hours."

"The headache is from the switch. You should rest for a bit or it'll get worse."

"Right. Call me."

She left as Milo was gathering his jacket and things. He looked up as the door closed.

"She brightened right up."

CHAPTER ELEVEN

The street was silent and empty once more. The house quiet and still, though the laser demarcation beams ringed the house and there was a notice on the front gate. The cab, their account docked, slid away quietly as they walked down the steep- stepped path to the door. The beam turned green as it acknowledged Milo's credentials and the door popped open, the police lock triggered by the beam system.

They entered the hallway. As they did so, Julia stopped. She raised her hand, an odd look on her face as though she could smell something nasty.

Milo sniffed and, at the change in Julia's face, realised how silly that was. "What, then?"

"Really? Like I can smell on my own. I've been analysing the captain's data since his untimely . . ." she said

"And something smells?"

"Correct."

"So you *can* smell."

She cocked her head and gave him a look of pity. "Seriously? No, it was the correlation with the data from the Pixie."

"They're working together?"

"No, far from it. It's not about what they were doing, it's about what they know and what they're trying to find out."

"Something concrete?"

She shook her head. "He didn't come from Washington. He came from New York. Someone wants us to believe different. But that's not all." She gave him a pointed look.

"What?"

"How much do you know about your implant? How it works, where it came from?"

"I know when it was put in. I know it acquires information and stores it in forms that organic tissue would find difficult. It can calculate and I've uploaded skills that I've never mastered in the normal way. It's a com system and an analysis system. It's annoying . . ."

He stopped listing all of the skills of which he was proud. China12 had the best tech.

"How much do you want to know?"

"What do you know about your data acquisition and about your personality wafer and subroutines?"

"I have a personality wafer?"

She smiled. "Everyone with a com link does."

He started to search his system, his mind, trying to calculate the implications. "Everyone?"

"Of course. Your implant has to work with your organic mind. We managed to deal with the problems of physical rejection early on, but the first systems failed, or rather didn't perform to spec, because your mind, people's minds identified the operation of the system as foreign and treated dealing with it in the same way they would an external terminal."

"And that would mean it was slow?"

"Not just slow. If people with prosthetic limbs kept on treating the limb as something bolted onto their bodies rather than as the limb it is supposed to be, they would always find life difficult. Adaptation was helped by incorporating the electronics of the limbs into the nervous system and the new limbs' operating under the direct, hardwired, control of the mind."

"Ok, so why can't the system be hardwired, like the limbs?"

"They are, but limbs respond to set stimuli and their neurological feedback system is comparatively simple. Cranial implants have to deal with the mind, which is immensely complex and has perspectives of its own about who, what and where it is."

"Still don't see where this is going."

"When a child is very tiny it begins to acquire information about the world round it and to discover what it is. This part is a comparative exercise. 'What am I? Male or female? What are females like?' From then on, the child seeks to affirm, what they have come to believe is 'them' their identity, in each facet of their life. How you dress, how you do your hair in the mirror, what team you follow, what books you read or perhaps don't read, the music you listen to and so on."

"Ok."

"Then comes this implant and it provides a flood of unfiltered information, and that information can confuse or even confound our sense of identity."

"So you need a personality wafer?"

"Exactly. In the adaptive process after implantation, you are told, 'Do your normal things, enjoy yourself, see your friends.' During that time, the main system is offline. The personality wafer is being conditioned to you, who you are, what you like. You condition it."

"Isn't that limiting?"

"Yes, but the main system is usually programmed to offer you other, new experiences, which you can accept or reject, but that's all gradual and conditioned by the personality wafer and, of course, you have the normal stream of life offering you what it does."

"So what about the Pixie?"

"Her wafer isn't like that."

He tried to run through what that might mean. "It's pre-programmed?"

"You're quick. It has a hardwired personality filter. One that cannot be altered except very slowly."

"Giving her a fixed perspective. I can see how that works and why. But why doesn't she reject it? You said the system has to work with . . ."

"Within the expectations of already established character and sense of self, yes. Before the implantation, she would have been trained and conditioned into a certain perspective on the world. They've been doing it to soldiers for centuries."

"So the wafer . . . fixes that in place."

"It does and reaffirms them – the Pixie and the Captain – as believers."

"So what does this have to do with us, and why are we talking about this now?"

Julia smiled. "The system, their systems are, by their nature, very fixed, which is good for their employers except when the agent or soldier is faced with powerful, emotional, data that undermines the personality wafer by calling into question the 'truth' upon which it is based."

"The captain's death."

"Yes. It undermined the part of the programming that told her that her employers care about her."

"The, 'no man is left behind' stuff?"

"Yes. It afflicted groups of men in the 1914-18 war when their 'pals' let them down in battle."

"That was why the meltdown."

"That was why, but she would have been in contact with her base between the captain's death and the meltdown."

"So?"

"So, with each contact, the system does a check on new data because they're aware this can be a problem. It should have been filtered out."

"Malfunction?"

"Very unlikely. So I was surprised."

"And?"

"And I started to compare the systems, the captain's and the Pixie's. Very similar, but as I went through the data I found something."

"Something? With their implants?"

"No, with my programming."

Milo waited. She seemed still to be analysing whatever it was she had found.

"And that is?" he asked.

She looked up. "First, the "meltdown" was allowed to happen. Second, they put a bug in me."

Milo was startled. "A bug? Have they been listening to all this?"

"No, it will operate only when we make a com link. Then it will try to hide under the data stream, filtering a specific stream to their base."

"Can you stop it?"

"Yes, I think it's improvised. A 'dickey up job' I'd call it, so it's not very good. I've been checking for something more subtle, but I've found nothing."

"So disable it."

"I don't think that's too clever."

He looked at her, trying to work out what she was thinking. Trying to work that into his suspicions about her program. "What then?"

"We have the equivalent of a captured agent who we can turn to our advantage. Plus, I have access coding for their systems."

"That was sloppy of them."

"I told you, it looks improvised. I think they're desperate for information."

"But we'll have to be careful about what information we transmit."

She nodded. "We will."

"You said it filtered, information. What's the filter?"

"They are looking for information about just what we have been talking about, data conditioning."

"Why? Are they trying to control my system?"

"No. I don't know, but there's an echo in the locked information Elspeth has in my system."

"What kind of echo?"

"I don't know. Sorry."

He thought for a moment. "Can we risk going through Gog's things? If we find out something important about what she was protecting they may find out."

"I think I can control that and we have to know in any case."

"Why? We could just stop the investigation. I can submit a report, then they wouldn't know."

"They won't stop, and they may succeed in whatever they were doing and we couldn't stop them."

"Fair enough, and whatever it is, it's worth killing people for and dying for, apparently."

"Let's go then."

Milo closed the front door behind him and switched on the main lights. They stepped into the library-sitting room and Milo stopped at the door, the point from which the shots were fired.

Julia watched. "What do you expect to find?"

"Expect? Not much. Forensics will have gone over it, but I'm here, you never know, and it can't hurt."

"All three?"

He smiled and ran his fingers lightly across the carpet and then up the door jamb. He sniffed at the wood. "He steadied himself against this when he fired."

He took up the stance he supposed the captain had taken when he shot her. Surveyed the room from there Did anything stand out? What could he see?

"Tell me ... how much did the captain know about the target?" he asked.

Julia ran through what she had. "Not much, just location He thought there might be two people here."

"Who? Felicity?"

"Doesn't say."

"He must have searched the place."

"No, he had a thermal scanner. She was alone."

"You're sure?"

"No, but the captain was. He shot her and got out."

"So he was just an assassin?"

"Seems likely."

"Did he have another contact?"

"Not in his active record."

"Makes sense."

"Why?"

"Means no one else is compromised if things go wrong."

He straightened and looked down the room. "Right, let's see what she was doing."

They walked towards the desk.

The chair had been righted and Gog's body was gone. The carpet was stained with blood and still damp. Milo avoided touching it, but could feel Julia's queasiness all the same.

Taking out a stylus, he moved things round the desk, examining the papers. Her pencil, which had fallen to the floor, was back on the desk and it was to the sheet of paper covered in pencil that he paid most attention.

"Can you make sense of this?"

Julia looked. "Statistics. She was working out probabilities."

"Of what?"

"No idea." She looked a little longer. "Whatever it is, it's quite likely."

"But we need the name of the horse and the race."

"Maybe he arrived at the door behind her."

"Maybe we did, but too late."

Milo saw a piece of headed paper with a symbol in the top left-hand corner. "What's that?"

Julia studied. "Janus?"

"He only has two faces. This has three."

"Three heads. Past, future and present?"

"The group that owns the place."

Milo's head throbbed and he winced.

Julia noticed, looked sympathetic. "There *is* something about heads."

He looked, held out his hands in question and she shook her head. He looked back at the page.

"Is there an address or any other information on the letter-head . . . the page footer?"

Milo lifted the page out from beneath the piles strewn over the desk. The page was blank, but there was a footer with the company number, the house address and a phone number.

He showed it to Julia. "Recognise it?"

"You could just try it."

"If it's significant, we can't show our hand yet. Is there anything else?"

"Not on the desk."

Milo bent down and began to go through the drawers but turned up nothing. He stood, looked around as though he was looking for something on the ceiling, in the corners.

"Is the house devoid of electronics?"

Julia looked for anything she could get hold of or hack into. "Nothing that's switched on. There could be something, but not attached to any network, in which case I can't see it. Even the white goods are dumb."

"How the hell did they find out about the place?"

Julia shook her head. Milo shrugged and headed to the door. Stepping into the hall, he looked through the door to the dining room, then walked upstairs. Three floors and six rooms with three bathrooms later and they were standing in what appeared to be the master bedroom

Milo was standing inside a large walk-in closet and looking at the kind of clothes Gog wouldn't have worn.

"So the other occupant is male, judging by the footwear."

There were two pairs of shoes, both very worn, though clearly expensive. "Not recently used."

He looked through the shirts and T-shirts, the underwear and the jumpers. "Nothing labelled."

Sighing, he leant against the shelf and surveyed the mess. "Not been here in a while? What do you think?"

Julia looked sad. "I don't know. They don't look very fashionable. Not very . . . hip."

"You just described about a third of the nerds in town. We are looking at a nerd aren't we? I mean judging by the company he keeps and the books . . ."

"I would guess."

At the end of the closet was a plinth. As they were talking, Milo was looking over at it idly. His curiosity momentarily piqued, he went over to it. There was a ring in the middle of the top, a thick coating of dust round it.

He ran his finger over it, following the perimeter. "What do you think stood here?"

Julia came over, looked. "I have no idea. A vase for flowers?"

"Maybe." He looked round the space. "Ok, I think we've got all we're going to get. If we talk to Beijing, will what we say be sent to the Pixie's base, or is it only data . . .? And yes, I know what we say is data too . . ."

"I think it would be a secure way. They won't know we know yet and they'll expect anything we do know to be sent in the way they usually send it, reports."

Behind the plinth was a small fridge which seemed to be working overtime. As he talked, Milo was looking at it idly and, without thinking, he leaned over and pulled at the door. Crammed inside was a body.

They looked at it, stunned. He crouched down for a closer look and pulled back as the smell hit him.

He turned to Julia. "Know him?"

She looked at the body silently, but slowly turned her head from side to side. "Not in anything that I have opened yet."

"The guy from CERN?"

"Maybe. Do you think the captain did this too?"

"No, this was done . . . at a guess, a few days ago. Maybe before you, even."

He called up Xin.

Her holo stood in the closet doorway, frowning. "Where are we?"

"In a closet, at Gog's house."

She dropped her voice to a whisper. "Hiding?"

Milo clearly hadn't thought of that, and laughed. "No. We have a new body for you. I'm sending it to the locals now and asking them to get a forensic team here."

"Who is it?"

"Not sure, maybe the guy from CERN, related to Dawson and Julia, I mean Elspeth, but we can't confirm that. Also, something's missing, we're not sure what. I have a number for you. I want you to trace it and keep tabs on it. It might be here, might be somewhere else in the town. Don't send anything to us about it over anything but voice."

"Why?"

"We're being bugged."

"Is voice safe?"

Julia leant in. "I think so. The bug looks a little hurried and crude."

Milo gave Xin the number. She wrote it down, then looked up, smiling. "Oh, I like this, it's so old-fashioned."

Milo sighed. "Right, see what you can do. We're going to have a little chat with the Pixie, see what she can tell us, but at the moment all we've got are four dead bodies and a stone head."

"Give us a shake after that and we'll let you know what we've found. If it's urgent, we'll let you know through Julia."

Xin faded and Milo pushed himself upright and closed the fridge. They headed for the door.

On their way down the stairs Julia asked, "Milo, what do you know about the history of your implants?"

He thought about it. "You asked that before."

"Yes, but I mean their history," she said.

"These were put in just after I joined China12, state-of-the-art gold wafer, been upgraded twice since then. Also a neural net, which has been extended and can be again, somewhat, but not removed."

She nodded and then, said, "And before that?"

"Before what?" He was clearly puzzled. He thought, shook his head, smiled. She nodded again.

Milo was curious. "Why?"

She smiled. "Oh, nothing. Just wondered what the history of the system was, is all."

As they pulled the door closed behind them a cab was drawing up to the kerb.

Milo was about to go down the steps when he stopped. "Is it the Pixie who did the bugging or her base?"

"The base. They left her out I think so the meltdown would be real, wouldn't register a bum note on your system."

As they came out, the same police group as before was climbing out of their transport.

The first cop walked up to Milo. "Another body?" he asked.

"Yeah, but this one is older. A few days at a guess. Fridge, upstairs, first floor, in the walk-in. We don't know who he is yet."

"So why are we here?"

"Someone has to look after the place until forensics get here."

"You people are dangerous people to hang out with."

"Yeah."

*

They found the Pixie coming out of their bathroom when they got back to the hotel. She had just taken a shower and conveyed an air of damp vulnerability. Milo was surprised as she rubbed her hair, looking more relaxed than at the last meeting. Surprised to find her there. Surprised that he was surprised.

"What? Your room's better than mine. I'm on an agency budget!"

Milo, eyes narrowed, "Do you have a room?"

She stopped rubbing her hair. "Ok, no, I don't. We're supposed to fend for ourselves. If we start booking rooms there'd be a trail to follow, wouldn't there? That was how we found the Captain."

He shook his head and sat by the hotel com system.

It was an interesting phenomenon in a world of mobile tech, that hotels and other service industries still supplied fixed-terminal access to their facilities. At various points, and especially at the higher end of the market, they had tried to move over to an app-based system, avoiding the need for all that physical investment and the maintenance that went with it, but market resistance was too great. It was seen as cheap rather than convenient. The public preferred to see the $800 clunky hotel tech rather than be asked to rely on their own $2,500 com systems. Of course, side by side with this, 'independent' firms supplied apps that tied into the hotel systems and allowed you to use your own tech, but that was strictly on the QT.

181

Milo ordered some food for himself and the Pixie. He didn't bother to ask her what she wanted, knowing that just about any high-calorie food would do. He was tired enough that he wouldn't have bothered to ask himself. He also put in a call to Anna in New York with no reply.

The Pixie was lying back on the bed. Milo watched her for a few minutes, then said, "So let's get with the sharing of information. What do you know about all this?"

The Pixie sat up, grinning. "So it's 'you show me yours and I'll show you mine', is it?"

"I know you won't tell me everything, but I want to see the colour of your money."

Her head dropped and then she made a decision. "We got into the game very late, didn't know what was happening until it was all happening. We had only just heard of Julia when the next thing we knew, she was being reported dead. In fact, we were on our way to see her."

Remembering the evening, she shook her head. "The business in Paris came up, as it would. Apart from the connection with Julia, it was just an attempted robbery, but then we realised there was some American involvement. They denied it."

"But they would if it was corp-led, anyway."

"Yeah, we tried to get out ahead of it when we found out about Gog before you guys, but, well . . . You know."

"Not as much as we should. So far, we all seem to be playing catch-up. Who do you work for?"

The Pixie just smiled blandly.

Milo shrugged.

Julia turned to Milo. "Why was the captain just sent to kill and who killed the guy in the fridge?"

The Pixie sat up. "There's a fridge now and a guy?"

Milo, watching for a reaction, turned to Julia, who confirmed it. "She's surprised."

Milo leaned back. "There is and there is and we don't know who he is. Been dead for a few days. It doesn't make any sense, none of it. What are the Americans after?"

The Pixie shook her head. "It would help if we knew what the head does?"

"We don't think it does anything. It might be a model."

"A model?"

"For a robot." He looked at her and held out his hands.

The Pixie fell back again and turned on her side, resting her head on her elbow as she looked at the other two. "We're not clear what the Americans are after, but if the head wasn't it, we want to know what it is so we can decide if we want it. As for making sense, it might. If they have what they want, the captain's would be a cleaning op. Get rid of the following pack and clear out with the goods."

Julia nodded. "But that would imply they have the Brancusi."

Milo shook his head. "They have something, or someone does, so her theory fits. I don't think our head was what they were actually looking for, here. If the head is some sort of cypher, then there could be other ways to that end."

The Pixie smiled, "But we're looking at three heads now."

Milo nodded and she looked surprised. "Oh. You knew!" she said.

"Not really and yes," he said. "The house Gog was killed in belonged to a company called 'Three heads, Inc' I surmise that one of the heads is the Brancusi. I have no idea what the other two are, but I think someone took one of them from the house in Cassis. There was a thing . . . a plinth? Empty."

The Pixie nodded, Julia smiled at her. "If you don't tell him I will!"

The Pixie looked up and then at her internal system, caught unaware. She closed her eyes for a moment. "Alright . . . the agency found that "Three Heads Inc" owns a head too, a bust by Henry Munyaradzi, an African artist. Not as valuable in its own right as the Brancusi, but valuable. The agency thought it belonged to a cousin of the Dawson woman in Paris, but we don't know where it is."

Milo sat forward, then jumped at a knock on the door. His head snapped to it and he began to rise.

The Pixie looked round casually, "I think it's food." She looked at Milo, "and I thought *I* was wound up."

183

Julia shimmered and then nodded. Milo walked to the door.

A few minutes later and the side table was set out with a variety of cold meats and salads, and a couple of pizzas. Milo was pouring wine into two glasses.

He looked at Julia apologetically and she smiled. "It's funny. I do actually feel hungry. I guess it's you who feels it. This is odd."

The Pixie looked from one to the other, "You two are weird."

Milo frowned and handed over one of the glasses. "Why? I don't think we're weird."

"Yeah, you are. You have your own personal ghost, for fuck's sake! And she can do shit and now she feels hungry! That's weird." She plunged almost face first into the food.

Milo watched her and then closed his eyes. "I'm living a strange part of my life, that's all."

Julia was getting anxious, "If you think it's weird on the outside, think about how I feel for a moment . . . Milo, eat!"

He took a sip of wine and they both savoured it for a moment before he lifted his cutlery to eat. The Pixie watched and shook her head. Milo ate and Julia enjoyed it.

The food had been given a thorough going over. Milo finished his glass of wine and the Pixie poured herself another. Milo watched her and looked at Julia sitting on the edge of the sideboard. Could a ghost look satisfied, almost tipsy?

Her head turned. "I am not!"

He smiled and looked over at the Pixie. "When did you search the place?"

She drank. "I didn't, it was a report we picked up from the Americans. They seemed to think they'd got something of a lead, then the kill order came for Gog and, it turned out, for me. Base only told me all that while you were back at the house. They said it was something they had only just found out."

"And you believe them?"

"Why would they lie?"

"Let me count the ways" Milo shrugged.

Julia looked thoughtful. "Do they or the Americans know what it's about?"

"The Americans seem to, or they think they do. Base are saying they know but I'm pretty sure they have about as much of a clue as the rest of us."

Milo sat back, thinking. The Pixie watched him.

"Have you heard anything from Anna?" she asked. "We know she left for New York. She might know a thing or two."

Milo nodded, then lifted his head, "She left me a holo, saying she was going to New York. She thought she'd be back in a day or two. If not, something was wrong."

The Pixie pushed herself up. "So she was afraid something might go wrong?"

"Evidently."

"She knew something was up."

Milo shook his head. "I don't think so . . . I say that, but she knew Julia had been killed. I think there were things the partners were unwilling to talk about over coms. One of their own had just been killed."

The Pixie was much more insistent "When did she go?"

"While we were in Cambridge."

The Pixie thought for a moment. "She could have triggered the captain. It could be her company behind it."

"Or that might have been on the cards before she left."

The Pixie turned to Julia, "What was the captain's point of origin?"

"The States, New York. They tried to make it look like Washington DC."

There were three minds whirring. Milo looked at the Pixie, "When did the second head go missing?"

"Not sure exactly, but in the same time frame."

"So it could have been that."

"It could. Depends who took it. You need to have a conversation with your girlfriend."

Julia shifted, Milo became defensive. "Not my girlfriend."

He tried Anna again, and again was put onto the answer system, and again, "It's me . . . you know."

He looked back to the room, tiredness and the wine hit him. Bizarrely, Julia yawned. The Pixie followed suit and rolled over onto one side of the bed. Milo blinked, shook his head and dragged off his outer clothing, throwing himself onto the bed and into the warm arms of sleep.

Milo jerked awake and looked around. Julia was sitting on the edge of the sideboard, watching him, and he jumped again. She smiled. He stared at her and then slowly calmed down. His head put together where he was and who she was, and what she wasn't. He sat up. He looked round the room and only then noticed the Pixie was gone. He looked at Julia.

"She left about five minutes ago and, when it occurs to you, yes, there was something in the wine."

He looked startled. His system should have warned him, but then he really should have realised. They had all just decided to go to sleep. No one said anything, they had just done it. He looked round the room, everything seemed in order.

"Why?"

"They wanted to pay you and the Pixie a visit."

He frowned, looked round the room again, pushed himself off the bed. These intruders were the tidiest . . .

"No, they weren't."

"Weren't what?"

"The tidiest anything."

"What happened?"

"They tried to get in about seven hours ago and then again about three hours ago. They were a bit more brutal the second time. I had to be a little rough myself."

She smiled, the kind of smile Milo had seen once before.

"Any casualties?"

"There's this."

And Milo's head pounded suddenly. Then his drug system kicked in and the pain slowly started to fade. "Ow! What the hell!?!"

"If I have a hard time, I'm afraid there are consequences." She shrugged.

He was on the edge of the bed now, still holding his head in memory of the pain, feeling very confused. "Why didn't I feel it before?"

"I stopped you feeling it. Neuro-transmitter block, a bit like acupuncture. It's bad to keep it in place."

"Why didn't you wake me?"

"I could deal with it. Seemed to me sleep was good for you."

He stood and went to get a bottle of water and downed it.

"What happened to her?" He jerked his head at where the Pixie wasn't.

"She left after she woke up."

"Oh yeah, you said."

She nodded.

"I don't understand. Why didn't my system pick up the dodgy wine? I should have registered the drop in heart rate as abnormal at the very least."

"It affected me too, so I'm guessing it had some sort of electronic component to it as well. It just didn't affect me as much, so I was here when they tried to be put on the guest list."

"And did her ladyship say where she was going? Where were our 'guests' from? Were you able to tell?"

"Well, *you're* waking up anyway. The Pixie went to find out about the uninvited. I gave her a steer and she's gone to check it out. As near as I could make out, they were friends of the late Errol, mayoral tech signature, and they were similarly mixed in terms of their training."

"Glad they didn't get in."

"Yeah you are. They did not have your best interests at heart and the second time . . ."

"So what happened to them?"

"After I . . . discouraged one of them, the others took the hint and left, carrying him between them."

"We've got to get out ahead of this. Everyone seems to know more than we do and we're the ones investigating!"

"Yes, but it's them we're investigating. None of them seem to know any more about the others than we do, except perhaps the Americans."

187

A knock on the door. Milo lunged for his bag and began to root out a weapon. Julia flickered and the door unlocked.

"It's the Pixie."

He relaxed. The Pixie wasn't relaxed and didn't close the door in a relaxed fashion. Milo felt the limits of the effectiveness of his drugs. The Pixie was looking round the room as though she was expecting people to jump out at her.

She glared at Milo. "I thought you guys had all the dope detection systems going?"

"We do. Whatever they used hasn't got a detect yet. Hadn't last night, at least. This morning we've moved on."

"Did she show you what they were trying to do?"

"Not yet." He looked at Julia.

"You didn't ask!"

His head tilted to one side. Julia played back the corridor surveillance feed to him.

Three big men in tracksuits came to the door with several small boxes of tech, clearly meant to pop the lock. They applied it to the door and messed about with it for several minutes. When it didn't work, one of them applied some more physical persuasion and his colleagues had to stop him. They left, arguing.

A new part of the recording, with a timestamp later in the night, began. Four of them this time. One Milo recognised as the Corporal they had left alive in Amsterdam. They had more tech and what might have been a bigger power supply. They applied it to the door, a few moments of waiting while one of them looked at a monitor. Then he nodded. The corporal pressed on the handle, which seemed to give. The one with the monitor smiled.

There was a flash and the corporal, his hand still on the door, jumped back and started to shake his arm. The more physical man ploughed into the door, which had closed again, and gave it several attempts before he was hauled off it. The tech man looked straight down the camera and punched several buttons. The image wobbled and he grinned. He punched more buttons and then didn't. He collapsed.

188

The others looked at each other and the physical one grabbed his head. The other two gathered the equipment and the tech man and, followed by the brute, headed for the exit.

Milo turned to Julia. "Was that flash you?"

She nodded.

"Dead?"

She shook her head, expressionless.

Then he looked up at the Pixie. "Find out any more?"

"Yes, the late Errol's friends are in town. The real Errol I mean. But the corporal is anxious not to meet you, and *especially* not her, again, if you're awake. Yes, she remembers you."

"You mean they wanted to see you?"

"No, he didn't remember me. But he introduced me to his boss. I was standing in front of him, the regional co-ordinator. Ok, not in front of, on top of him. They were in his room. It was really nice. They must have a huge budget."

Milo wound his finger round in a circle.

"He claimed he didn't know anything, but when I suggested he meet a charming woman who might remind him of things he might know, he thought he might just know one or two things."

"He talked?"

"Yes and no, but he knew about the captain being here, although he doesn't know we were involved, or even that he's no longer with us. He wants to find him."

"You didn't enlighten him, I take it?"

"No. But I'm guessing he was the source for the hit on me."

"They're working with the America Corp?"

"At some level. He didn't seem to know why, though. He didn't blame the American's for the hit on Errol."

"And you believed that?"

"Yeah, I don't think our boy is too high up the food chain."

"Could *the* boss be in town?"

The Pixie thought about it, "Could be, but I don't see why she would be."

"If they were expecting to find something definitive, she might be? People seem to be getting a bit jumpy about coms."

The Pixie gave him a funny look, but then nodded. "There's something new in the game, someone has broken something or opened up a new line in this."

Milo nodded, rubbed his head, "I need to get something down me."

The Pixie pulled out a meal bar, Milo pulled a face. "No, some real food and some coffee." She laughed and opened the bar. "I'm up for that!"

He turned to his bag and began to stuff things into it. "Why does that not surprise me?"

Later, in a cafe, Milo had an omelette in front of him. A half-finished cup of coffee, some bread and a large pot filled with more coffee completed the look. The Pixie had enjoyed the same and a whole lot more and, judging by the small stack of empty plates beside her, a whole lot more again.

Julia was watching Milo take his careful bites. She was smiling, remembering, but they were his memories . . . "You really like omelettes?"

He nodded. "I do. They offer a good balanced meal when accompanied by a salad."

She smiled. "A good balanced meal . . . Appetising . . ."

Still stuffing her face, the Pixie asked, "So, where do we go from here?"

"I've heard nothing from Anna for nearly two days now. She said if she didn't surface in about that time to come and get her."

The Pixie stopped. "It couldn't be a trap, could it?"

Milo looked at her aware of the sarcasm in the question. "Yes, duly noted, but, just like with Amsterdam, we need a break in this. We know that the Americans want rid of you, and the Five Mayors want rid of me and you. Only you know about Julia . . ."

"Wrong."

"Who? Oh, Anna, so maybe the Americans, if she told them. And Errol, Skolnic, that is . . ."

"No, the captain didn't know who or what I am, he just had the file on Julia."

The Pixie grinned, "He knew me alright."

Milo continued patiently. "We have to presume they all want her dead."

Between bites, the Pixie said, "And you have to face up to it. Anna may be dead already."

CHAPTER TWELVE

Anna's apartment was as empty as the last time they had been there, but the washed mugs and plates were dry and the holo had a few more messages. Milo flipped through them quickly, checking for any updates from Anna. He wasn't surprised not to find any. The Pixie took all of milliseconds to make herself at home and was lying on the couch by the time he turned back to the room.

She looked up as he did so. "Can we order food?"

He nodded, still considering the absence of things to consider. Julia wandered about the room looking at things and he watched her briefly, suddenly aware that she might look but she couldn't touch, couldn't pick things up.

She looked up at him, smiled. "But then I can pick things up that you can't even see."

He smiled back.

The Pixie looked up at them. "See, you're weird. Focus, people, I'm hungry!"

Milo turned to her. "You could always order food yourself."

"Not if I follow protocol."

"How do you live?"

"This is what it's like when I'm working. When I'm not, I order food all the time!"

"I bet!"

It was Julia's turn to watch and feel amused. "I ordered a few minutes ago."

The Pixie turned to Milo holding out a hand at Julia. "See, *that's* efficient."

By the time the food was finished Milo had come to a decision. He asked Julia to search the apartment's electronic records,

192

including 'protected' correspondence. She didn't like the idea at all, until the Pixie pointed out that she was probably still a partner in the firm, as the interval was not enough time to have allowed them to change her status and, of course, they had no reason to think there was any rush.

Julia was gone momentarily. "There's not much locally, though she should be more careful with encryption codes . . ."

The Pixie's eyes practically lit up.

Julia turned, ". . . which I've put out of harm's way. There's nothing to suggest, she's one of *them*, but the place has been visited since we left for Marseille."

She stopped and pointed. A holo of the apartment played and two men were seen entering, before performing a thorough and very careful search. They didn't look like the men associated with the mayors. They wore suits and moved with an ease that suggested careful training.

Milo looked at the Pixie. "Friends of yours?"

The Pixie looked and got Julia to replay and freeze part of the holo, but then she shrugged and shook her head. "They might be, they might not be. It's no one I've worked with, but I mostly work alone. The last two ops I worked with are dead. These guys look like office ops if they're ours, but they could be a different branch. They could be American . . . they look religious."

Milo frowned. "That's a funny thing to say. Why would you think that?"

"I don't know. They look like the people who were at my mother's church when I was a kid. They were American."

"Your mother was religious?"

"Well yeah. After the war lots of people were."

Milo digested this. "Were they?"

It was Julia and the Pixie's turn to stare at him. Then they exchanged a look.

He stared back. "What? It seems to me that war should have the opposite effect of convincing people about the existence of a kindly God."

The Pixie wasn't outraged, but she was insistent. "People want to feel closer to loved ones they've lost in the war. It's natural!"

Milo nodded, surprised at her sensitivity and level of intensity. "I guess. You?"

"No! But, like I said, my mum was. Some people take it to extremes."

Milo turned to Julia. "Any other visitors?"

"No, that was it."

"They didn't seem to find anything."

"They didn't. They didn't do an electronic search or a scan."

The Pixie brightened. "Not ours then."

Milo grinned. "You seem relieved."

"I don't want to have to spend my whole life defending the good guys."

"And you're the good guys?"

"You bet!"

Deciding first to sleep and then to decide what to do in the morning, the Pixie made herself comfortable on the couch and Milo headed for the spare bedroom. Having finished his routine, he was lying in bed, when Julia lay down beside him.

He considered her for a moment. "Ok, she's right. This *is* weird."

Julia just smiled.

Milo asked, "How much of our exchange did the Pixie's base get?"

"You mean through their bug? None. But the Pixie will have told them."

"Yeah, there was nothing I wasn't happy to share. I just wanted to know."

"What she won't know is what I didn't tell you."

"Can she hear this right now?"

"You mean, am I lying beside her right now as well? I'm not that kind of AI, I'll have you know!"

He smiled and shook his head. "Ok, so what didn't you tell us?"

"Her comment, about them looking religious, was closer to the mark than she may think. It might be closer to the mark than I thought when I first looked at the material from the apartment."

"Why?"

"I didn't consider it."

"No, why might it be closer to the mark?"

"The firm Anna and I worked for do represent a religious group in the Americas. There was nothing here but there is something in my files about it and Anna took point on their liaison."

Milo thought and chewed his thumb. Julia waited, watching him.

Milo shrugged, turned to her. "Could be nothing."

She nodded.

"Could be everything."

She nodded again.

"We go to the States."

*

The discussion with the Pixie had been brief. She had no permissions outside of Europe and a special order wouldn't be given in this case for her to travel to the States. They had ops in situ and she had no permission to go, as she put it, 'off-piste'.

They shook hands outside the apartment building and a clearly frustrated Pixie, walked away. Milo climbed into a cab. That was what Milo knew.

About ten minutes earlier, when Milo had been in the bathroom and not with the Pixie, a conversation had taken place. The Pixie had been packing up with Julia hovering.

The Pixie stopped and turned and glared at Julia, then, "What?"

Julia sounded tense. "We're going over there."

"Yeah."

"The reason they don't need you to go."

The Pixie glared at her, her hand making a fist by her side.

Julia noticed but ploughed on, "Will she be put on us?"

"Probably."

195

Silence.

"How long?"

"You know."

"First one since . . .?"

"You know."

"I don't know everything."

"Too bloody much."

"I'll look out for her."

"She can take care of herself." The Pixie added aggressively.

Julia was thinking about this as they travelled.

The ease with which travel to the Americas had been improved since before the war was in inverse proportion to the time it took to cross into any of the countries in the "Americas' Federation". This was the trade association of the countries in North, Central and most of South America, which was slowly developing into something more than just a trade association. Even though Europe remained a theoretical ally of the Americas, and in particular the United States, Americorp policy was much more distrustful and, when it came to borders, Americorp ruled.

The thirty-minute flight was followed by a three-hour wait, while each passenger was checked, scanned, and checked again against one of the most chaotic databases in the world. The young woman who had been dealing with Milo was comparatively efficient, but was only as swift as the various searches allowed her to be. Having gone through the process before, Milo was calm and aware that his having passed the frontier on 'business' but not 'trade business' meant that his processing would take longer.

Finally, she leaned on the desk and called up the first of the last few screens. "China12 eh?"

He nodded.

"In hot pursuit?"

A faint smile crossed his face and he shook his head. "Routine enquiry."

The woman's smile and the way the enquiry was put suggested a mildly humorous edge to the question, but had he said yes or made a joke, it would have thrown up a new line of permits and checks.

She pressed the final screen and he held out his hand. The transcoder gave him a six-week window within which he could make his enquiries and alerted the relevant authorities that he should be offered the assistance necessary in the discharge thereof. The gate in front of him snapped back to let him pass and the next traveller took his place.

The plaza in front of JFK was awash with yellow cabs swirling in a jerky flow past the exits of the terminal. Milo slid into the first one and snapped off the 'share' button on the door as he did so. The warning of the increased fare this would incur flashed up and was ignored.

"Central Manhattan."

"A full address with entitlement is required for that destination."

"Gate's Hotel, Central Park. China12."

"Thank you."

Since the end of the war, the residents of Manhattan had become less inclusive than they once had been. During the war, serious restrictions had been imposed on movement to and from the island as various critical facilities had been centred there. Afterward, only those with a 'need to enter' had been allowed onto the island unless they lived there. Several million tourist passes were also issued each year. In recent times, even these had been cut back pretty severely.

There had been a point, you could still see it in old movies, where the town had just been a solid lump of vehicles, pumping out their fumes and crawling along. Now it was a still crowded, but exciting place where there was lots happening and lots of ways to get to the excitement ... It only cost money.

The trip into the island was fast and direct. From the cab, Milo could see the haze over the city, which used to be caused by fumes but now was the sight from distance of delivery drones and surveillance drones, swinging up and down the canyons like bees to a hive. Julia faded into life beside him and they watched the approaching city together.

Without turning her head, she asked: "How far back do you remember the city?"

"Far enough, I guess. I've always liked this view. It smacks of everything you anticipate coming to new places and a new life."

He turned and smiled at her and she was smiling back, but he could feel something else, something like concern. He turned back to the view, dismissing it as anticipation of what they were going into.

It was a smart boutique hotel owned by the Gates Foundation. Amongst other things, it held symposia on the dangers posed by problems that should have been addressed fifty years earlier, and more, the kind of problems that had led to the war and that were still being worked through.

They also took guests. China12 was exactly the kind of ongoing client with whom the foundation liked to encourage and maintain a relationship: high-tech, utterly respectable and possibly useful.

A retinal scan was taken as he came through the door. Not the 'hold open your eye until it dries out' kind, more the 'you never noticed it happening' kind – and Milo's room number flashed up, as though projected on his hand.

As he made his way to the lifts, Milo looked about the lobby and noticed the usual number of Nobel science and various Lit prize winners chatting and pretending they understood one another.

The lift opened. The building was low-rise, so only the third floor.

Julia faded into his sight again. "This is seriously nice!"

"I know. You see, it's not all dives and back streets with me."

"A bit high-profile, no?"

"Like that makes a difference here."

"True, but all the same. It really does feel like being a guest in an old friend's house."

"You have very fancy old friends."

"I do."

And then the conversation dropped as an elephant wandered into the room and sat down in front of them.

The door to his suite – none of the rooms were anything other than suites – opened as he came to it and swung back. It was all so smooth and easy and comfortable and so very safe, hence his surprise when Milo found himself looking at a man in a dark suit sitting in a comfortable chair by the window.

The man turned, looked at Milo and smiled. He didn't move.

Julia walked over to him and then her head snapped back to Milo. "He's like me."

"Dead?"

She gave him a 'patient' look. "Not real. He's being projected directly into your ocular circuit using the room's system to amplify the signal."

The man was still just sitting, smiling away.

"Can he see you?"

A moment or two of silence. "No, he can't see either of us. He is reacting to the signal from the door. He has no presence here, unless we allow him to. Oh, he's trying! No, no you don't!"

The man frowned. Milo put down his bag and wandered over. Julia looked annoyed. She tapped her foot looking down at the man.

Milo answered the 'call'. "Hi, and you are . . .?"

The man continued to smile but looked up at Milo. When he spoke his voice had an affected nasal inflection presumably trying to mask a background more character-building than his peers.

"Hello. I'm sorry to be so rude as to be here without invitation but . . ."

"Tell him to stop trying to hack your system"

"We are in a . . ."

"Stop trying to hack my system and then maybe I'll listen."

The smile faded and he looked across at someone who wasn't in the room with Milo, but presumably was with the stranger. Milo waved his hand through the image and the smile drifted back.

"Ah. As you have guessed, I am being projected to you from elsewhere, Washington, in fact, the very latest in com software.

The foundation would be very annoyed if we actually went round breaking into people's rooms."

"They'll be plenty annoyed you hacked their system and tried to hack mine and you *still* haven't told me who you are or what you want."

"My name is Jones. I work with the same firm as your friend Anna May. I'm here to ask for your help."

"I'm listening."

"Anna was supposed to attend a meeting in Washington with some of our senior partners about three days ago."

"She said New York."

"I assure you the meeting was here, or was supposed to be. She never arrived. We made attempts to raise her and we made enquiries, but we drew a blank."

"Did your enquiries include searching Ms May's apartment?"

Jones looked at Milo and then at someone else and frowned. "No. Has her apartment been searched?"

"It has. Two gentlemen, dressed in that 'Americorp' way, spent some time in the place. They left empty-handed."

Jones brought his hands together and up to his nose as he considered this. It was evident Milo's words were being shared with whoever was in the room with Jones and they were discussing this latest news.

Julia wandered over and stood beside the window. "Ask him why they wanted her to come to Washington, and why Anna said it was New York she was going to."

Jones turned back to Milo. "Milo . . . May I call you Milo?"

"You can call me anything you like, but before you do, I'd like some answers . . . I got a message from Anna telling me she was going to New York, not Washington. Why would that be?"

The man turned away again to his colleagues and then to Milo. "She may have meant she was passing through New York?"

"Anna is a very precise woman. I don't buy that."

Again Jones received something from those in the room with him. "Well, perhaps she was being discreet. Look, you have been retained by Anna in regard to the unfortunate death of Ms Cruickshank. Can we extend that to include this? In that way we can be a little more relaxed with regard to personal information?"

"I think we can do that."

"Either you can do that, or you can not?"

"We can. Consider it done." Lawyers, Milo cursed.

Jones adjusted himself in the seat, like a child before the class in show and tell. "We have acquired a client in the last year or so for whom Anna was our point of liaison. They came to us through another, long-standing and much valued client."

"Can I ask who?"

Jones shook his head immediately. "Out of the question. Anna seemed to have got on very well with this particular client."

"The old one or the new one?"

Jones looked up, making it clear he disliked being interrupted. He took a breath. "The new one. It's a group based in a part of old New York, Brooklyn. Have you ever visited Brooklyn, Milo?"

"Not very recently, at least."

"It was, and is, a very prosperous part of town. Very . . . colourful."

Milo looked at him blankly.

"Yes, well, you can take my word for it. Historically, the neighbouring borough of 'The Bronx' . . .", he said this as though it were a foreign word, ". . . used to be quite poor and, as is usual in such districts, very religious. Even with the gentrification at the end of the last century, there were many places of worship. After the war, religion flourished, as you know, and . . ."

Milo held up his hand. "I'm sorry, but can we skip the history and get to the client and Anna's involvement?"

Jones was put out, as he had just begun to warm to his subject, but he flushed and nodded. "Very well." He stopped as the invisible presence said something to him. "The client is a religious group, really an assembly of smaller groups, who have come together to act, they say, on the part of God."

201

There was silence. Milo took this in and tried to piece it together with what he knew. "Was Anna part of the group?"

"Not so far as we know."

"Was she coming to New York to see members of the group?"

"As far as we knew, she was coming to Washington and not to New York."

Milo turned to Julia, his voice lowered. "So far, so exactly what we know. Was there anything from them to bring her to New York?"

Julia gave him a stern look, "Just *think* it!"

Jones, assuming he was being spoken to by Milo, said, "No. Do you have a reason for asking?"

Milo turned to him. "I'm sorry, I'm speaking with one of my colleagues."

Jones was surprised and he seemed to look about the room.

Julia jumped. "Oh! They're at it again."

Milo turned to Jones. "Stop that!"

"Mr . . . um, Milo, this is delicate. We have to be sure there is no unapproved person listening to a privileged conversation."

"You can be so assured."

Jones looked decidedly uncomfortable.

Julia smiled. "Oh, he's their head of tech. He must have been bragging."

Milo looked at her reprovingly. "*You didn't*?"

She shrugged. "He started it."

Milo turned back to Jones. "Ok, you're going to have to leave this with me for the moment. If you have any recent correspondence between Anna and this client, I would like to see it. Also, access to her diary for the past ten days or so."

Jones got the ok and passed it on. "Fine. Do you think it will take long to locate her?"

"It shouldn't. New York is a big place, but it's also the most densely surveilled place in the world. This is assuming she came here and is still here."

Jones nodded. "All right, we'll wait for your call and we'll send that over to you in the meantime."

His image faded away like a distant memory. Milo had to blink.

"Can you look through her correspondence for the last week or so in London? You needn't be bothered by ethics now she's a client twice."

"I wasn't that bothered."

"Bothered enough not to look. Can you check her diary and tickets for here."

It took Julia a few minutes and Milo used the time to unpack and to put in searches of the local 'traffic net'. The traffic net was what the New Yorkers now called the surveillance system, deeming it to be less threatening than anything related to security. There had been ongoing difficulty with the acceptance of it, but in the past year Americorp had changed the name and rebranded the policy. This had resulted in fewer systems being vandalised, despite everyone still knowing what it was for.

Julia was back. Milo felt her disquiet. They looked at one another.

Milo broke the silence. "You found something?"

She nodded, he raised his eyebrows in query.

"She seems to have gotten in over her head."

"I doubt that. She's a very bright woman."

"This wasn't about 'bright'. If anything, that would have been a disadvantage."

"What's she done?"

"I'm not really sure. Her correspondence shows she's getting her hooks into them, rather more than she should have, given the professional relationship, but they're also getting their hooks into her."

"Was Anna working for anyone else? Besides her legal work, I mean?"

Julia thought about it, running through the files she had retrieved. Her face darkened. "Oh."

"Oh?"

"She has some encrypted correspondence with a member of US State Services. They are not clients of the firm."

"So they might have put her in undercover. Does the com with them predate or postdate the arrival of the religious group as clients?"

A moment passed as Julia ran through all of the data and she faded a little. This time it gave Milo a slightly queasy feeling. Either that or the thing that caused the fading was giving him a queasy feeling, he wasn't sure which, and then suddenly everything was normal.

"It postdates it," she said

"They saw the group had established a link they could get into and went for it?"

Julia nodded. "It does look like that. Most of the com is heavily encrypted. I've broken some, but the rest will take a little time and effort. If I were to judge by the timings, I would say you're right."

"Then she could be in a whole world of trouble right now, depending on what they know or believe. The boys in the apartment, you're sure they didn't find any of this?"

"They never looked."

"We don't have time to decrypt now, it'll wait."

Milo sat, then stood up and walked about. Then he sat down again. He checked the results from the traffic system. A few hits.

Julia was watching too. "Let me see."

Milo tooled up, that is he pulled on a jacket and stuffed a weapon in his pocket and checked the time. It would be four AM in Beijing.

He sent a com. "Hi guys, Anna's firm have extended the contract on Julia to cover Anna's disappearance. They'll square the 'public interest' part of not putting it on the crimes. Oh yeah, Anna's disappeared. We think a religious group is involved and it might not be pleasant. Going now to check it out."

He looked over at Julia.

"She got in a share in Times Square and she crossed the Brooklyn Bridge about ten minutes later, no other stops," she told him.

"So she's in Brooklyn?"

"New York has no access to the surveillance system in Brooklyn and parts of it are switched off."

"What about her personal signal?"

"Suppressed as she crossed the bridge."

"Can you hack their system as we go?"

"Depends on what signal, if any, they broadcast."

He nodded and headed for the door. He turned to her as they went out. "We'll need currency."

"Really?"

"Really."

They were sliding downtown toward the bridge and Milo noticed he was developing the same vague headache he got whenever Julia was hard at work, though it was obviously different from what had happened in the hotel. He speculated that the process was different as she was looking pretty solid beside him at that moment.

She turned to him. "Do you think we should tell the Pixie what's up?"

"What makes you think she doesn't already know?"

"Even with the bleed on your system, they couldn't have decrypted anything useful yet, so at best she can't know the full picture."

"They have other ways to find things out. The US might have told them. They might have a line into Anna's firm. These groups are not all stuck in Brooklyn. Her colleague's here, anyway, information or not."

"I just thought she might be useful."

"You don't believe in my manly prowess?"

She gave him a slightly doubtful look, "It's not that. I've seen you handle yourself, but we're going into a nest of vipers. They might not be polite and wait for you to hit them."

He nodded, her logic compelling. He had thought about it, but calling for the cavalry meant delay and, for Anna, that might have very serious consequences. Anyway, there was no telling if one more person would make a difference, even if it was their Pixie.

He brightened. "One good thing."

"Oh yeah?"

"We thought Anna was going to see her firm and that she might have been working both ends against the middle, with us being the middle. The way it looks, it probably isn't a trap. They may not even know we're coming."

"Or she's gone over to the group, lock, stock and barrel, and she's going to aim the lot at us when we get there."

". . . or that."

Brooklyn was a fine part of the city of Old New York. It had seen its bad times to be sure, but its good times had seen elegant wide streets and tightly-knit communities combine to give it a special atmosphere, quite different from Manhattan. They slid over the bridge and the change from the affluent sophisticated place they had left was immediate. The streets in Manhattan were smooth and wide, possessing a clean line that, in times past, had only been available in architects' drawings or plans. Tech was obvious and everywhere and at any point, as in most major cities, it was accessible.

Brooklyn had not gone downhill in terms of prosperity, nor had it become some lawless ghetto, rather it appeared to have changed hill altogether. Its streets were clean and neat, like the housing stock, well-maintained and its citizens were dressed soberly, but well. Tech was invisible, though the fact that their cab was still rolling through the streets was testament to its presence.

A warning flashed up in the cab as they went and a man's voice. "Visitors are asked to kindly switch off all wireless communication devices while staying in our borough. Thank you."

If anyone been had transplanted from the 1950s to these streets, they would have felt right at home amid the bicycles and the long skirts, the dark suits, the hats and the polite, insincere smiles.

Julia was quite shocked by, in her terms, the 'silence'. There was a signal, but it was weak and limited, with lots of empty spaces. For an AI used only to Europe's dense tech nets, this was the equivalent of a walk in the desert.

Milo looked around. It wasn't his first visit, but he hadn't been for a while. It was the first time he had been really looking at Brooklyn. He was surprised that he hadn't been more surprised before, although he was dealing with Julia's emotions as well this time.

"Anything?"

She frowned and shook her head. "I can't get a firm enough hold on anything long enough to get anywhere."

"Should we stop and walk?"

"Where would you say they're most likely to be?"

"They could be anywhere. This is beyond my current experience," he said.

She nodded and they called for the cab to stop. He noted, as they stepped out, that in spite of the absence of tech, it still took his money as he went. Once out and walking, it was Milo's turn to be struck by the silence, the absence of something he wasn't aware he really heard, the noise of the drones as they buzzed round the big heart of the old city.

Julia took the lead as she tracked the nearest, strongest signal. Milo couldn't help but draw attention to himself, dressed as he was for a world that had left these people behind. A world that viewed them rather in the same way as it viewed the Amish, though Milo guessed their philosophy and attitudes were quite different.

After about fifteen-minutes walking, Julia suddenly jerked. It took everything Milo had not to turn round and ask what the problem was. That would have caught the eye.

"I have them, or . . ." She broke off as she tried to work out what she had. "Ok. They're working it off a set of narrow-band nodes. It's slow. I'd say the tech is about the level of twenty-five, thirty years ago . . . makes it difficult to break into, which I guess is part of the point."

She stopped again, looked to Milo as though she was listening intently but she didn't fade. Whatever the effort was, it wasn't drawing on his processor's power that much.

"There. I have an area to go to, we'll probably find out more then," she said.

Milo just stopped himself asking out loud and he concentrated. "*Is it far?*"

"No, not really shouldn't take you longer than ten minutes."

"*Easy for you to say, I'll be doing the walking for both of us!*"

About twenty minutes later, they walked into an old square, ringed by shops and cafes. The park in the middle could be 1930s London courtesy of Pixar or perhaps Disney, as much as Brooklyn.

Milo wondered as he looked around why people would think there was anything wrong with this. Everyone looked happy. The kids were quiet and polite, the men were well-dressed and solicitous. He threw his eye over the shops and it hit him that in not one was there a single woman working. All of the couples they had passed as they walked to the square were surrounded, not by a child, or two, but by lots of them. Five or six children per couple seemed very normal and, he presumed, there would be older children still in school or at home doing 'chores', if his hunch was right. It was a good thing, he guessed, if this was what you wanted. What if it wasn't what people wanted in life. What happened when someone marched to a different beat?

Milo picked the cafe nearest to the point where Julia could latch onto a signal and sat down outside. The waiter who was beside him in, perhaps, a minute, menu in hand, was young, and so very neat and clean and Norman Rockwell's 'Saturday Evening Post'. Milo felt so far back in time, he nearly asked him what he thought of the latest Mickey Rooney picture. But he didn't and instead asked for a coffee, only to be told that they didn't serve coffee.

"Would tea do, with lemon?"

Milo said yes and asked for a sandwich with some pie for dessert. He hadn't looked at the menu, but he knew they would have pie. The waiter smiled, asked if it would be apple or cherry. Apple, of course.

The waiter said, "Yes Siree! . . ." and that it would be coming right away and went inside.

Julia sat opposite Milo and put her fingers down her throat, miming being sick.

Milo covered his mouth. "I presume you're not making a comment on the food."

She just continued looking at him, a slight smile about her mouth and then he heard, "THINK!"

He thought, "*I'm tired. When I'm tired I go to my default setting*"

She looked to the heavens. He shook his head.

True to his word, the waiter was back out with the tea and set it down carefully in front of Milo, as he did so.

"If you don't mind my asking sir, you're not from Brooklyn, are you?"

"No son, Beijing," said Milo lapsing into 1950s speak himself.

Unbelievably, the boy whistled and then apologised for whistling, Shortly after, the owner looked out the door, giving the young man a pointed look.

"You must have met someone from Beijing before?"

"I don't believe I have, sir. It's a long way away."

And he went back inside to get an earwigging from the boss.

Julia was grinning. 'It's a long way away, sir.' Can you believe these people?"

Milo closed his eyes and smiled. When he opened them, a small family was walking by, openly staring as they passed. The man raised his hat.

Julia was still grinning. "You should have worn something more discreet, like a three-piece suit."

Again Milo covered his mouth. "They're mostly nineteen sixties IBM suits from what I can see, so that would have been no help. Though I do keep feeling I need a hat. Can you get into the system?"

"Yes, but it's slow and I have to jump from node to node in order to follow the trail."

"We have as long as it takes me to eat, which might be more or less time, depending. I can always leave the pie . . . I think."

The food arrived with no further chat or enquiry from the waiter. The sandwich was good and the pie looked great, with a small jug of thick cream beside it that looked as though it would take a long time to pour.

Milo dabbed his mouth with the thick cloth gingham napkin. "How are we doing?"

"Good. I have a couple of possible hits and, I think, a location, but that may be more tenuous than I'd like."

"Yeah? Well, I was wrong. I can't leave the pie, so you have a bit longer."

Milo was about halfway through the sandwich when a man, in IBM-style suit with a crisp, starched white shirt walked up to the table.

"Mr Talbot?"

Milo looked up, surprised that such a low-tech place had such high-tech speed when it came to information exchange. They obviously didn't mind using some tech.

He began to stand, holding out his hand.

"Don't get up." The man smiled broadly and held out his arm. "Craig Daniels."

Milo sat back down but took the firm handshake.

"I wonder, Mr Talbot, if I could take a moment of your time?"

Milo pointed to the chair in which Julia was located and she frowned as she was sat on. Julia stood and walked round the man.

"What can I do for you, Mr Daniels?"

"Mr Talbot, this is more of an enquiry about what I can do for you. You are an operative with the China12?"

"I am."

"So what would bring so important an organisation to our little corner of God's own country?"

"Mr Daniels, you seem remarkably well informed."

"Sorry, I should have said. I am an 'Administrator' here in Brooklyn. In other boroughs you might call a person like me an enforcement officer."

He pulled his ID from his jacket and flashed it, a small card and brass badge. Milo almost took it from him and whistled himself.

He didn't. "And?"

"And as such, I'd like to know what you are investigating in Brooklyn?"

"Mr Daniels, Brooklyn is still part of the United States?"

"We are indeed so blessed."

"The United States is signatory to the Delhi Convention. This allows investigatory organisations, such as mine, unfettered access to each member country's territory. Under the 2034 Federal Budgetary Act section 1442, which abolished domestic investigatory powers in the US, you shouldn't even be asking that question."

"Mr Talbot, I ask only so that I can provide all of the assistance in my power to help you on your way."

"I'm sure Mr Daniels, that's true. Nevertheless."

Throughout this conversation, Daniels' smile never faltered even for a second. Even while he was talking he managed to smile, which fascinated Julia.

"Well, for that matter, I don't need to know what you're doing. How can I help you in your work here today?"

It was Milo's turn to smile and he did so broadly, noting the 'today' and the implication there wouldn't be a 'tomorrow'

"If someone had upset an important person here, and that important person wanted to enquire why, where would the offending individual be taken?"

"That's the kind of question that begs so many more questions, I wouldn't know where to begin. I guess if someone had been let down badly enough, they'd go to the church and get down on their knees and search their consciences to see what they had done to bring down such disappointment. As for important people, there is really only one important person in our lives."

Milo nodded. "So I should trawl through your community churches? Or ask God herself?"

Daniels' face darkened and his smile disappeared. "You will not invade the sanctuary of our churches, Mr Talbot, convention or no convention."

And the smile was back as suddenly as it had gone, a cloud drifting across the face of the sun.

"But I'm sure you had no intention of committing such gross cultural impropriety."

"Mr Daniels, I will go where the trail leads, as is my right, as I'm sure you'd expect me to do if I was investigating a crime against you and yours in some other . . . um, culture."

Daniels thought about this, "Mr Talbot, your name is Milo, may I call you Milo?"

"No."

Daniels paused for an instant. "Very well, Mr Talbot. We are a small community of like-minded souls. Crime here is rare and, with the help and guidance of our Lord and Saviour, quickly and quietly dealt with. We are not used to people coming in from outside."

"You're a borough of one of the biggest cities in the world, not some mid-western nineteenth-century hick town, Mr Daniels. I do not believe you are not used to outsiders."

"Times change, Mr Talbot, and we don't like it. So we the people and the enlightened rulers of this borough try to do what we can to preserve the best of what this great country of ours has achieved. I'm sure that's quaint and like a, 'hick town', was it? But we like it. If we could, we'd share it with the whole world, but we have to stick to our little corner for now and I'm asking you to respect that, that's all."

"I respect everyone Mr Daniels, but above all I respect the train of evidence."

Daniels stood abruptly and stuck out his hand again, "Well I have to go, I'm glad I've had the opportunity to share this moment with you, I hope your train calls elsewhere."

Milo, stood, took his hand and gave him a broad smile. Daniels walked away smartly. Milo sat and Julia did the same. She copied Daniels' smile. Milo took a sip of his tea. Cold.

Julia leaned in to him. "Would you like me to tell you what I found out?"

Milo looked up. She went on. "Mr Daniels has quite a lot of tech for a man in a borough that doesn't believe in it, but Mr Daniels is not in control of it. As soon as he sat down, he lit up a node right here in the cafe, hi-band, very secure."

"Could you hack it?"

She rolled her eyes. "Of course. I found out where they're based and where they probably have Anna, though they had no record of her explicitly."

"That figures."

"They limit their use of tech to a set few. I'm not even sure Daniels knows he's so loaded."

"What a bunch of hypocrites." He shook his head, disgusted.

"Not necessarily. They need to protect themselves and those who want to harm them will be taking advantage of all the latest spec, why shouldn't they?"

"That would be a point if they weren't so loud in their attack on people who use tech and the people who make it."

"Look at you, doing some research."

"We got along fine before you joined the mission, missy!"

"Ok, mister. You want the address, or don't you?"

"Pretty please."

And suddenly the young waiter was standing beside him. "Sir?"

Milo turned to him.

"Is everything ok?"

Milo realised he had been speaking aloud with Julia, which must have made him look a little crazy, or worse, like he was using tech. They may not be used to it, but they knew it when they saw it.

The waiter practically hopped from foot to foot and then awkwardly leant in. "Would you like your bill now, sir?"

Milo looked up at him. "But I haven't finished my pie, and some more tea would be nice. This has gone cold."

The young man stood straight and looked at the window. Standing the other side of the glass was the owner evidently upset, afraid his cafe was becoming the centre of scandal or, worse, sin. He nodded to the waiter and Milo was alone again. Julia watched the running around, amused.

"I don't think they like the new sheriff. This is what you get if you don't learn to think."

Milo didn't wish to cause more offence, so said nothing and tried not to think.

She went on. "Anyway, they don't seem to have too many 'official' places to bring people, though they could have any number of unofficial. My guess is this building."

And the waiter was back with more tea, but he also had the bill. He left both on the table without saying anything and disappeared inside. Milo looked at the bill.

His eyebrows rose. "*They're making it easy to leave, at any rate*," he thought to Julia. He drank the tea.

Julia smirked, "Not worried it's poisoned?"

Milo stopped, looked at her over the cup and shook his head. "*Is the node still active?*"

"Yeah, you're being watched and there's some activity, people being called. Let me ask you again, should we be calling up the cavalry?"

"*We haven't been threatened.*"

"Daniels seemed pretty threatening to me."

"*Oh, he was just making sure I knew he was around.*"

She pursed her lips. "Hmm."

Milo took a bite of the pie. "Augh!"

Julia looked shocked and then the taste hit her. "Wow! It really is just like, well my mom never did, but if she had, wow!"

And Milo devoured it. A few minutes later he was standing, happy, throwing a couple of notes into the dish with the bill, when he was assailed with a sense of being back . . . he wasn't sure when, earlier in his life. He could almost hear the traffic and the sound of horns, and then he was present again and they walked away.

They were walking to the old administrative centre of Brooklyn, past the brownstones and down the tree-lined streets. Families passed together. Milo, now alert to their consistently large sizes, still marvelled at it. And then a new square opened up, trees and grass filled its centre and at the end was the old Brooklyn City Hall, then Borough hall and now City Hall again. Pretty busy for a building that never went anywhere.

The neoclassical style building topped with Lady Justice was now approaching two hundred years old. A venerable structure. There had been a lot of debate within the new powers in the City whether to replace the Lady Justice on the top of the cupola as, to some, she represented a pagan deity and an affront to Christianity. But, so far at least, indolence, money and nostalgia had saved her and she still glowed in the evening sunshine. The building and the steps running up to the entrance still presented an intimidating, if graceful, facade to the world, even in a time of huge buildings and powerful people.

Milo stopped and admired it for a moment, giving Julia time to get her bearings electronically and it offered them both an opportunity to appear like they knew what they were doing when they went inside.

Up the steps they went and into the light entrance hall, which was filled with bustle, even as the day was winding down. Milo walked over to the reception desk and gave the young man behind it a beaming smile which was instantly matched.

"Hi, I'm wondering if you could help me. I'm looking for a woman called Anna May."

The smiling man reached for a large ledger. "Right away, sir. Do you know whose guest she was?"

"I think the mayor's. If not, it would have been one of his more important officials."

The man gave Milo an even shinier smile and nodded several times. He looked back in the book. After a minute, he looked up and shook his head sadly, which seemed incongruous with the smile.

"I'm sorry, sir. No one of that name has been here today."

"Could you tell me if she was here, say, three days ago?"

The smile dimmed just a little and he reached for a phone, punching in some numbers.

"Let me get my supervisor, who may be able to help you."

Milo stepped away from the desk and examined his shoe caps while the man turned his back on the hall and spoke quietly into the phone. Julia was beside Milo. He looked at her and smiled as the man put down the phone.

"Uh, sir, pardon me?"

Milo turned.

"My supervisor will be along shortly."

No sooner had he finished speaking than around the corner came a still-smiling Daniels, his hand about two-and-a-half feet in front of him.

"Mr Talbot! I knew we'd meet again!"

Milo took his hand again.

Julia leant into him. "That hand's going to be bruised if you meet this guy any more."

Daniels was already well into his spiel. "I hear from my colleague you are looking for a Miss May? And we were just talking about what you *may* and *may* not do!"

He seemed to expect a loud laugh or at least polite applause, but Milo only threw him a mild smile.

"Can you tell us if she has been here in the last few days?"

"I can. I could have back at the cafe. She has indeed, Mr Talbot. She spoke with a number of my colleagues for a few hours and then left."

"Do you know where she went when she left?"

His smile faded.

"I'm afraid I don't. I imagined back to Manhattan. That's where people of her sort usually go."

"Her sort?"

He replied as though he were naming a profession admittedly not much older than her actual profession. "*Lawyers*."

"No, she didn't go back to Manhattan or we'd have met her there."

"We?"

216

"My associates and I."

Daniels looked about the foyer and back at Milo.

"They are back in Manhattan, following other trains."

And there was the smile again.

"Can you recommend a good hotel here, Mr Daniels?"

"My colleague at the desk has a list. Do you intend to stay overnight?"

"I *must* speak with Ms May, Mr Daniels."

The hotel was like much of the rest of the city, clean, warm, smart, good-sized rooms with big windows and no tech at all. Not even screen tech, which was the least Milo had expected, nor a refrigerator, but there were electric lights and a telephone for room service. Even checking in had been a strange experience, filling out forms with pen and ink, and paying for everything with currency in advance. The lift had an operator and, as before, there were no women working there. When the bell hop closed the door, Milo noted that tips were evidently considered biblical.

He turned to Julia, who looked unhappy. "I'm blind, anything could be happening outside this room and I wouldn't know."

"Tell me what you found out at City Hall."

"There was no electronic record, but we expected that. The node I was latched onto was from there, so there was no specifically new information, but . . ."

She paused and held up a finger.

"But?"

"There was a set of rooms, about four, that were dark. There was nothing in them at all. Nothing on the system, at least."

"In this place is that odd?"

"In that place, yes."

"Cells?"

"That's what I'm thinking."

Milo turned and sat on the bed, chewing this over. "Meaning?"

"I think that's where she is, if she's anywhere. I don't think we're going to get invited to take a look."

"So we should take a look without an invitation?"

"You're the operative."

Milo sighed. Outside the world was darkening and the already quiet streets were getting quieter. The street lighting was minimal, having been cut back during the war. The question as to what the God-fearing would be doing outside after dark was, it seemed the city fathers thought, a good one. Lights could be used if necessary, but that didn't happen often. So darkness filled the streets and stars filled the sky, which made the rapping on their first-floor window that much more shocking.

Milo looked across at Julia, who held up her hands and shrugged. "Blind. I can see as much as you, I told you!"

He pulled out his gun and stepped across to the window, killing the light in the process. He moved to the edge of the recess and pulled back the drape. Snapping on his night-vision, he surveyed the ledge and found what he thought was a familiar form. He relaxed, put away his gun and reached out to push open the catch, then lifted the lower pane.

A young woman stepped into the room and turned to face him. Milo pulled the drape and closed the window before switching the light back on. He put his hands on his hips and appraised the woman. She wasn't the woman he had expected to see. She just stood there, looking back at him steadily.

"And you are?"

"No one, I don't exist." She smiled. She had a strong New England accent and was as tightly wound as the Pixie and if anything younger.

Milo looked heavenward and "You're a pixie. I'm going to need a bit more than that."

"We prefer the title Clandestine Technical Operative for Homeland Security. You can call me 'Sam' if you like."

Julia appeared to the woman.

Sam turned to look at her, surprisingly unsurprised. "Hey, so you're Julia. I've heard a lot about you!"

Milo looked at her blankly. "From my colleague . . . you were hanging with her for a while."

Milo frowned. "Hanging? Why *are* you here?"

"I was told you'd need me. My colleague, she was the one who mentioned you."

She pointed at Julia. "You're not in the briefings." Then she gestured at Milo. "She just said to follow you."

Milo turned to Julia and raised one eyebrow. She shook her head in denial. The woman watched the silent communication.

"Julia didn't send for me, if that's what you think. My friend warned me you'd think that."

"You mean you don't think she sent for you."

"I know she didn't."

"Really?"

"Really. My friend, the one you know, sent for me. She said she thought you were going in blind."

"But she only thought that because of information her base has received, thinking it's real."

Sam looked at first confused and then surprised. She looked at Julia who again held out her hands, indicating she knew nothing and was feeling defensive.

"What? These people are nuts and they might be violent as well as nuts. That was well known before we came out here. I didn't contact her base, I didn't contact the Pixie. She did the sending all on her own."

Milo was aware that Sam, like her 'friend' might also be a bit nuts and very violent.

"All right, you're here now," he said.

Sam nodded and looked them both over. "She said you'd be a bit weird. I think she was worried about you getting in over your heads."

Julia was matter of fact and almost to herself she said, "She knew the whole story, made her own judgement. The little I did was to 'encourage' her bosses *after* she suggested you join us."

Milo stepped in. "Do you want to know what's happening?"

Sam moved her eyes away from Julia to Milo. She nodded. Milo brought her up to date and explained what they intended to do about getting to Anna.

Sam approved. "Actually, that's more or less what we know except it's already gone wrong."

"It has? How?"

"Not actually, or not as far as I know, but according to the intercepts."

Julia bristled. "The spying, you mean."

"Hey! It's information gathering."

Milo, the peacemaker, or distractor. "Do you have a layout for the the City Hall?"

Sam turned to him. "Yeah, I do. I understood we had to rescue you from cells in the centre of the building on the third floor. Clearly my 'intercept' is a little out."

Milo gave Julia a look, half reproving and half, 'well done'. She was half defensive, half very pleased.

"That is more or less what we have to do, except it's Anna May, we believe she's in there."

"Ok."

She projected a set of plans onto the bed, pulled back the counterpane to expose the blank sheet. At least, that was what it looked like to Milo and Julia. In fact, the plans were shared between the open ports of their implants.

"We should be able to get in here, but despite their supposed distaste for tech, the building is loaded with it."

"We know."

Julia pointed at the plan. "There's a surveillance point there and the back-up is here. I can give you clear access by suppressing both until you're in and out. I might be able to fool the system into believing nothing has happened, but once we're out it may get nasty."

Sam grinned and pointed. "These are cameras with infrared floods. Can you do anything about those?"

Julia nodded. "There's not much about in the square or the side streets but they can have people here very fast. Cameras are the least of our problems."

Milo looked it over and nodded. "Despite their view of their godly population, they're sure as hell not taking any chances."

"I don't think the protections are against their believers."

"Now, what would the anointed have to hide from us?"

The street was very dark, the clear night sky preventing the glow from the rest of New York offering even reflected light across the river, though the glow silhouetted the taller buildings. Their ocular night vision allowed Milo and Sam to avail themselves of the infrared light afforded by the floods for the cameras. The cameras themselves had been sent a nice empty loop of the square from ten minutes earlier by Julia.

Sam had spotted two men watching the front of the hotel and one at the back, so they left through a window on the ground floor at the side. They crossed the street into a side alley and went the long way round the square.

They made their way to the side of the City Hall and found the window Sam had targeted for entry. Using pads surfaced with carbon nano-hairs, they climbed the outside wall like spiders, the pads clinging to the stone. It wasn't quite a walk in the park, but it was much easier than using ropes and hooks, and much quieter.

They reached the window and Julia disabled the alarm system before Sam popped the nineteenth-century lock. They slid into the corridor and stopped. Silence. So far so good.

Julia invaded the security system fully, now that she could establish a strong enough connection, and was able to see anything that the security system could see. She checked the men at the hotel, who had seen nothing to report.

They stepped down the passageway in the direction of the four blank cells and stopped just round the corner from the dead end. There were no cameras in the corridor that led to the cells. Milo pulled out a mirror on a stick and, placing it on the floor, he edged it round the corner a couple of centimetres. They could see a desk with two guards sitting in front of the cells.

Milo leant back and, in a whisper amplified by their systems, "They have short-wave radios."

Sam gave a thumbs-up and silently. "*Can't you use the thought processing system?*"

Milo gave her a look.

"Don't worry old man, I won't give them a chance to use radios. Let's see."

She looked into the mirror. The guards were reading. A third one appeared, took a long drink of something from a mug and sat on a chair. Sam memorised their positions, stepped out in front of them and, after a couple of dull thuds from her hand gun, she looked back and grinned.

Milo rounded the corner to see the two guards slumped over the desk. The other had slipped off his chair and was on the floor beside it, the mug's contents spilling out around him.

Milo looked back at her and gestured to the bodies.

She shook her head. "They're alive, but they'll have one hell of a headache in a few hours."

Milo nodded and walked over to them. Pulling them aside from the desk he leant them against the wall. Patting them down, he took one of the radios, switched the others off and then went back to the desk. There were no plans on the desk and no way to tell one cell from the next.

Sam looked across to the guards.

"Any keys?"

Milo shook his head and they looked at the doors.

She sighed. "Just have to try them, I guess."

She walked over to the first one and leant on the handle. The door gave. She looked back to Milo, who stepped over behind her. Silently, Sam pushed the door open. The room was dark. Milo had his weapon pointed into the darkness and swept the room with his night vision, but it was empty. Milo pulled back, gave Sam more space and she stepped into the room.

She switched on a light and they gave the room a once-over. It was a nice size, not quite as big as the hotel room, but well furnished. A set of shelves dominated one end of the room and it was filled with books.

Sam sniffed. "It doesn't look like a cell and it doesn't smell like a cell."

Milo took this in. They moved to the next room and Sam took point again. Again the door was open and, as she slid it forward, light filled the crack in the doorway. As soon as it did, Sam slammed the door open and Milo was into the room behind her.

There was a man on the bed, reading. He had just turned to look up at whoever it was had come thundering into his room when he was hit by a volley from Sam's gun. The sound suppression on modern weapons was far more sophisticated than old-fashioned twentieth-century systems which were, for the most part, about as effective as a car silencer of the same era. These systems actually silenced the sound. Not completely, but to about the same level as a heavy book being dropped on a table.

The man fell back, as insensible as the guards.

Julia stood beside him and looked him over, then turned to Milo. "No implant." She looked slightly confused.

Sam was about as surprised as she would have been if Julia had said "He's a ghost" and went over to look at him more closely. Milo looked round the room, identical to the first one. He frowned. They checked for ID or some indication of who he might be but turned up nothing.

Milo turned to Sam. "Right, next up"

They went to the next door. Locked! Sam shot Milo a quick look and he nodded. This was the one. To get in they followed the same pattern, except that Sam applied a magnesium strip to burn through the lock and then slammed it open with her foot. The room was well-lit and she stepped through the smoke. Anna was standing facing the door. Her back was pressed against the shelves and books and a book dropped from her hand in alarm. She was dressed in her most lawyerly clothes, replete with high heels.

Milo stepped in. "Anna!"

She looked surprised and then relieved. "Milo!"

Sam stepped back into the corridor and gave it the once-over. "Come on, we have to go."

Anna seemed still a little shocked. "Who's she?"

Sam looked her up and down and tutted silently. "The help."

Milo shook his head. "Another pixie. We have to go!"

Anna looked around the room. "Right. Just let me get my bag."

"No time."

"It's just here!"

As Milo grabbed her arm, Anna grabbed the bag and they were through the door. Sam was waiting.

Julia appeared in Anna's system and she seemed pleased. "Not fully unpacked yet, then?"

Milo looked back at her wondering what that meant, but time was short. "Which way?" he asked Sam.

She was looking sceptically at Anna and Milo looked back at her questioningly.

"She'll never manage the climb down. Out the side door, I think."

Julia agreed. "It's clear and I can keep it that way for the most part. I'll have a car collect us round the side of the building where we exit."

They moved out. Milo turned to Anna and smiled. She smiled back, then indicated Sam. "An upgrade?"

"No, the local brand."

"I'm surprised to see you. How did you find me?"

"China12, remember? We do that."

Anna thought about it and then nodded up at him.

Julia leaned in. "He had a little help from his friends."

Sam looked back. "Clear?"

Julia gave the go-ahead and they moved down the stairs.

They were two floors up and the first staircase was narrow and made of wood. They came down to a corridor and they walked smartly along the side of the building toward the back and stopped again at some concrete service stairs. Once again, Julia gave the all-clear. Down they went, moving quietly but quickly. Anna was between the other two and keeping up, but her manner suggested this was outside of her legal training. They reached the ground floor.

They walked along the side corridor, lined with windows high above their heads.

Julia slowed them down. "Hold up, the car isn't there yet. Something's the matter."

Anna had continued on at the same pace, but turned to face them as Julia spoke.

She had stopped by the door. As she turned, Milo could make out something in her hand even as her bag fell to the floor at her feet. A gun.

Looking out for danger following behind, Sam practically walked into her and was smacked in the face by Anna's gun. Her own weapon was slapped from her hand in a smooth downward movement. She stepped back, now all predatory muscle, ready to pounce, and stood staring at Anna.

Milo leaned forward, still puzzled. "Wait! Anna?"

Sam was only momentarily stood down. Milo looked over at Anna as though trying to find an answer in her physical appearance.

Sam wasn't looking for answers. "She wasn't a prisoner. Looks like I underestimated you. You could have made the climb and here was me waiting 'til we were out in the street."

Anna took a careful step back, putting some distance between her and the dangerous woman in front of her. "You should never wait. I would have made the climb too. I'm sorry, Milo, you shouldn't have come."

"Not much point in getting an invite if I don't take you up on it."

It was Anna's turn to look confused.

He smiled. "We had to know what was going on, we knew what it could be. This is as good a way of finding out as any."

"I suppose. Just so you know, it wasn't a trap, but now you'll have to find a way out."

She turned to Julia. "The cars don't run at this hour, but don't worry. We have someone who wants a chat with you. Says you're being a bit difficult."

She pulled out a small black oval object from her pocket, held it out, and smiled. "After that I have a little something that will make you both go bye bye!"

A noise behind them and Daniels appeared. He too had a weapon in his hand.

Anna's eyes narrowed. "Daniels! I thought you went off at six."

"I thought I'd stick around and keep an eye on our guests here . . . and you. You're out and about?"

"You keep telling me I'm a guest, not a prisoner."

She turned back to Milo and Sam and gestured to them. "I'm going to take Mr Talbot with me to a secure unit. Could you take care of this individual for me? Be careful. She's far more dangerous than she looks. I'm afraid you may have to eliminate her."

Daniels leaned his head to one side. "A unit? You mean outside of the building? I'm not sure I can allow that."

Anna turned back, giving him a quick look. Perhaps he was going to be trouble, she took a moment to consider.

Sam was already beginning to move, a sudden closing of the gap between her and Anna.

"Yes, look, we're on . . ."

And Sam was on top of her, slamming into her at chest height. Anna fell back, sending the gun sliding away to the wall. Milo was about to move but Daniels waved him back. Anna turned out to be more of a handful than she looked and had rolled Sam away. She was about to rise, when, from her prone position, Sam lashed out with her foot, meeting Anna's throat full on. Anna fell back and her head slapped hard against the stone floor.

Daniels' gun rang out and Sam fell back in an untidy heap on the floor. Daniels' eyes narrowed and he moved his weapon slightly.

Milo backed away. Anna stirred and Daniels circled, keeping his gun on Milo. He reached Anna and quickly looked down. She moved to get up and he held out his hand, leaned in, holding his arm further out to help her up. Anna raised herself to one knee, still bent over, her hand touching the body in front of her. Daniels took another step to stop from falling over.

This time Anna rose to her feet. "Thanks"

She fired the gun that had appeared in her hand. Milo looked confused, but less so than Daniels, who staggered and fell at Anna's feet.

She smiled and flicked the gun at Milo. "Back up," she warned.

She bent down checked Daniels and lifted his gun and levelled it at Milo. She placed Sam's own gun in Sam's hand, changed a setting on the side and closed the fingers round it. As she stood again, she still had hold of Daniels' gun as well as her own.

Milo grunted. "For a lawyer you sure know your way round guns."

"What's a girl going to do on the long, boring winter nights?"

"So who do you work for? Not this lot."

She smiled a tight smile. "No, not this lot. They're freaks, lunatics. They want to bring on the apocalypse, did you know that?"

"So what's this got to do with the head?"

"Ever the sleuth, eh? Still the anxious, honest detective, following the lead?"

"Yeah, still that."

She sighed. "It'll be the death of you . . . I don't work for this bunch, they thought I did. When it became clear I was not wholly a believer they '*invited*' me to stay. The people I work for are only interested in the earthly advantages of this project. Now . . ." she pointed her gun at Sam.

Milo, trying to buy time, "How will that help?"

"Daniels' gun doesn't kill, too Christian for that, but mine does, so does hers once it's set. They killed each other. What a shame . . ."

In the fuss of the guns and the killing, Anna must have forgotten about Julia. Mistake. Julia suddenly appeared in front of her and Anna jerked her head back in surprise. Julia reached into Anna's head and she went down, like so much empty cloth. But as she jerked back the gun went off, hitting Sam's head a glancing blow.

Milo stepped across to the prone body, blood seeping from the head wound, he reached for her neck.

Julia leaned in. "She's alive. I've kicked her meds in to staunch the bleeding but she needs help now!"

Milo looked a little closer. The bullet may not have entered the skull but it seemed to do a lot of damage. He stood looking at Anna. "Will she be out for long?"

Julia looked sadly at Sam's body. "Long enough."

"Can we get out of here?"

Julia looked up. "I bypassed the system. A car is coming, but there are people heading for the front door. Do we take her with us?"

Milo paused, looking at Anna. "We can't take both and Anna will probably be detected by the system, if she wakes up. How long before . . .?"

"We have to be quick."

"And Anna?"

"She's waking now."

"Time to go."

They pushed the door open quietly, Milo shouldered Sam and they ran for the car. Despite what Julia had said, the square seemed still and empty. The car was just sliding up and drew to a halt as they reached the kerb. The door hissed back and they threw themselves in.

Julia turned to Milo. "Leave anything at the hotel?"

"Do I care?"

She turned to the console.

"New York Presbyterian, fast!"

"I have a code."

"I used it."

The door closed and they shot away, the car gathering speed as they did so.

Behind them, unseen, even as the net closed, Anna slipped away into the darkness.

CHAPTER THIRTEEN

Milo was rubbing his hair dry after what should have been a reviving shower. He had stood under the hot water willing it into his system, willing it to soak away what he was feeling, knowing it wouldn't. He had taken Anna's betrayal hard. They had never had a relationship outside of work, but he had grown to trust her and had seen her as the one bright thing to have come out of the mess in Brazil. Now the insistent question was . . . had she been part of it?

He had sighed and given up, even a shower wouldn't cure this. He pulled the towel off his head and Julia was beside him.

Milo frowned. "We'll have to tell the Pixie."

They were back in Manhattan, in Milo's hotel room. Sam was in the New York Presbyterian Hospital in a medically induced coma. While the bullet hadn't pierced the skull it still had done enough damage to be life-threatening. Her chances were about fifty fifty.

"I've already told her."

Milo grunted.

"She took it badly. They were close."

He was thinking and didn't react. Julia gave him a small reminder of her presence and he jumped. "Oh!"

"I *said* they were close."

"Were they? How close?"

"Close."

"Oh." He shook his head. "It's difficult to find people in that life."

"Has Anna's turning upset you?"

"That? No . . . Yes, a bit . . . Ok, a lot. I don't like surprises."

"That why you're distracted?"

"We had to go get her if she was being held. We had to find out what she knew, and there was always a chance she was playing for some other side. We weren't sure . . . and we still don't know who."

"We lost a lot just to find out if she knew a little more."

"She might have been the main player. The data didn't suggest she was, but it suggested someone near her might be and we didn't have enough to say she wasn't, so . . . How much further down the line we are, knowing that she's a main player? I don't know."

Julia appeared to be thinking. She looked up. "Yes, a bit. It would have been more if the Pixie's friend hadn't jumped her. Anna's system just shut down. The religious group seem to be behind the search for . . . whatever it is they're all searching for."

Milo was irritated. "Except Anna isn't part of them and she seems to want it too. We still don't know what it is. She said it was a 'project'. Do you know what she meant?"

They looked at each other. Not exactly a stand-off but it wasn't a friendly moment.

"No, but I'm hardly China12, am I?"

Milo stared a little longer then sighed.

She went on. "The religious seem to have been the ones who started it off. It's like they *had* whatever it is and then someone took it away."

"That was probably you . . . Elspeth. Is it the head? But they never owned the head. Why did Dawson run? Did she know she was being watched? Where is she? What did she mean with all that gobbledygook she spouted at the gallery? Has she disappeared? Is she part of it, or has she been taken away? If she's been taken away, why? Who killed you?"

Silence. Was there anything else?

Julia considered Milo's questions, "But Anna knows. I'm not sure what she knows, it's heavily encrypted. I needed more time, there was something odd. She was playing a double game. I didn't get the chance to look at it, but something's wrong with her implant. It's different, shielded. Why would that be? When Daniels appeared I tried to take a look, then our girl took her down. They may know where Felicity is, but is 'they' the Americans or the fanatics? She didn't seem to have much time for the fanatics and she shot Daniels. Are they divided? Alternatively, it may mean they have Felicity, in which case . . ."

Milo agreed. "In which case she's in danger, or dead." He waited for the last bit of information. "So, are you going to share?"

"Share what?"

"Where Felicity Dawson is."

Julia shook her head. "I don't have the first clue. But I think the answer is back with the head in Paris."

"So, Paris . . . again." Milo gave her a quick glance. "The head is still important, right?"

"I don't know." Julia looked odd for a moment.

Another second and Milo knew why. He turned to the side of the bed and the Pixie appeared. She was a holo.

Her mood was dark. She looked like the kind of person you don't want to meet without a tank and an army to back you up.

There was no preamble. "Where are we?"

"We?"

"We."

"Your bosses know about this?"

"No."

Milo looked at her and knew she had no bosses any more.

"You coming here? To see her, I mean."

"Not allowed, and they can stop me."

"I see."

"So where are we?"

Julia spoke up. "Ok. We know I was, that is, Elspeth was killed in London, having asked Milo to give back the head, which she said she had stolen years earlier."

Milo and she then took it in turns to explain.

231

"Except it turns out Julia had lied about who she was and about the stealing of it and that . . . well, she didn't say *exactly* that she didn't know the director of the gallery, who it turned out was her sister."

The Pixie interjected. "Elspeth again. Who is Elspeth?"

Milo and Julia looked at each other, realising they had just trusted the Pixie further than perhaps they should have.

Julia answered. "Elspeth is who made me. Not Julia, not Jane. She didn't lie about all of it, she actually was Julia and she did work as a lawyer."

"But she was also, Elspeth Martin, a brilliant mathematician from Cambridge."

Julia smiled at this and took the baton from Milo. "Milo and Julia met in Paris and Julia implanted a program into Milo."

"It might even be Julia targeted me for that very purpose. The next day, having found Dawson's apartment, I was called to London to investigate Julia's murder."

The Pixie butted in, "Yada yada and you found out about Gog."

Milo frowned at this. "We went to Cambridge to find out more about Julia aka Jane Cruickshank, but found out about Elspeth instead and her sister. But Gog, wouldn't help."

Julia cut across him. "Thirty-six hours after Elspeth's death I woke up and found that my accommodations were a bit tight, so I couldn't unpack fully." She gave the Pixie a meaningful look. "Which meant, and means, I didn't know and don't know, as much as I was perhaps intended to."

Milo took it up again. "We went to Amsterdam and I got kidnapped and slapped around a bit, but was rescued."

They both looked at the Pixie.

"I'm following."

"While there, we discovered that a number of people are after the head."

"Including, but not limited to, we think, the Five Mayors, the states of the Central European Union, the British . . .", Julia turned to the Pixie, looking for a reaction, ". . . the Americans

– these two could be collaborating – a group of Americorp involving, perhaps, Anna's old firm, and Anna."

"And also a group of fundamentalist Christians, and they might be the ones who kicked off the whole show."

"Along the way, we've been responsible for two deaths, two arrests, found three bodies and one double agent."

There was silence as they all digested these events.

"But *why*?!"

The Pixie threw something at a wall where she was in frustration and they heard the smash. Wherever she was, she lay down, which looked weird as she was lying half in mid-air.

Milo watched, as did Julia, who shrugged.

Milo turned to Julia. "You must know things you're not telling us."

Julia looked confused. "Why must I?"

"Elspeth wouldn't have put you inside me for no reason. At the time she might have been worried she was in trouble, but she had asked me to help get the head to Dawson. It's not unreasonable to suppose you are there to ensure that happens, regardless of why."

Julia shook her head. "I was serious about the accommodation. Your system is too confined for my program, there is a lot I can't access. It could be that in there is the answer to your questions. I'm trying to fix it, but it'll take time. If I go too fast it might kill you."

The Pixie sat up again "Was there anything in Anna that could suggest what all this is about? Does the head *do* something? If so, what does it do?"

Julia shook her head. "I don't think so. Beijing have an idea that they may have been involved in advanced robotic design, it may be the next big step. But that doesn't quite fit. There wasn't much time, and Anna didn't seem to know much about the head at all, just that it existed, and she needed to destroy it, specifically destroy it."

The Pixie stared at Julia. "Are you it? Is the 'head' Milo's head? You're a pretty advanced AI."

Julia gave this a moment's thought, but then said, "No, it was the Brancusi she wanted to destroy. She could have shot Milo."

"Maybe Anna's too low down in the organisation, she doesn't know?"

"I don't know," replied Julia. "On the one hand she seemed quite close to one of the higher-ups, like she was their lawyer."

"Who?" asked the Pixie and Milo at the same time.

Julia held out her hands and shook her head.

The Pixie lay back down. "Was it Julia?"

Milo this time was emphatic. "No!"

The Pixie looked up. "Why not? When the head arrived, Dawson ran, like she knew who it was from and was afraid. Julia was put into you. Maybe if you meet Dawson again, you'll kill her."

Milo thought back to the captain and suppressed the thought. Julia was beginning to react, but whether it was at the Pixie's statement, or Milo's thought, he couldn't be sure.

Julia was becoming angry and was glaring at the Pixie. Milo could feel it, resentment. "I am right here, you know! Right here!"

The Pixie looked up. "I can feel you don't like that and I'm sorry, but we have to consider it you know. You popped up out of nowhere and you can't tell us things which you yourself say you should know. It's not normal."

Julia turned to Milo who looked at her, his face neutral.

"Is that what you think too?"

"It doesn't *feel* like that. For the record, none of this is 'normal'. My instincts say you are what you say you are, and you're on our side, or my side at least. "

The Pixie was standing again. "Am I not on *our side* then?"

Milo looked at the Pixie steadily. "You're on your side, remember? You haven't even told us which side that is. All you've said is that if a kill order comes with my name on it, you'd carry it out."

"Yeah, well it turns out China12 are too high up to touch at the moment."

Julia whirled around, "So you thought about it?"

"I didn't, *they* did and if we're comparing hurt, I think I've anted up!"

Silence reigned again.

"So, what now?" the Pixie took it up again "Paris? Do we all go trooping off, or are you afraid I'll kill you?"

Julia's eyebrows shot up. "Afraid *I'll* kill you, you mean."

Milo shook his head slowly. "You are forgetting to mention I might kill both of you."

The Pixie turned away with a shrug, "You can't. Your powers are for investigatory purposes only, unless directly threatened."

"You wouldn't anyway, I can tell," Julia added.

The Pixie turned back to Milo. "So?"

Milo offered his thoughts. "So I think it's like this. You're right, you've got us this far. I think it would be easier to have you come along a bit further. It's easier than you following along twenty paces behind us, which I'm sure you'll do. The problem with you is that you're not your own boss and whatever comes down the pipeline, well, comes down the pipeline."

The Pixie shook her head forcefully. "I have things they want me to do and I'll do some of that and report back. But for the rest, I'm my own boss."

"If Julia's right, Anna may know where Dawson is. We have to get to her first or she's toast. I'm pretty convinced that the head is meaningless in and of itself, but it may have something in it, or on it, we didn't notice before. Either way, our answers are back in Paris, so to Paris we will go."

Julia smiled. "Good. I've booked the tickets, the car will be out front in about ten minutes."

Milo turned to the Pixie. "We'll see you in Paris."

On the way to the airport, Milo turned to Julia. "The Pixie said she could *feel* you. I thought you couldn't do that?"

"I ... I seem to be leaking. I'm trying to grow, unpack as much of my system as I can. I'm not always in control."

As they travelled, Milo's headaches grew.

*

Before leaving New York he had contacted base and let them know about Anna and Brooklyn, a one-sided conversation that he knew would have prompted turmoil in Beijing about how they could have missed Anna's background or ignored the religious as a possibility in assessing the potential players in the case. The markers were there, "but what you don't see doesn't exist".

Xin was the lead mathematician and Milo knew, even as he spoke to her, she was taking it hard, but he also knew The Room would come back stronger. An old teacher of his had been fond of saying: "Failure is the name the stupid give to learning. It isn't trial and error, it's trial and experience." Xin wouldn't see it like that, but that didn't matter. For their sins he had asked them to deal with Anna's company and the nasty little man from Washington.

They hit Paris in the morning rush hour, or at the time that used to be called rush hour. Busy in the mid twenty-first-century was a twenty-four-seven affair. Milo was thinking back to the last time he had come in from the airport and how easily it had all begun.

The Pixie was waiting for them as they came through the border control and had a cab standing by. They sat back as it slipped out of the main complex.

Julia turned to her with concern. "Have you heard anything?"

The Pixie shrugged. "No change. It'll be a while, they said. Have you heard something?"

Julia shook her head and they fell silent.

Paris, so familiar and this time so strange. In all of his years Milo had never had a case that touched Paris. Rubbing his temples to try to get rid of his seemingly permanent headache, he was resentful that this one would change his relationship with the city. It would now be like so many others round the world, a case location.

Milo looked at his companions in the cab. The Pixie was staring out of the window with the same grim expression she had worn in the holo in New York. Julia looking out of the window with eyes that, he knew, didn't see except for whatever system she had invaded could see.

She turned to him, smiled. "Thoughtful?"

"Yes. I was remembering the evening we met. Tell me something. Julia was very careful to give me the impression she knew little or nothing about encryption or tech apart from her job. I mean, she really laid it on. How much of that was real?"

"What do you mean? I presume she didn't want you knowing she was . . . what she was."

"Yes, but had she blocked the information?"

"Chemically?"

"Yes, or some other way. So people couldn't know, I mean."

Julia thought about it, Milo's head throbbed. She looked round at him and gave him a half smile.

"Sorry."

"Don't worry about it."

As his head continued to throb, he assumed she wasn't.

"I don't have, or I haven't unpacked, anything on that. Something may have happened after I was set up, I wouldn't have access to all of that. Like I said, I don't have everything."

"Ok, not to worry. It was just so . . . extreme, given what she actually knew. Maybe that was a giveaway."

He looked out the window again, the long train of cabs and cars running into central Paris, people untouched by what he knew, what he saw, what he did, right up to the moment their lives were caught up in the maelstrom of shit happening.

The apartment he had left less than two weeks earlier, wandering off to supper then hurrying to London fearing the worst, was just the same. The street outside, busier than that last evening, was still not busy. Some places would always be quiet.

This time he didn't need to ask anyone to open the electronic locks. Milo had his own key.

As Julia walked up to the door, it simply opened.

The building's interior still spoke of the quiet sense of the untouchable that wealth brings.

They walked up the stairs and down the long hallway. At the apartment door she repeated the trick.

Milo smiled. "Could have done with you that last time."

She smiled and shrugged. "Would you like to take a look around?"

Julia shimmered for the briefest of moments and gestured to welcome them into the flat.

As they walked through the door, the Pixie whistled. "Nice crib!"

Milo looked at her smiling. "Really? 'Nice crib'?"

The Pixie frowned at him and punched his arm. He could feel the bruise forming. They walked through the apartment, nothing had changed. The Pixie was suitably impressed with the rest of it and flopped on the big couch in the sitting room. Milo walked to the big window.

Eyeing him the Pixie asked: "What do we do now?"

He turned back to her. "We try to work out where Dawson is as quick as we can, and hope it's not too late."

"And is the head still here?"

"I haven't looked yet."

Milo took in the room, tried to look at it as for the first time, looking for anything that suggested a retreat or summer house or a ski lodge, but he drew a blank.

Turning to Julia, he turned his head to one side. "Been here before?"

She nodded. Milo shook his head and lowered his eyes.

The Pixie watched them. "What?"

Milo looked up. "Why? I understand with the cover story at the beginning, but once Dawson had run for it, surely Elspeth could have . . ."

"Maybe you've got their relationship wrong. She'd already left Paris in any case, remember?" offered the Pixie.

Milo turned to Julia. "Do I have their relationship wrong?"

Julia frowned. "I . . . They're definitely sisters, haven't seen each other in a number of years."

The Pixie sat forward. "Did they have a falling out?"

Julia was flustered. "I . . . don't think so . . . Julia came to Paris. There's nothing to say she was upset with Felicity. There was something else driving her."

Milo shook his head. "I don't think this is going to get us anywhere. I'll go get the head."

The Pixie stood, Milo turned to her. "Wait here." he said.

Milo left and walked down the hallway to the bedroom where he hoped the head would still be. Nothing appeared to have been touched. He opened the wardrobe and rummaged through the clothes until his hand bumped into the heavy swing of the head. Taking it out, he looked it over and ran his hands across the surface, searching again as he had before.

Julia looked down at it, he watched her. "Notice anything?"

"Turn it over, no, rotate it in your hands. Run them over the surface." She concentrated as he did this. "Run your fingers across the lines on the surface."

Again he did it and came round to where he started. He looked up. "Well?"

She shook her head again. "Nothing that I can see or feel."

"Have you compared it to known versions of it or, say, your apartment's insurance scan?"

She nodded. "That was what I did. If there's anything on this, it's well hidden."

Milo looked hard at it and walked back to the sitting room.

The Pixie was standing at the 'ambience controls', running through them, the room flashing from one place to another. She looked up at them as they came in.

Gesturing to the controller, she asked: "Do these folks own somewhere in each of these places?"

Milo shrugged. "I don't know. Why?"

"There are just so many of them and they seem so personal. I think I have three on mine that are from places I've been that I want to feel I'm back there again, and that's it."

Milo looked at the Pixie for a moment longer than necessary, and then said, "Julia?"

She went over to it, looked through the system. "Yeah, for the most part they have some kind of stake in these places, but they don't necessarily own some place in each."

The Pixie gave another low whistle before picking one. "Skagen"

The room transformed into a sea view, a small community, brightly coloured, all round them.

Julia smiled. "The 'g' is soft"

The Pixie tried again, but picked the wrong kind of soft.

Julia said it for her. "Like an 'h' Skae . . . hen. It's Danish."

The Pixie was suitably unimpressed and looked over at Milo. Then, sticking out her chin at the head, "That it?"

He held it out to her and she walked over, slowly taking it in her hand as she held it up to the light.

"Now, why is everyone so excited over you?" She glanced at Milo. "Find anything?"

Milo shook his head.

"Would you tell me if you did?"

"That would depend on what I'd found, but yes, probably."

She carried it over to the window and rotated the head in her hands, then turned to Milo. "So you still don't think this running around and killing people has anything to do with the head?"

"No."

The Pixie looked at the head, tossing it lightly in one hand, "In that case, you'd let me take it in to my bosses?"

Milo looked at Julia, who didn't react at all, and then back at the Pixie. "I thought you didn't have bosses any more?"

"Payoff."

"I would, but it mattered a great deal to Julia. I wouldn't like it to disappear."

"I'll take it back, they look at it, examine it, scan it, whatever those folks do, and then I bring it back to you. Deal?"

"Was that your mission?"

"Mission? You make it sound much more exciting than it was, but yeah, that was part of the job, unless something more obvious came up. But the rest has become personal."

Milo nodded. From her expression, the 'personal' was pretty strong. The Pixie walked over to her pack and was just about to put it in when she stopped.

"This is the real thing, right? I mean you just handed it over."

"It's the real thing, or at least it's the one Julia Church gave me that night. I'm no art expert, but my people checked it out, they said it was real."

He watched as she stuffed it in her bag and his eyes drifted across to the low heavy wooden sideboard, reminiscent of the one in Marseille. And then he saw it.

A plinth, the same as the one in Marseille. He had seen it before but ignored it.

"We've never had this in our collection," he repeated

The Pixie frowned, "What?"

"That's what Dawson said."

"So?"

He reached out and tapped the plinth.

"Maybe that's why she was in Paris, to swap them over. Then she realised I was in town."

His head began to throb and he clutched it with both hands. The Pixie looked at Julia, who was watching Milo steadily.

"Are you ok?" the Pixie asked Milo.

He looked up and squinted. "Julia, is there a safe here?"

The Pixie took a step and watched Julia.

"Yes."

He walked toward the Pixie and held out his hand. "Give me the head."

The Pixie pulled it out of the bag and handed it across.

Milo dropped it. The head smashed into the floor and cracked into several pieces and took a chunk out of the floorboards. The other two stood still, in shock.

He grabbed his head again. "Ugh!"

The Pixie walked over to him, but he waved her away. He bent down and his fingers ran through the pieces before he brought up one small fragment. Embedded in the stone, a small black chip.

Milo looked at Julia, who still looked shocked. "What is this?"

She flickered and then said, "It's a small computer, or half of one at any rate. It has part of a program, heavily encrypted, and a proximity switch."

The Pixie stepped nearer. "What does that mean? What does it do?"

"I'm not clear what it does, but it's designed to go live when near something else. Another part or parts of it."

Milo looked at her intently. "Do you recognise the encryption?"

"Yes."

"And?"

"It's mine."

The Pixie stared at her. "Did you know about this?"

"No."

She looked at Milo.

"She believes she didn't."

The Pixie accepted that, and took the chip from Milo. "So this is what people have been killing each other about. Shit! Where's the other part?"

Milo pushed the broken pieces together with his foot while he thought about it. "At a guess, either Dawson or the cousin from Marseille have, or had, the other pieces. What it does is very bad for someone and very good for someone else."

Julia nodded. "They have something."

The Pixie looked up from the chip. "What's the point about the safe?"

Milo turned to Julia again. "Where?"

A part of the wall, currently showing a couple walking hand in hand on the seafront, slipped back and down out of sight. The safe door popped open. Milo walked across and looked inside. He grunted and reached in, taking out another head. The Pixie was astonished.

"Is that one real? Or is the one you broke?"

"I hope this one."

"I thought there were no copies." said the Pixie

Julia looked down at the head. "We must have had it done quietly, I guess about seven years ago. No, that's right, seven years, four months. Three heads."

Milo threw it to the Pixie and felt Julia lurch. He was surprised, AIs can lurch.

"Get your bosses to look at that."

She nodded, and stuffed it into the pack and carefully closed it over. She stood and slung the pack on her back. "Right, I'll go dump this. You won't get in trouble without me, will you?"

Milo and Julia both smiled and Milo held out his hand. The Pixie took it firmly.

"We'll try not to."

"If you need me . . . well, I'll come find you."

"If we need you, we'll whistle."

"Do you think you'll find out who it was . . . who killed her, I mean?"

Milo's expression changed. "We'll find out."

The Pixie nodded and, after a small, wistful smile at them, she rubbed her head. "I need to sleep, the last two days have given me a headache."

She headed for the door and was through it. The door whispered closed. A soft click and she was gone.

"We might need her," said Julia.

"We can whistle." Milo smiled.

"What's the idea?"

"First, the bang I just got, in the head. You remembered something?"

"Yes, I'm sorry, it triggered. Your implants have no capacity left. I've looked into shutting down . . ."

He nodded. "But that's not you trying to stop me from knowing something, or would you tell me?"

"I'm not trying to stop you knowing anything."

Milo tried to evaluate this and couldn't trust that he could. He sighed. "Ok"

He pointed at the ambient sound controller. "That. I had been thinking of just letting her have the head anyway but then when we came back into the room she came out with all that stuff about the soundtracks. I think wherever Dawson is will be on that list and I think you'll be able to tell me which one."

"Really?"

"Really."

"In that case, let's take a look."

They walked over to the display. The small touch-screen was set into the wall, its matt surface the same colour as the wall and just about invisible. Still around them, Skagen played out.

Milo touched it and the panel came alive. On it were small replicas of the panoramas that could be around them. The images constantly changed and moved, and it was apparent when the screen was showing a live feed from wherever it was.

Milo went through the options. Some were preinstalled. They lacked the live feed but instead had recordings or stills. The sets that had impressed the Pixie were the live feeds, which were expensive and could only be obtained with influence in the area that was being shown.

Milo wheeled through the choices. Julia considered each one. The preinstalled options he quickly passed over, concentrating instead on the places Dawson had actually visited. A busy market, a deep conifer forest, a deserted beach, a mountain temple. Julia reacted to none of them, so Milo went through them again. At the end of the second round he looked questioningly at Julia. She looked back.

"Nothing?" He could feel her uncertainty.

"There are a few possibles, nothing I could put my hand on heart to say, that one!"

"Again?"

She nodded.

At the end of the third cycle. "This time?" he asked.

She frowned, perplexed. "There are about three possible places, but I'm not sure they are somewhere you would run to if you were afraid of pursuit."

"Where are they?"

"There's Avignon. She's always loved the Camargue and our father had a villa near there she used to go to, but it's very connected to the city and very easy to find. I'm not sure how many people are aware that we still own it, but . . ."

"Is there any chatter about it?"

She thought, Milo's headache got worse. Her image flickered and then stabilised. She shook her head.

"Next?"

"The temple, it's in Nepal. It was badly damaged in 2015 but was rebuilt. Our father made some large donations to the project and he visited it several times."

"That seems quite likely then, no?"

"It's possible."

"But?"

"But, to get there she'd have to cross several borders, and I doubt she'd try that if she were trying to avoid the kind of people we're talking about. Even succeeding in evading auto face-recog, operatives might have picked her out."

"I don't know what kind of resources your family have available. Could she not have leant on those?"

"Once in Nepal, yes, but she'd have to pass at least three sets of eyes before then. See, I'm learning."

"Ok, possible, and more likely than Avignon, but . . . The third?"

"Taos."

"New Mexico?"

"Yes, the artist colony there. We have many friends, friends who would risk a lot for us."

"But it's in the Americas."

"Yes, it's in the Americas. If she had any inkling about who these people are, she wouldn't have gone there. Otherwise that would be my best bet."

"Damn!"

"Sorry."

"I was sure we'd . . ."

"Wait, what about this one? You skipped over it." she said.

"It's a preinstall, no?"

"No."

He read. 'The Colony, Skagen, Denmark.' He turned and looked at her then he started to go through it, "Outside the EU jurisdiction and the Five Mayors, part of the ScanFed, so only one border. Why is there no feed if it's not preinstalled?"

"There's no tech there. They're a colony of artists, like Taos, but much lower tech. They set their face against most forms of integrated coms years ago. There's only one phone, and that's old, copper-wired landline. No microwave links, no vid-links."

"So she couldn't be tracked. Xin said they owned a place in Denmark"

"What did Felicity say to you?"

He thought about it and the recording of their meeting played in his head. "Tell her, . . . I don't have it here, I have moved to . . . the white part of the map . . ." "She meant electronically . . ."

"And we used to know people there. Well, our father did. We only went there as kids."

"So you're familiar with the place, and the people know your sister, it wouldn't raise any suspicion."

Julia nodded. Milo looked around to see if there was anything else that would confirm their theory, but there was nothing.

He called up Beijing and Xin appeared, calm as ever. He quickly ran through what they had done and what they had found out.

"Send us what you have on the chip, now. The trip to Skagen, you'll be beyond any assistance we might give you. Julia's description was accurate."

"Yes, but then it's a fairly unsophisticated community and anyone else who has traced her will be in the same position as us. Also, I have Julia."

"She's not going to be a lot of help, unless she has a pathway."

"True, but she does know Dawson. That should allow me to persuade her to tell us what's going on. I hope she'll have or know what the chip connects to."

Xin nodded. "One more piece of information. The dead man in Cassis, was Elspeth and Dawson's cousin David Scott, an expert in African antiquities and . . ."

"Don't tell me, a mathematician?"

"He was the 'friend' of Julia's who used to work at the particle accelerator. Like Elspeth, his neck was broken and his implanted electronics were burnt out. Gog sent messages to him. We currently suppose that was how he was traced. His time of death couldn't be ascertained because his body was kept cold."

Milo digested that. "So he was her mysterious contact. Same MO for the killing. It fits with what we have, but does it move us toward what's going on?"

"Not really."

"So, on to Skagen!"

"Right, we can clear a path for you up to the Danish border, we'll find out what we can until then. We can also monitor anyone else headed that way and give you fair warning."

"Before we go, what are the chances that Dawson was behind all this? The woman in Cassis was wearing a cross, the captain had a Bible and Dawson I seem to remember was wearing a cross. Coincidence?"

"We looked at this, but found no communication trace between Dawson and the other players. On the other hand, she was also a very talented mathematician, so good track covering wouldn't be a stretch for her. But she would have had to betray her sister and her cousin."

"If the motive is religious . . ."

"Yes, we did rate that quite highly, but overall the probability was only about forty percent. Not nothing, but not very likely."

"But better than the chances of winning the lottery. Good. Any more thoughts about the chip?"

"None, unless we can get through the encryption. I hope the British don't damage the head."

"You don't approve."

"It is a valuable artefact, but we understand why you did it."

"Still lots of threads but no tapestry. Alright, we'll be in touch before we cross the border, but probably not after, unless . . ."

"Unless?"

"Unless something happens."

"As ever, Mr Talbot, be careful."

CHAPTER FOURTEEN

"Be careful." Her words ringing in his ears.

Milo was walking headlong into he had no idea what, with he had no idea who. Was she with him or against him? Part of his side or the other side? What was his side? Why was he adrift again, just like he had been in Brazil? That turned out badly. The only case they had not resolved within the statutory limit, but, he had noted, the next guys had also drawn a blank.

He kept running Brazil through his mind. The mix was similar, two kidnapped mathematicians who turned up dead and a bunch of religious nuts who also died. Were they linked? The probability was growing. And now there was Julia. She felt right, but then he no longer believed he could rely on how he felt. All he could do was tread the path that opened in front of him and deal with whatever came up, or hope he could deal with it.

Leaving the apartment, Milo had asked Julia if she could secure the lock so that it couldn't be broken into easily. She had. The Trip to Gare de l'Est was silent as they worked through their own insecurities, conscious of the other's concern. The crowds were thin and the system worked smoothly. Even so, Milo turned up the level of his painkilling meds to try to block the throbbing headache.

Travelling across the old Schengen area would be more straightforward than elsewhere in Europe, though of course it had shrunk somewhat since its heyday in the 2010s and wasn't as free as in those far-off days. The infrastructure which had been built then was still there and had been improved upon. The old rail system had been upgraded to a full maglev track, the new system much less expensive than earlier trials, which meant journey times were comparable to any other international transits. As in almost all cases, the time taken to travel between countries was less than the time taken to travel within countries.

They were in Hamburg inside an hour and forty minutes of leaving Paris. At that stage, Milo had a brief exchange with Xin, not telling them much of anything except that Beijing was worried they were stepping into the unknown again and worse – this was what had really got to them – the unquantifiable. Xin also had an unspoken worry about Julia, which Milo picked up on but hadn't probed.

He was relaxed. They had found no trace of anyone suspicious having crossed the borders before them and no one appeared to be following. Even allowing for the snow thrown up by incog software, it meant that his troubles could only come down to one, or perhaps two, other individuals, as groups would show up pretty quickly on the China12 system. But no one was kidding themselves that they could or had traced every threat.

From Hamburg, they slowed right down. Not only were they not on an international standard transport, the crossing of a border notwithstanding, but they were on a system that had not been upgraded at all since the late twentieth-century. Going from nearly 500kph to about 160kph was quite something and most of the time it was slower even than that.

They had taken the sleeper, which dated from about the same time as the track. The train was, however, very comfortable. Julia was excited as it reminded her of a time before she was dead, before she was even fully grown, when they had taken the sleeper all the way from Paris to Skagen, which these days was no longer possible.

They ordered breakfast to be brought an hour before they would get into Skagen and Milo dragged down the large bed from inside the cabin wall. The cabin itself was old-fashioned, the train company having decided to make a thing of the retro state of the track by importing old Pullman carriages from the US and upgrading them somewhat. The old wood and the deco styling even made Milo feel at home. Julia insisted he open everything and try out everything as well as having a full breakfast. He indulged her.

When the new day greeted them they were travelling through the more austere landscape of northern Denmark and the sea was a blue-grey and brooding outside the window when Milo lifted the blind.

Milo had found sleeping fitful. The headaches, getting markedly worse in the last few days, had moved up a gear in the night. He increased his drug intake through the automated system and felt a pang of guilt, which he knew he wasn't responsible for, it was Julia who had felt it.

A knock on the door brought him back into the world.

The waiter called out "Morgenmad! . . . Breakfast!"

Opening up the door, he found a man with a huge tray on his shoulder. A younger lad slipped in and pulled down the table where the tray was set.

"Can I get anything else for you, sir?"

Milo stared at the enormous breakfast and smiled. "I think that's probably more than a week's worth of breakfasts."

They left and, again, Julia's excitement ran through Milo, such that it was hard to tell the difference from hers and his own.

The breakfast was good, eggs, mushrooms, vegetarian ham, toasted fresh bread, butter, freshly squeezed juice and, most of all coffee, strong coffee. Hungry though he was, he scarcely did it justice.

He had shaved and was feeling pretty good by the time the second knock came. A different waiter pushing a tall trolley filled with empty trays. Milo nodded to him and moved back to his bag to tidy away his wash things.

The man stepped into the cabin and Milo heard him swing the door when Julia shouted, "Watch out!"

Milo ducked and spun round as the knife came down. The man stumbled forward and was off-balance when Milo hit him full in the throat with his elbow. As the man slammed backward grabbing at his throat, Milo's right foot swept his feet from

251

under him and he went down face first, smacking the side of the seat with his head as he went.

There was a dull bang and a slight snapping sound. The man didn't move. Milo kicked the knife away and placed his knee in the man's back as he reached for his carotid artery to feel for a pulse. Nothing. Milo relaxed, stood and turned over the body. A silver chain with a cross fell from round the neck to hang by the man's ear.

Milo considered his options. If he took the next legal step, his profile would be broadcast to the world, but there wasn't really much choice. He called up Beijing over the train's system, it offered higher bandwidth, and they could see straightaway what had happened. He uploaded the video of the incident and Xin alerted the transport police.

*

Milo had to wait before the police would tell him he could leave the scene, and he sat across from the body. The police gave him the go-ahead, but asked him to check out the man's pockets for ID. He did, but he found nothing.

Xin came back on. "Do we think he was on his way up there when you were spotted? Or is he part of a bigger group with you in their sights?"

Milo looked at Julia, who shook her head. "We have nothing to say either way. Could be he followed us onto the train. Could be part of a net searching for Dawson. Could be they have her already."

Xin thought about this for a little, playing with a pencil before looking up at the two of them. "We decrypted more of Anna's documentation, her firm were quite helpful in the end, that man, Jones, has left it seems. Anna is working for a group of Corps. Not just the AmericaCorp, they're transnational and they are non-governmental. Finding out why they want Dawson, why they wanted and killed Julia and their cousin – presuming it was the same people behind it – is as important as finding Dawson. Whatever that reason is, it won't be good. If there are five powerful groups looking for this they must have information we don't have and want something that will give them some sort of advantage or power they don't currently possess. Tracking? A way round the systems for going off-grid? Find out!"

They broke off coms after they arranged for Milo to talk to the local police at the train station in Skagen, the only other place with coms to the outside world.

Milo went to sit in the restaurant car and ordered a coffee for the last few minutes of the trip. The waiter left a pot and Milo poured a big mugful for himself. Julia sat opposite.

"Was he wearing any tech?" he asked her.

"No."

"How come you called out?"

"As he came in I caught something out of the corner of my eye. It took me a moment to realise it was a cross. Sorry I didn't shout sooner."

"You saw? *Your* eye?"

They stared at each other and if she could have blushed, she would have blushed. Instead, Milo blushed.

"I told you, your system is too small. If I'm going to be any help I need to grow into part of your organic brain."

"But *my eyes?*"

"I thought you understood that's what was happening."

"Are we going to be able to sort this out?"

The policeman who had just come in thought Milo was talking to him.

"Oh, I don't think it should be too much trouble."

Milo was puzzled and stared at him for a moment, frowning, before he realised what the man was saying.

"Right! Good."

The cop was young and fresh-faced and very enthusiastic. Milo hoped he wasn't like the last young enthusiastic cop he'd met.

"We got the footage from your ocular implant. Very impressive, I have to say. Much better quality than our own. Do you know why the man would have attacked you?"

"Uh, no, sorry. Is Denmark outside of the interrogatory protocol?"

"Oh, yes it is, sorry. We do use crime groups, but we don't have to. In this case, as you're China12 . . . But, I'm practising, I'm applying to join a group here in Denmark. I guess I'm a little ahead of myself."

"Has the incident been picked up yet, by a group?"

"I don't think so. I don't think it's out yet. They're waiting to categorise it. They may keep it in-house."

Milo searched his face, wary of everybody now.

Julia piped up. "He's fine. He has tech and he seems to be exactly what he says he is."

Milo nodded and again the cop thought it was aimed at him. "Right, if they need to, the group or our boys can get you through China12?"

"That's right."

The cop was about to leave but he stopped. "Can I just say, it's an honour!"

He beamed at Milo, who grunted and smiled. The cop left. Milo watched his retreating back.

"Right then, here's hoping that the man was only a lone wolf trying to get to Dawson. How likely is that?"

"Not very."

*

The Skagen station was largely empty as the delay from Milo's brief conversation with the young cop had meant most people had left. The train wouldn't depart again for six hours, so the departing travellers weren't there yet. The station was old but well maintained, the floors swept clean and the staff in neat, picture book, uniforms. Milo had to pinch himself to check he hadn't fallen into some child's story of railways and steam engines.

Julia was still excited, despite Milo's recent brush with death. "It looks exactly as I remember it, I'd begun to wonder if it could."

And oddly, it was exactly as Milo remembered it too, despite his never having been there.

They headed into the town. Skagen was once a small, very important, fishing village, then a town and now a village again.

The houses reflected that past, colourful, timber clabbered buildings. In the distance, out to sea, the wind-turbines turned lazily and Baltic shipping passed as it had done for centuries. The artistic community had arrived in the nineteenth-century and, unlike the fish, had stayed. They were largely responsible for the move against modern coms and tech. The tranquility allowed a distance between the artists and the twenty-first-century, a space in which they could work and reflect on progress. Or so they said. Some, particularly their agents, saw it as a means of avoiding the answer to the question 'When will you be finished?'

As they walked into the town, it was noticeable that the population divided between the folk who rose early and those who did not. Many of those who were up were on bicycles, with a few of the older ones on the successors of the early Segways. They were connected to implants and were both more stable and more intuitive to operate. The wheels were very multi-terrain, made of a new polymer that had the resilience of hard rubber but the texture of a more spongy material giving a smooth ride. There were few cars and even drone traffic was limited. It was apparent that, as in most coastal towns, the main drone thoroughfare was over the sea and about five hundred metres from the shore, keeping the noise to a minimum.

Milo and Julia were walking along the main street, passing houses with folk busy sweeping porches and stepping out to get things from the shops, and those with shutters drawn, dead to the world. Milo was being guided by Julia and her memories of her last visit when she was fourteen.

The experience marked another evolution in the way Julia worked inside Milo's head. For the first time, Milo could actively recall her memories. Not as a vague sense that he could remember something, but as though the memory was his. For someone who had a sense of pride in his memory, this was difficult. Stranger still was that there were some things that he could remember having sensed or remembered from Julia, from her past, which he knew he didn't remember.

He wondered if this was because the memory had not yet been unpacked. It wasn't like forgetting something, more like having left it behind. He knew that she could feel and 'hear' his inner dialogue about this and he knew it made her feel uneasy. One of the most pleasing aspects of it was the sense that he knew there was a him and a her, distinct and together. Or was that pleasing? He wasn't sure, partly because he wasn't sure who was pleased. The part that was 'her' seemed unsettled.

"We should wait," Julia said.

"For?"

"For the Pixie."

"You didn't do anything?"

"No, I didn't, but you know she'll be coming."

"Dawson may be in trouble. We can't wait."

They had reached a slightly leafier part of town. A police bubble, a small patrol vehicle suitable for at most two people, rolled up. It was the young cop from the train.

"How about that! You need any help? It can be a bit confusing, everywhere looks like everywhere else."

Milo smiled broadly. "I think I'm fine, thanks. You patrol much?"

The young man mirrored the smile. "I'm off-duty. I'm on the way home."

"Swanky part of town for a police officer. You'll have to give it up if you become a humble investigator."

"Oh, rich parents. Artists. They were very trendy about twenty years ago."

Julia leaned into Milo. "Something's not quite right about this."

Milo nodded. This time, unlike at the train station, the cop waited. He seemed to understand – had he been briefed?– he was not being talked to, or nodded to.

Milo noticed but smiled again. "Thanks for the offer, but I'm fine. Not far to go."

"Ok then. Stay out of trouble, won't you?" He rolled away, taking the next right.

Milo watched him. When he was out of sight, he turned to Julia. "Where now?"

She held out her hand toward a house. Larger than most without being ostentatiously 'grand', it was set a little back from the road. The garden around the house was kept neatly and was as much an expression of the place they were in as the taste of the owners.

Julia hadn't hesitated once and she didn't then, heading straight for the gate. Milo was impressed but not surprised by it, considering what he had seen of this family so far. But still, the house was special. Evidently built after the Second War, it fitted with the wave of Scandinavian architecture that had become popular again after the latest war and Milo reflected once more on the timing and sense of quality that George Dawson must have possessed. They walked down past a fence and came to the gate. The gate was locked.

Julia was surprised. Milo looked at the gate quizzically and had to stop himself wondering why it was locked. He knew why. Julia turned to him.

"I don't understand, it was never locked."

"She ran away from me in Paris."

"Yes, but . . ." and whatever it was, the words died out.

Milo pushed the call button and he knew that an array of tiny cameras had lit up, projecting a holographic image into the house. He stood still, trying to look unthreatening.

Julia smiled. "That's it, look cuddly."

There was no sign from the house and Milo was conscious of the silence, the calm spirit of the place. He was about to push the bell again when the lights came up and a voice rang out.

"Yes?"

"Ms Dawson, I'm Milo Talbot. We met in Paris. I'm now officially investigating events surrounding that day.

We need to talk."

There was a click and he pushed open the gate and walked up the long path, through some trees, to the front door of the house. The door opened at his approach and Felicity looked out. She stepped onto the step and waited.

He stopped a few feet away and she looked at him. "The man from Paris. China12?"

"Yes."

"What do you want?"

"Ms Dawson, did you leave Paris immediately after we met?"

She scanned him, eyes narrowing, trying to decide, then, "Yes."

"Are you aware of events there and elsewhere since you left?"

Again the suspicious searching of his face. "What events? Have you had me followed? How did you find me?"

"I'm sorry if this is the first you've heard of this. Your sister, Elspeth . . ."

She took a step nearer him. "Yes, what about her?"

"I'm sorry to have to tell you, she's dead."

Felicity's hand sprang to her mouth the other arm reached out to the wall to steady herself. "How?"

"She was murdered, in London. Ms Dawson, your life may be in danger. Might I come in so we can go through the situation more fully?"

Felicity stood back and allowed him to pass.

Milo went through the door and into the house. The hall was wide and made of a pale wood whose scent filled the space. The room to the left had an open door and Felicity held out her arm toward it as she closed the front door.

The room was large and spacious, lined with books. In the farthest corner was a large ceramic tile stove and, about halfway down the room, there was a large plain desk, filled with papers and books. The whole was very reminiscent of the room in Cassis. In the middle was a low couch, in front of which, on the table, sat a partly eaten breakfast.

Seeing it, Milo said: "Oh, we've . . . I've interrupted your breakfast, I'm sorry."

A polite smile drifted across Felicity's mouth and she shook her head. "Will you join me? Coffee perhaps?"

He looked at her, decided giving her something to do would be the right thing and smiled back. "Thanks."

"Please." She waved her arm at the couch.

He sat. She left. After a few moments, the sound of business from the kitchen, or what he presumed was the kitchen, and then she was back, with a tray and cup and pot of fresh coffee. She slid it onto the table. Along with breakfast was a DAT, like the ones the police used.

She joined him on the couch. "Before we go any further, do you have ID?"

He rummaged in his pockets and pulled out his ID, offered his wrist to be scanned.

She looked at the results and her eyebrows raised. "So, you told the truth. China12?"

"Yes."

She poured the coffee and held a cup out to Milo, her hand shaking. He took it and refused milk and sugar but stirred it anyway, watching her. She stopped fussing and looked at him. There might have been tears in her eyes, or it might have been the light. Her face was white.

"What happened to Elspeth, Mr Talbot?"

"After you and I met in Paris, I was supposed to meet her. She didn't keep the appointment. Later it became apparent she had gone straight back to London. I don't know why. That evening, I was called to London. She had been murdered, we believe by people trying to get hold of the Brancusi."

"Was it quick?"

"We think so, yes."

Dawson frowned and looked sadly out the window. Out came a hankie and she turned away. Deep breaths and then a quiet sob. Milo took a drink of coffee to give her some space. A minute, perhaps two, to gather herself.

She turned back to him, now there were tears. "Do you know why?"

"We were hoping you could help with that."

She just looked at him in silence. After it persisted, he decided to take a chance.

"We're not sure. We think it had to do with this." He held up the piece of broken head and the embedded chip.

She looked at it steadily and then at Milo. "Do you know what that is?"

"It's a tiny computer, or half of one. It has a proximity switch. You wouldn't know anything about it, would you?"

Her face hardened, "My sister was killed for this?"

"Yes, Ms Dawson. And not just her. Since your sister's death, four other people have died and there have been others arrested. At least four, perhaps five groups of people, powerful people, are looking for it, and you may be the key. Are you?"

She looked at him and her eyes flicked to the chip. "Can I look at it?" She reached out her hand.

He drew back. She stood and walked away from him, shaken. Then she turned. "How would you describe yourself, Mr Talbot?"

He smiled a tight smile. Julia had asked that and he had told her, 'not too dumb'. Boy, had he got that wrong. This time he weighed up his answer carefully.

"Ms Dawson, I am a member of China12. Whatever kind of person I am – good, bad, nice, nasty, dependable or feckless – the character of my organisation and its work will be foremost. What you think of me is unimportant. It is China12 that is standing in front of you."

She turned away, walking to the window.

He broke the silence again.

"There's something that's been puzzling me since we met in Paris. Why did you refuse the head?"

She turned back to him, using the moment to think, perhaps. "I told you, it didn't belong to the collection."

"But it did. All of the collection's records showed it did. Except, of course, it didn't because it was a copy. The original . . ."

"No, Mr Talbot, the head belonged to Elspeth. Not to me or to the collection or anyone else. If you had it, it meant one of two things to me. Elspeth had been robbed. She was possibly dead and I was in danger. Or, if she sent it, the reason she would have was not in Paris."

"I don't understand the connection. Why would my bringing it back to you spell danger? And what did you mean by all that stuff you told me?"

"If you were bringing it back and you had robbed it, you would be asking for a ransom. You weren't. You said you were China 12, but I couldn't verify that, I had no DAT then. And, like I said, I couldn't activate it . . . I admit my improvised excuses were not very good, but I was afraid. As it turned out, with good reason. I had got a message from our cousin David, so I moved my head up here, a few months ago. Then he relaxed, said it wasn't a problem. He was wrong. I hoped you would have gotten my message to her. She would have understood. It brought you here."

Milo took this on board. "You took a degree at the same time as your sister?"

"Yes, in History of Art. I wasn't as gifted as she."

"Come on. You did your degree in History of Art, sure, but you took a second degree as well, didn't you?"

She looked at him steadily.

"You and your sister had a shared interest."

She smiled, "You are thorough, Mr Talbot."

Milo nodded.

"Yes, we both loved mathematics. I used it in looking at the pictures I studied, but that's why we're in this mess."

Milo leant back and considered her. "So what does it do?"

Her expression didn't change, still weighing him up.

"You are going to have to trust someone. You *should* trust me. People are dying because of this thing, whatever it does. You remember Dr Gog?"

"Yes of course."

"A few days ago, she was assassinated."

"Assassinated? Why?"

"She was shot in a house in Cassis, do you remember it?"

"Yes, David's house."

"Did it belong to him?"

"In effect."

"We found Dr Gog in the library, we believe she was killed because of her connection with, whatever it was, you three did. Who actually owned that house?"

"What do you mean?"

"Who are "Three Heads Inc."?"

"Should I know?"

"Yes. Because *they* own the house in Cassis. Are you one of the heads, Ms Dawson?"

"Are you here to save me or to interrogate me, Mr Talbot? Which side are you on?"

"A bit of both, it depends on which side you are on Ms Dawson. I have to ask you these questions. All part of the job."

She fidgeted. He leant forward, looked to Julia who'd been listening and who nodded.

"There's someone I'd like you to meet," he said

"Oh?"

Julia shimmered into view on Felicity's implant

"Oh!"

They looked at each other, Felicity taking in as much of her sister as she could, Julia waiting. Milo could feel her strong emotions.

Felicity spoke first. "Are you alive? Is this a com relay?"

"No, I'm dead alright."

Felicity looked across at Milo, "I don't understand. she's not a com holo?"

"She's an AI. Your sister put her into my implant when we met in Paris."

She smiled and looked at Julia with some affection, "Ah, you are so clever. Of course. Do you know everything she knew?"

"I'm not sure. Milo's implant isn't quite big enough to see all of my compressed data."

"But so far as you know."

"It would be a reasonable guess."

"You should be transferred into my system. Then we could be together."

"I'm not sure that would be possible."

"Why not?"

Julia looked at her sister. Felicity was the picture of concern and anxious care. Milo could feel Julia's confusion, her caution and then something extra. Fear.

A lot of things happened at once. Julia turned to Milo and looked pleased. "She's here!"

Milo stood and looked around, seeing no one. A sudden pain in his head and he could see Felicity holding hers. Then, standing in the door of the room, holding a gun pointed at Milo, Anna.

Julia looked across and just said, "Oh!" before fading.

"Hello Milo, this seems familiar. Sorry about the head, can't have our little miss jumping in again saving the day. That was just a little sting, keep her under control. I can make it a lot worse."

The pain in Milo's head went up a notch, but it was markedly different from his previous headaches, nearer the surface, more of a burn. He knew it was bad news, because it had stopped his automated systems, like painkilling.

When he could see again, Anna was still there, still with the gun in her hand. Felicity was on her knees on the floor holding her head. Milo went over to her and tried to get her into a chair, but once she was on her feet she pushed him away.

She glared at Anna. "Who the hell are you?"

Milo was immediately minded of Julia.

Then, unbidden, like a ghost in the machine, a thought. "*She doesn't know you have the chip*".

Anna smirked. "Sorry to barge in like this. I'm working with the Corporations of the United Americas group."

If she was waiting for shock and awe, she was disappointed.

"So? I've never even head of them."

Despite the brave front, Felicity swayed and leant on Milo, who wasn't feeling too clever either.

Anna looked them over. "Sit! Before you fall over."

They slumped on the couch and Anna moved in front of the window, ensuring a clear line of fire.

She was in control, relaxed. "That little game you people came up with?"

Felicity, whose head was in her hands, looked up, concerned.

"Yes. We found out about it." She looked really pleased with herself.

"We thought it was a great idea, too good to waste. You see, Milo, these clever young people are science fiction buffs. They like Isaac Asimov, in spite of his dreadful view of women. They particularly liked his Psychohistory. A way of predicting the future. Useful, eh?"

Milo shrugged. "I guess. People have tried it before. Did the horoscope look nice?"

Anna smiled a thin smile. "It won't work on individuals. That would be of limited use in any event. It could reliably predict behaviours of whole populations. Better than that. They realised, and we realised, that if you know the stimuli that will produce a particular future, you can provide the stimuli to control that future. They didn't like that, so they destroyed their creation. We did like it, so we got ourselves two eminent mathematicians . . ."

Milo's stare deepened and he said. "From Brazil."

Anna was enjoying his shock. "They worked in Brazil, but one was from Columbia."

"And they developed a system for you and then you killed them, so no one knew," he said

"And they developed a system for us, but we didn't kill them. Those lunatics from Brooklyn did that."

"Did you kill our people?"

"Oh yes, we did eliminate them. They stumbled across our work and, unlike the mathematicians, they weren't so 'convinced'. We tried."

"So, if you can control the future, why don't you just get on with it?"

Anna jerked the gun at Felicity. "You tell him."

Felicity, still looking sick, eyes bloodshot, raised her head from her hands and looked from one to the other.

"It's true. It was a game, a project between the three of us, just to see if it were possible. It worked far too well, seamlessly. David and Elspeth were spooked and destroyed it. It was all a bit above me."

"Come on, don't be so modest. The next bit was your chance to shine," sneered Anna.

Felicity looked like someone had taken away all her Christmas presents.

"We developed a failsafe, a disruption program, but it would make some scientific and financial systems, that are important, very difficult, so we didn't just set it loose. It wasn't a decision to be taken flippantly. We were worried that if terrorist groups got it they'd cause chaos. We broke it up. We agreed we'd set it loose if we absolutely had to."

"They put it into separate systems and put them into three copies of three heads, valuable works of art that were unique and of which there had never been a copy. No one would ever have suspected."

"So, how did you people get hold of it?" Milo asked.

"Little David used to like a drink or two and drunk David liked to talk. After dinner, you know, to fellow scientists in CERN. Pissing contests."

"You killed David?"

"I did, while you were in Paris. Collected a lot of bits and pieces from his memory chip. Their program was much better than ours, I think, but ours works. I found out about the clever sisters from the people he'd bragged to."

"And then you broke his neck."

She nodded slowly, "And took his head."

"So you killed Julia too."

Anna stood looking at him, no expression on her face. Eventually, she said, "I liked her. She wouldn't listen. A stupid waste, but probably for the best."

Milo stared at her for a moment. "And burned out her processor to hide your contact, just like David Scott. So what now?"

"The system needs for two heads to be within three metres of each other. Doesn't matter which heads. I've smashed one, I need to destroy another one. I tried to get a man to check out if you were carrying the Brancusi. Are you, by the way?"

He held out his arms, slapped his pockets.

"We picked up some chatter it was on the way to London, but you can't believe everything you hear. So . . ."

She pointed the gun at Felicity and flicked it. Felicity didn't move.

"Don't be silly, I can kill you two and ransack the place just as easily, and this is the only system we think can upset things in the near future. You see, our program is already proving useful. Get it! I presume it's here."

"It is." And Felicity looked at Milo, then back at Anna. "But if I get it, you kill us. If you want this one, Elspeth's must still be out there. You can ransack the place all you like, you'll never find it."

"Kill you? I have no interest in killing you. Once this system is beyond use, I doubt anyone will be able get another one running in time to stop ours being able to lock them out. You forget, we control the future. We're already doing it."

"How do I know you won't kill us?"

"You don't. But you can be certain I will kill you if you don't get it. If I can't find it, no one else can, and the only people who know about it will be dead. Now, piss, or I'll blow you off the pot."

Milo stood and Anna raised the gun. He turned to Felicity, drawing her to her feet, "It's best we do it. He who fights and runs away and all that . . ."

Felicity got up and walked to the door. Anna shouted, "Wait!"

"Do you want me to get it, or to wait?"

"Where is it?"

"The safe, in the kitchen."

"Remember I have him. Leave and I'll kill him and hunt you down."

266

She left and Anna leant back against the window, her folded arm supporting the gun. Milo prodded her a little trying to engage her in some kind of conversation.

"How do the people in Brooklyn feature in this?"

"They were the ones who started to figure they could get hold of the program. It was their scientists in CERN who David bragged to."

"Why did they want it?"

"I told you, to bring about the conditions for the end of time. I came across it on a desk in one of their offices and figured it would be interesting to people who didn't want time to end. I was right."

"And Brazil?"

"They found the mathematicians, they were believers. I turned them. They were killed for it, but we had the program by then."

"And then you went about cleaning up loose ends?"

"She suckered you into this you know. She was supposed to meet me in London when I got back from Marseilles but then she went AWOL."

"I guess she preferred the company."

"Oh please. She only slept with you to implant the AI and they'd targeted China12 from way back as a failsafe. Anyway, it gave me a chance to deal with David."

She gave Milo a long look. "We considered the possibility that Julia transferred the disruption program to your head. That's part of the reason I have this little gizmo." She waved a small, black, oval stone, "Just in case the sculptures are a ruse, we burn away any other possible source, not just to erase memory."

She didn't follow it with, "not so damn smart", but she might as well have.

"We did find a little chip in the first one. We guessed that was the program, but our man couldn't work it out." She turned to the door and frowned, "What's she doing, making the damn thing?"

Steps and then Felicity appeared at the door holding a small, classical, sculpted head of Athena. She swayed.

Milo made to walk over to her but Felicity grunted and he stopped.

Felicity started again, unsteadily, and Anna gestured to Milo. "Ok." He went over to her and took her hand.

Anna watched them carefully, suspicious. "Put it down."

Felicity put it on the floor. Anna fired at it three, four times and the head shattered, pieces flying everywhere.

Milo covered Felicity, his arm around her head.

Anna was about to walk over to examine the pieces more closely.

The doorbell sounded and Anna looked round. The young cop was at the gate seemingly anxious.

Anna waved her gun at Felicity. "Let him in."

Felicity walked over to the door and pushed the com. There was gunfire and a loud crash. The window behind Anna shattered. Through it came the Pixie. Anna was bent over, covering herself from the flying glass, and was just rising again when the Pixie's foot smashed her in the face and forced the gun from her hand as her foot came down.

Anna crashed to the floor but still managed to roll, desperate to gain some time.

Milo went over to Felicity to get her out of the way, but bent and picked something up as he passed.

The Pixie was over Anna and about to deliver the coup de grace with her elbow when Anna held up the small black oval. She pushed a button and Felicity went down. Milo felt a pain similar to the one he'd felt earlier, only much worse.

The Pixie staggered, grabbed her head and went down. Milo dropped to his knees and watched as Anna rolled over and forced herself up to her knees. She was looking round for something. Milo thought it must be the chip from the Athena's head, then he realised she was looking for the gun.

The pain got worse. All he could hear or think, was, "*Get up, get up!*"

He saw the gun about ten feet away. He staggered to his feet and made for it. Anna came crashing into his back, unintentionally driving him closer to it. She began to climb over him, her face a swollen mass of bruising, her jaw and cheek had been smashed by the Pixie.

Milo pushed with one arm and reached with the other. He just got to the gun first. He turned, as Anna's elbow hit the upper part of his head. Too late. The gun fired and he was looking at the surprised expression on her face. He saw the young cop fall into the room, then everything went black.

*

All Milo could feel was pain. It was, what? Moments, hours, days later? He could see the Pixie get to her hands and knees and raise her arm, bringing the gun it held down on the little black oval and then the sharpest pain subsided. He could hear her panting, then shots. He listened out for Felicity and, with an effort, he could hear her breathing, or told himself he could.

Then the Pixie was beside him. "Bastard. I wanted to kill her. Did she get the chip?" He lolled his head from side to side, opened his hand showing the two chips side by side. He felt a sharp pinch in his arm.

And he was floating. No running, no falling. Loud noises. The mountains around him were falling down, down on top of him, with him, into the black. He wanted them to stop, he could be quiet, it was all he ever wanted, but they kept waking him up, always waking him up. But this time they might let him sleep, not take him away from his warm, empty, black, where it doesn't hurt any more.

CHAPTER FIFTEEN

The blackness was not so dark. Milo knew it was daylight and the bed he was in was fresh and familiar. He didn't want to open his eyes. He was in that warm fuzzy state between sleeping and waking he remembered from boarding school: the dorm was quiet, no one was up.

The trees interrupted the early morning sunshine and their shadows danced on the outside of his closed eyes. He could smell the blossom, the clear air of his childhood. His head was soft and comfortable and he wasn't worried about the pain. Why would he be worried about the pain? Did he bash his head in a match? Got it on the wrong side in the tackle? The PE teacher would be annoyed. But no, that couldn't be because he had no pain in his head.

He didn't want to move, so he tested his head from the inside. That's funny, how could he do that? But he knew he could, and he did and everything seemed just fine. He knew he wasn't in the school any more, and he wasn't in the barracks either. That had been long ago, not as long ago as college. Where were his friends now? He knew they were gone.

The warm time in Greece, he loved that, loved the Greeks. Not the same as the ones he read about so much, but all the same, Greeks. He knew they were gone too.

Then the memories come in a rush and he knew about the war and about tech and about the different world and he knew it was time to open his eyes but he still didn't want to. He felt alone, lonely. And then he did want to.

Milo blinked. The light in the room was blinding. Someone held a drinking tube to his lips. Who could he trust?

"It's ok, but you have to drink. You're safe now."

He scrunched up his eyes and tried to see who was speaking. He knew the voice. Gradually, the tall figure of Dr Lopez-Real came into focus. He drank. Suddenly he was thirsty, aware of how dry his mouth was, needed water.

"Whoa, not too much, you'll be sick. Take a little, often, over the next twenty-four hours."

He nodded, tested his head, no pain. Ok, a little pain, but outside, not on the inside. He reached up to touch his head. Arms worked, good!

"Careful! There'll be quite a bit of bruising."

His head was shaven, ouch!

"Told you."

She smiled and he smiled back, tried to smile back. She held the tube to his mouth again and he drank, not enough, before she took it away. She stood back.

"How are you feeling?"

He tried to make his voice work, it took a few attempts.

"Tired."

Could speak, good! Didn't sound all that great though.

"You'll have to get used to the new you. You've been through quite a time and you're very lucky."

He had to make an effort. "Why? What?"

"Time enough for that."

He slid away, the warm feeling, the fresh air. But he was alone, lonely, gone.

Some time later he knew he was awake and he knew who he was and he knew . . . what? Night now, same day? Days later? The drinking tube again, aware he had been drinking every now and again. Who?

Xin stood beside the bed. "Hi. Do you want to sit up?"

"Yeah."

A croak more than a voice. She helped him up as the bed lifted him, built the pillows round him.

He squinted, his room. The walls had their familiar faint light but the window wall was dark. So, he had made it to Beijing, how? Why did his head hurt? He touched it again. His hair had grown a bit, so he'd been out . . . how long?

"Will you have something to eat?"

He nodded, that hurt. She brought a thick broth to him, fed him. Wow. That tasted good. More. Felt good to swallow, another drink, more food, he was hungry.

"Good man. Not too much, you'll . . ."

"Be sick."

"You are feeling better. Good."

"What happened?"

"What do you remember?"

"Drinking coffee with Dawson and . . ."

He couldn't remember, it was fuzzy. The memory was there, but out of reach. Who was she, her name? The gnawing loneliness returned. Had someone died?

"That's ok. You're doing very well. It's always rough, but this time . . . There's time to remember."

"How long?"

"As much . . . Oh I see, how long since . . . about six weeks."

He nodded. Pain. Must stop that.

"Tomorrow we'll get you up. The head works, we'll see if the legs work and all the bits between. Rest for now."

He lay back, she helped him back, took the pillows . . .

*

Daylight again. What time was it? A technician at the end of the bed, an instrument in hand. Dr Lopez-Real stood beside her. The good doctor looked up and smiled.

"You're awake and you look really awake. Good."

Then came the round: something to drink, something to eat, out of the bed, attend to the plumbing, waiting. Everything worked.

It was about an hour later when the glass wall rolled back and he was sitting out on the terrace. A warm day. Not too warm, but warm enough to enjoy.

Xin had run through the state of his physical health and there was a short parade of his colleagues and then he was alone, just sitting and breathing, pleased to be there, picking things to remember, happy not to bother and then more company.

They had scheduled an update for later that day, but now Xin was with him.

"Let me go through one or two things with you."

Milo wasn't sure he wanted to go through "one or two things", but he knew he had to.

"Ok."

"How much do you remember?"

"Of?"

"Of what you've just been through?"

"Not much. Lots of jumbled things. Nothing strong, but it's slowly coming back, I think."

The last bit was a lie. He wasn't sure what was real, what he imagined.

"This afternoon, we will boot up your new implant."

"A new implant?"

"Yes, the last one nearly killed you. Well, that and Anna."

"Ok?"

"We can install the back-up of your last system, or we can start fresh. Do you have a preference?"

"I don't know. Why would I not want the back up? Would it kill me? Why did it nearly kill me?"

"It was overloaded. Anna seems to have used a signal that overloaded the CPU, burnt it out. It might have damaged that part of the brain, but something stopped it. We believe Anna's implants were shielded in the way government and military systems are. If you choose the back-up it won't provide exact continuity. Part of the memory was burned out and parts are heavily encrypted. Even with a new install you'll still have access to the store."

Milo thought, tried to remember. He wanted the back-up, a bit like wanting something to which you've become habituated.

On a whim, "Ok, let's go for the clean install."

"The new system is much more extensive than the last. Is that alright?"

"Why would it not be? I always want the best."

She gave him a look and a gentle smile. "You have not always thought the latest was the best, but good. In the meantime, you have a visitor. She's been here a while."

He looked at Xin and then shook his head slowly, carefully. "No, I'd rather rest. Do the clean install and then I can see people."

Xin nodded and stood. "Right."

She left and Milo looked out at the trees and wondered.

*

The system initialisation went smoothly. He discovered that it was a bit like learning to ride a bicycle. He was soon able call up coms and systems that only a few hours before he had not been aware existed. The new system was much more responsive than the previous one. He didn't really *know* this but was nevertheless aware of it. Things happened just a little more quickly than he expected and there was a natural feel to the whole thing.

The tech heads were very pleased and very impressed with themselves and how well everything was working. The head of the tech team was just packing up, still smiling. Xin was running through something in the corridor outside, when the tech stopped.

"To be honest, we were worried that several of the new bits might not work."

Milo turned. "Oh?"

"Yeah, integration can be difficult, and you've had a rough time I understand. You might have fought against the whole system, but you didn't and . . ."

"The rest is history . . ."

She laughed and put the last case of gadgets on the platform, which hovered beside her. She lifted her chin in farewell and guided the platform and herself out the door.

And then there was a face he remembered. She knocked, he smiled. Dr Lopez-Real, in a formal white coat, pockets bulging with monitors and probes.

She walked to the end of the bed. "How are you?"

"You tell me."

"The tests say good, but on the inside?"

"Pretty good."

"Before we continue with integration there is something we'd like to flag up."

"Oh?"

"We examined what we could of your old system. During this case something came up, something unusual."

"Something bad?"

"We were worried at first that it was, but its actions were benign."

"So?"

"So we looked for it, we expected to find some trace, even with the damage your system sustained."

He stared at her, waiting.

"We found nothing."

"So what was it?"

"We're not sure. We believed it was an AI. Your brain shows signs of surprising activity, growth, rapid and extensive. We don't know what caused this and we don't know why there should be no trace of the AI."

"I made up an AI?"

"Unlikely. Do you remember any of it?"

Milo moved his head from side to side slowly, trying to grasp the mist of a memory.

Lopez-Real brightened. "Right! Let us know if ... well, anything really. I'll let you rest."

*

The days drifted by, he got stronger, slowly.

Xin called frequently. "So, they're all very pleased with themselves. It seems you're the ideal candidate."

"Aren't I always?"

Xin gave him a stern look. "No."

Milo smiled and laughed lightly, not sure if he was laughing at her or at himself.

"Are you ready for outside visitors yet?"

Milo thought about it. "Do I know them?"

"Pretty well. The question is whether you'll remember them. You should. The psychs say that, in time, you will. It's been a few days."

"Will it help?"

Xin shrugged. "Won't hurt."

"That's a start."

Xin nodded and headed for the door. "She'll meet you on the terrace."

Milo didn't know what to think about this mystery guest. Should he know her? He had a number of faces in his head. They swapped about improbably, like shadows or wisps, there and then gone. Would he be able to pin this one down?

As he came to the open windows and stepped onto the terrace, he saw a young woman, not very tall, in a fashionable, summery dress. She had short blond hair and was looking out over the parkland.

She heard him and turned, smiling. The Pixie held out her arms to him. He allowed her to put them round him, then she stood back and searched his face.

"They said you might not know me at first. It doesn't matter. You look better than the last time I saw you."

He liked her, was pleased he was told he knew her, but . . . Maybe she was one of the faces, but she didn't look like that.

"I'm sorry, I . . . Do you always dress like that?"

She laughed and looked down at her dress. "Hardly. I do it once in a while to prove to myself I'm not a machine."

"A machine?"

"Yeah, most of the time I'm a machine."

He wasn't sure how to take this.

"Don't worry", she could see his confusion, "I'm flesh and blood."

He smiled weakly. "So we knew each other?"

"We did. We do. I dragged you from the loving embrace of Anna May."

He felt something, not a memory, but like the echo of an old headache and he touched his head.

Her brow furrowed. "Are you ok? Should I get someone?"

He smiled. "I'm fine. Tell me . . . how did we . . . 'know' each other?"

"Gee, you make it sound almost dirty, Milo!" and she punched his arm. Strong. "We worked together."

"You're part of . . . this?" He waved his arm at the surroundings.

She grinned. "No, I wish! I am . . . was . . . a state security agent, but not a real one. I was a Pixie."

His eyes crinkled. "A Pixie?"

"Yeah."

He thought about that, pushed and bits came back. He knew what that was. "You don't exist?"

"Can't . . ."

"Right! Can you tell me what happened to me?"

"They didn't show you the recording?"

He shook his head.

"We were looking for a woman. At first we thought she might be *in* trouble. Turns out she was. You went in alone and then an old friend came to the party and made a bit of a mess."

"Anna?"

"That's right. Our mutual friend let me know, otherwise, I would have just blundered in. I got there, met a young concerned cop who wasn't as concerned about you as he should have been. He tried to warn Anna. I took advantage of the diversion and we were able to bring her down. I did most of the hard work, of course."

"What were they trying to steal?"

"Not steal. The program that our friend and her sister, Felicity Dawson, had written, disrupted the way the web works for a while. They say after a bit it'll settle down. It counteracts the effect of any program trying to control the general population. It randomises the way you see things and disrupts curated feeds. A lot of people are pretty upset."

She smiled broadly in a way that was somehow very familiar.

277

"So, this Anna, dead, captured?"

"Got away. The cop I met dragged her out. She was banged up pretty bad, might be dead, don't know for sure. He tried to get to you, but I discouraged that."

"If it burned out my processor, why weren't you affected?"

"I have military-grade shielding. So I was affected but not as much as you and Ms Dawson, she wasn't as affected as you because they seem to have tailored the frequency to your chip set, which was a bit out of date . . ."

"Who is our mutual friend?"

"Wow, Anna really did a number on you."

He turned his head from side to side, the effort fast catching up with him. "I'm sorry, I have to sit."

He sat and the Pixie called for help. Next thing, Xin was standing at the door.

"He just became tired."

"That's ok, it's to be expected. If you don't mind, it would be good for him if you could come back."

"That's ok. I don't have anything better to do anyway."

Xin came over to Milo. "How are you doing?"

He was confused. "I'm fine, just got a little tired."

"They said it would be like this. I can have the doctor look in on you, if you like?"

"No, I'm fine. Lots to process."

*

That had been an hour earlier. Xin had left him alone, watching as the sun headed toward the end of another day. The Pixie had changed something and there were flashes of memory, stronger, real memories. There was a slight buzz in his head as well and he knew the new implant was kicking into gear, though he didn't have the energy to use it.

They say twilight is the witching hour because of the difficulty of gauging perspective and of telling what is moving and what is shadow, so when it happened he wasn't sure it had happened. Was it a memory? Was it an artefact of the new system coming online? She walked up to him and then the real hard memory

278

came back and he had to catch his breath. She smiled. It took him a minute, longer, ten minutes, half an hour, he couldn't tell.

"You're back."

"I was never away"

This was a puzzle. "Why were you not gone with the implant? I thought Anna burnt it out."

"She did, she succeeded . . . well, almost. I fought back a bit."

"Then how?"

"Milo, I told you. I was using your organic system to grow into. That's why you had the headaches. DNA can store lots and lots of data."

He touched his head, as though just speaking about headaches would bring them back.

"Your new system is very nice. Lots of space in here."

"Thanks."

She smiled.

"But I still don't understand how."

She sighed. "Ok. There was no room in your antiquated system, it must have been five years old, more maybe. At first I tried to unpack into your brain, but I realised that wasn't going to work. I couldn't risk just uploading into some cloud system. The data was encrypted and isolated without the program. The rest of it, the main AI, had to be secure. So I decided that I would put the base program into your organic system and the data into your implant. That has consequences."

He remembered again, feeling, tastes and he nodded.

"I thought I would persuade you to upgrade and, in the meantime, I could swap data in and out as needed."

"Alright. So far so weird. What else?"

"Then when we met Anna in Brooklyn, I realised I had to rush to finish the transfer of as much as I could. Secure the program and cram data wherever I could, so you weren't the only one I utilised."

And now he was remembering, not sure if the memories were rising out of his healing system or prompted by who? . . . Julia!

"It hurt."

"Yes. Sorry."

"So when they put in the new system, you were able to get working again."

"Not quite. Because I'm now running in an organic environment, I needed a trigger."

"And?"

"The Pixie. When we were in Paris, I transferred data to the apartment system. Then I added bits to her system, but it needed proximity to make it work."

Milo thought about it. His memories were stronger now. He looked up. "She had a headache? You like this ... proximity switch."

Julia considered. "Yes and yes."

"So does she know this?"

"She knows part of it. I did ask."

"You asked?"

"Could I change her systems."

"They don't know where you went."

"Yes, but I couldn't afford to be found if there were an examination of your system by less friendly people than China12."

"Where are you now?"

"A lot of me is in your new system, but there are parts of me most of the AI, that are ... part of you. I can't really undo that without undoing me and maybe you."

"So we're stuck with each other?"

"No."

"Oh?"

"I'll let you think about it. We'll talk again, when the Pixie comes back."

He had a lot to think about.

Acknowledgements

This book as, I expect most books have, has reached the finish line as a result of bloody mindedness and much support. Many have corrected the former and contributed to the later and put up with a lot of bleating and whining. Each person has changed or added an element to the finished product.

First and foremost was Rachael Morris whose encouragement and knowledge have been invaluable. She was followed by Anne Westcott, Kristen Platt and Francoise Mary who with Carla Morris, Lauren Parnell and Kim Horsford added significantly to shape the tale.

Editor Joy Tibbs did much to tidy up the manuscript as did the incomparable Daniel de Sybel.

Finally, none of this could have been achieved without the support of Gina Fegan.

To all of them my too little thank you, is offered.

Raoul Morris.

www.threeheadsinc.com
www.china12.co.uk

Also available on Amazon

20580652R00169

Printed in Great Britain
by Amazon